JANUARY 6

A NOVEL

NORMAN BREWER

While closely following some speeches, events and timeline of January 6, 2021, as widely reported in the media, this book is essentially fiction. Names, characters, plots, dialog, and other literary devices are the products of the author's imagination or are used fictitiously.

~

Dedicated to the United States Capitol Police officers who battled the insurrectionists.

PROLOGUE

Madam Speaker sat in the House Dining Room, a human shield. Right-wing extremists had positioned her cushioned chair in front of a tall window, heavy drapery blocking the sensational view of the National Mall. Armed men flanked her. A militia leader had warned the FBI that she and other hostages faced execution should a rescue be attempted. This is surreal, thought the Speaker. This can't be happening in the Capitol, in the United States of America. Unthinkable.

It was January 6th, 2021.

CHAPTER 1

Protesters cut away from the rally, first by ones and twos, then by determined handfuls, surging up Pennsylvania Avenue from the Ellipse. A call to arms echoed in their heads, an order from their President: "We will stop the steal."

The cadence of their footsteps imbued that call with action, finally giving meaning to the endless battle of words. The righteousness of their cause lent warmth against forty-degree cold. Above MAGA hats and stocking caps they waved their hero's red and blue campaign flags, those of the Confederacy, too. Their mid-day numbers grew, with marchers leaving Pennsylvania to feed onto Constitution Avenue or angle toward Independence Avenue at the south bookend of their target, the United States Capitol.

"Whose Capitol?" demanded a rugged woman wearing combat boots.

"Our Capitol," came back the only answer possible.

The charge of a rigged election had become gospel, propelling the belief that if no one intervened on that January 6th, the specter of a stolen presidency would be reality. The MAGA crowd felt chosen, the front line of what loomed as the decisive battle, a nation's way of life dangling in limbo.

"1776!" shouted a squat man dressed as an American revolutionary.

"1776!" came back the battle cry.

Well before the November 3rd election the President had sounded his warning: The steal is coming, with the manipulation of untried voting machines, unguarded absentee ballots never cast in such numbers, dead people voting by the thousands, outdated guardrails failing to contain the new threats.

After the election, his warnings mushroomed into a grievance of injustice, centered on the charge of voter fraud. He beat that drum even as court case after court case, audit upon audit found minuscule evidence of corruption. Across the country, election officials and judges – many his own appointees – refused to connect what he saw as obvious telltale dots.

But the faithful knew. There was too much evidence for it all to be false, too much for the mainstream media to explain away. Those reporters never had supported the President, never understood he is one of us, giving us voice against an establishment leaving us behind. The faithful knew, most of all, because the talking heads on Fox News and their media brethren told them: The steal was real.

A buxom woman in a light-weight blue parka and clamped down Texas Tech straw offered up:

"Now's the time, to stop the steal."

Defiant protesters embraced her call, their voices rolling toward the Capitol and back to the rally:

"Now's the time, to stop the steal."

Pressure on governors and election officials had failed to do the job. Mass protests in Georgia and Arizona and other swing states had not either. Neither had disrupting press conferences or social media postings. The most ardent of the faithful tracked down phone numbers of election officials and learned where they lived, threw garbage and bags of excrement on their lawns. Some of those now marching on the Capitol punched in late night threatening calls: "We know where to find you" and "We are coming." Families were terrified. Officials angered and shaken, but they stood firm. As weeks passed, the hoodlum tactics paled, seeming futile and pitifully childish.

Finally, saving a presidency came down to January 6th. The day Congress was to move the election out of reach became, in the minds of the desperate faithful, a last gasp to salvage victory. Such was the mindset of rally organizers, holding permits for tens of thousands of loyalists to gather. The mindset of militant extremists, stockpiling munitions and hatching plots both vague and dangerous. The mindset of right-wing media stoking conspiracies and stroking the cult's patriotism. The mindset of an exploitative President, leading the rhetoric.

Myriad post-election defeats had been pushed aside. The way forward was at hand. It was time to bludgeon the Vice President into doing his duty or Congress into doing theirs. The marchers' fealty was a given. Only courage was demanded.

"Revolution 2.0!" a protester bellowed.

"Revolution 2.0!" chanted the crowd.

Closing on the Capitol, marchers in the vanguard felt proud. They had answered their leader's call. Not only the White supremacists and militias now blessed with a long-awaited mantle of respectability. Not only those driven by a cause – from the Second Amendment to pro-life, from border security to cutting taxes. But blue-collar workers and small business owners and regular Americans alarmed by unwelcome changes bearing down on their communities – counterculture threats, confusion over gender. And, on the horizon, the unpalatable loss of majority status, a chasm widening with minority births and every immigrant, illegal or legal. The jobless and those struggling paycheck-to-paycheck – beaten down by a privileged elite and the Deep State, both ignoring their needs – answered the call. Conservatives fearful of a leftist agenda and burgeoning government came, and vaccine resisters pressured to conform in the name of Covid-19. The veterans and cops who found their pace out of step with the country's, their service all for naught.

Many protesters came from politically red states, driving, hitch-hiking, flying if they could. Or they paid the low freight charged by groups with patriotic names, hopping a chartered bus, two nights lodging included. Some drained scanty bank accounts for a one-way trip, unsure how they would get home. If that smacked of being cultists, fine. The President's survival outweighed personal sacrifice. As did preserving the American way of life. Their way of life.

Many came with lawful weapons – knives and batons and bear spray. But many also brought firearms and ammunition that, until registered, were illegal in the District of Columbia. Perhaps some brought firearms out of the back-home habit of carrying. But others – most? – came with an agenda, their own or one pushed by a militant leader. An agenda heightened by anticipation and imagination, by the prospect of a happening larger than themselves – fueled by hearing over and over again: "Be there. Will be wild!"

Ambrose Dancer hung with the rally, avoiding the spearhead of the march on the Capitol. He had an agenda, one more demanding than marching and chanting. And he enjoyed watching Republican lawmakers and a presidential son exciting the crowd, the President's lawyer leveling a war cry: "Let's have trial by combat!"

That fit Dancer's agenda. He had driven from Michigan with three other men from his National Patriot Movement, one of five teams he brought to the rally. Most extremist militias in Michigan hunkered along the Detroit-Lansing corridor; NPM was based to the west to avoid attention.

Years earlier, Dancer spotted the potential for White supremacy gaining a national foothold when a brash newbie, armed with a keen sense for the jugular and unfettered by a moral or ideological compass, methodically rolled over other presidential wannabes. One by one they fell victim to withering ridicule dumped on unguarded soft spots.

Ready to step up was the NPM, driven by the seditious intentions of Dancer and his younger brother, Alexander, both former Army Rangers.

Honorably discharged within months of each other, they had encountered a void: Dangers faced routinely as Rangers had proved addictive, and beyond the reach of civilian life. But at full strength was a rebellious itch, a compelling urge to lash out, spawned by overseas deployments that turned them against military as well as civilian authorities.

Ambrose Dancer's eight years in the Ranger's elite Delta Force had equipped him with skills on a par with Navy Seals. Dangerous missions made teamwork paramount, but his zest for solo operations earned him a reputation for staying cool, regardless of the threat. When treacherous villagers betrayed him to the Taliban, he took a bad-odds chance to escape, knowing death was certain anyway. He killed his three captors and made it back to his unit. Asked why he did not wait for a better chance, Ambrose said, "Ya gotta believe."

When superior officers pressed him to explain, he refused, then hotly recounted a mission months earlier when three soldiers in his patrol were killed. Air cover for their raid had been scrubbed at the last minute over fears of political backlash should civilians become collateral damage. "Somebody's gutless fucking decision turned my men into collateral damage," he screamed at a colonel. Luckily, the colonel had experienced something similar, and didn't take disciplinary action. Relieved comrades noticed Ambrose had gnawed his fingernails to the quick – clueing the pressure he felt.

Following his lead, Alexander reveled in the Rangers' small arms and hand-to-hand combat training. While a natural leader with no shortage of courage, he lacked the fervor crucial to surviving the rigors of Delta Force. Headaches were his pressure telltale, and harder to cope with than gnawed nails. The brothers served in Afghanistan and Iraq, though not together. Both shed blood and came to resent it. They were all-in for spreading democracy when first deployed, but Alexander, too, saw missions tamped down by political expediency or wishy-washy commands. He, too, watched colleagues die. Left behind was a sour taste for civilian as well as military leadership, and a disturbing belief that the problem was intractable. Talking when they could, the brothers discovered they shared a new-found aversion to taking orders. Severe discontent turned to opposition against the very flag they fought for. Agitated talks moved from bitching about missions to fiercely opposing left-leaning politics and government. Their politics shifted right, then to the extreme right.

Discharged, they learned in late-night crab sessions with friends about right-wing militias in Michigan. Cautiously making contact, the brothers found the groups' rebellious politics appealing, but most of their foot soldiers far from serious. Too often, field exercises or martial training disintegrated into sloppy beer fests the Dancers scorned as a waste of time – and dangerous. Toppling a government, or even reordering one, would demand professionalism and full commitment. Anything less and a militia or coalition of militias would be doomed, helpless as a lethargic fly in winter, when pitted against the power and resources of the United States.

If they wanted to be in a militia, it became clear, the solution was to start their own. Carefully, quietly, they recruited like-minded friends. The NPM's rolls slowly grew. The bulk of recruits were White men, as were the Dancers. A few were women and a smattering had been to college. Almost all knew weapons as lifelong hunters or from the military. Like the brothers, many were gym rats – hard, conditioned for a rebellion – and enjoyed martial arts. They eagerly absorbed killing lessons the brothers readily shared. Almost all were skilled with their hands – as blue-collar tradesmen – or with heavy machinery like bulldozers and backhoes. Alexander was a gunsmith. They mostly could pay their bills, but saw the prosperity of coastal states, let alone the American Dream, constantly jerked away by a tone-deaf establishment of liberal elites. Anger ran deep, feeding their full embrace of culture wars.

Ambrose's cavernous aluminum shop, where he maintained his trash collection trucks, was the NPM's headquarters. Set in woods well off a county highway, meetings drew little attention as disgruntled recruits signed up. Almost everyone who thought correctly was welcome if they practiced discretion and discipline. Those closely monitored standards weeded out beer-drinking weekend warriors.

Prized were the well-trained – current or former military and police, and those with medical know-how for treating casualties that one day must surely come.

Ambrose had insisted on the NPM keeping a low profile. But the brothers – mainly Alexander – did spend enough time at rallies and meetings of other militias to appreciate their poor standing with most people, usually to the point of disdain. Even staunch conservatives did not embrace anti-government groups, and certainly not White supremacists or those targeting Blacks or Jews or the LGBTQ community. But Ambrose saw how that could change. Racism and bias were latent among a large swath of Americans, ready to be exploited. That was clear, regardless of the election and reelection of a Black president. In fact, Ambrose reasoned, the deep antagonism unearthed by those elections revealed the promise of exploitation. All that is needed is the right leader – a strong unorthodox politician with an autocratic streak – striking the flint, supplying the spark. Millions will follow. No longer will militias like the NPM be on the fringe. We will be in the mainstream, he told himself with satisfaction. On the right to be sure, but still mainstream. We will be respectable.

The NPM was disrupted when Alexander fell in love, trailing a woman to her home in central South Carolina. By the time he had opened a gunsmith shop near Columbia, their relationship soured – but with an upside: He founded a chapter of the National Patriot Movement. The brothers' determination to change the system had expanded their base.

A few months into the new president's administration, Ambrose made what was to be a prescient call. "Hey, sergeant bro," he began. "I see how our old talks can be more than talk. Time's coming to raise hell."

Short years passed. A badly divided Congress hardened. The new President, not content with only flaunting the norms of his office, treated it as his fiefdom. He used "my" when talking of judges and departments including justice, where the very name demanded independence. He played the school yard bully without mercy, not only assailing titans of industry or congressional lions. Average Americans weathered brutal attacks from the world's most powerful man, too; a local union official in Indiana who dared question the President's claims of saving jobs, Muslim Gold Star parents grieving a son killed in Iraq.

Meanwhile, the NPM chapters slowly gathered more than four hundred soldiers, seeping without fanfare into nearby states. The brothers held on to their approach of aligning with other militants with caution and low-balling NPM strength. "We're just not ready," Ambrose insisted when asked to join missions he saw as futile mischief making. He most emphatically stayed out of the plot to kidnap the governor of Michigan, smelling failure and arrests. Keeping a low profile paid off. Not even the Southern Poverty Law Center, the premier, non-government tracker of domestic terrorists, had the NPM on its Hate Map. Neither did the FBI.

But NPM troops were restless. Loyal to their extremist roots, they saw violence as a worthy, even pleasurable, tool. They wanted more than talk and training sessions. The brothers did, too. They welcomed the President's unbridled attacks on his reelection results as fortuitous, an emerging opportunity as millions of his disciples were energized by his big lie. The brothers knew the election was honestly lost. Knew it did not matter how many voted for the President, it had not been enough. They knew the fraud charge was a straw man. The President's lawyers had been laughed out of court, repeatedly, his baseless lies, unfounded reports and conspiracy theories all rejected. Simply put, the President was exploiting his own people and worse, leading an unholy attack on democracy. The Dancer brothers knew all that but didn't care. Democracy in these United States could not be under attack, in their view, when it was already dead.

"Need evidence?" the Dancers would ask recruits. The powerful – politicians, business leaders, academics – my god, those academics! – stand mute as American ideals are violated, a socialist state created, opportunity drained from the working man into Washington's swamp. The powerful stand mute as borders are breached and police are attacked. Black lives matter more than White lives. We have lost everything from the statues of heroes to Merry Christmas to peeing with your own sex, for Christ's sake, the brothers fumed. But given the President's relentless courage, we are ready to take back our country – at whatever price.

Ambrose listened to a Southern congressman challenging the rambunctious crowd to step up for "kicking ass" time, as the sycophants finally gave way to the great man. He entered to thunderous applause that rolled on and on as he waded yet again through a discredited litany of states wrongly lost – Pennsylvania, Georgia, Michigan and Wisconsin, Arizona, Nevada. The faithful was charged anew when he zeroed in on his Vice President. How he must – very soon now – show courage, must refuse to certify some electors and send the fight back to key states in search of new electoral slates.

"We become President and you are the happiest people," he crooned in his clumsy style to deafening cheers.

Ambrose groaned when the President declared "I'll be there with you" walking up Pennsylvania Avenue, knowing that even if serious, the Secret Service would never let it happen. Ambrose wished it would. He tried to imagine such a spectacle – the President of the United States leading a mob marching on the United States Capitol, set on blocking Congress from certifying a new president – and he could not. He could see the confusion and uncertainty that would envelop the security apparatus, from the Secret Service to the generals. He could see a constitutional crisis, no doubt, but of what magnitude? It was beyond prediction. How would already divided Americans react? Would those who swore an oath to the Constitution bow in fealty to an individual? Families would be broken, and neighbors would battle neighbors. Violence not seen since the Civil War would engulf the nation. Of that Ambrose did feel certain, and he muttered, "Hit the street, Mr. President."

He sensed a stiffening of resolve as the crowd, hungry for victory and uncertain how to achieve it, was challenged: "...you'll never take back our country with weakness. You have to show strength and you have to be strong."

There was a sentence, "I know that everyone here will soon be marching over to the Capitol building to peacefully and patriotically make your voices heard."

But peacefully and patriotically in a single sentence were drowned out when the President insisted, "This was a LANDSLIDE." Peacefully and patriotically were summarily buried as he goaded a crowd pregnant with insurrection:

"Our country has had enough. We will not take it anymore..."

"We will never give up. We will never concede."

"And we fight. We fight like hell. And if you don't fight like hell, you're not going to have a country anymore."

As the crowd cheered wildly beneath banners heralding the "Save America March," the rally shifted its sight onto the Capitol. Not with a sharpshooter's accuracy, but an artillery round loaded with mini balls, spinning out of control.

The steady exit of inspired protesters took on urgency, a tense energy, when he finally was done. But the President did not walk from the podium to join the march to the Capitol. He walked to his SUV, for the short ride back to the safety of the White House.

No surprise there, thought Ambrose. He smiled as he spotted Alexander, red MAGA cap pulled low. They were near twins, of medium height, blocky, always clean shaven. Alexander could be counted on to wear tight-fitting blue denim shirts and jeans, while Ambrose favored loose plaid shirts and cargo pants. Their eyes met briefly, then they joined the horde.

CHAPTER 2

The brothers kept a discrete distance from each other, a precaution against the unexpected. A few paces ahead, Alexander saw a Three Percenter he had met just weeks earlier. More than Ambrose, he was inclined to seek common ground with others agitating for radical change, but he did not call out.

Alexander remembered the man from a gathering of militias in Richmond, purposely selected for its symbolism of cherished statuary and other Confederacy touchstones in Virginia. The meeting was called after the President marked his January 6th rally on everyone's calendar as the place to be. With much to plan for, key leaders insisted on secrecy and limited invitations to major groups. Only through an Oath Keeper friend did Alexander hear of the meeting in a rented warehouse and gain entry.

Fiery speeches, to the point of rabid, set the tone: January 6th was a huge opportunity to join forces, do something far larger than was individually possible – saving a presidency or, at least, disruption on a scale unseen since 9/11, maybe since 1861. Lasting militia alliances could be forged. The established order, from Congress to leftist judges to the media and swaths of big business, could be cracked, perhaps dismantled. Fear struck into millions of misguided liberals, recasting them as sheep for generations. "Woke" policies reversed, on gender, immigration, and whose lives matter most.

Alexander was all-in but did not see any of that happening without violence, starting at the Capitol and spreading to the city, then coast to coast, border to border. The rhetoric of the assembled militants buoyed him. Speakers preached bloodshed, engaging in chest-pounding declarations of killing lawmakers, judges, election officials who failed their duty. Set downtown D.C. ablaze, they urged. Riot. Wage random attacks in suburbs, shattering homeowners' comfortable cocoons of safety. Box the President into using the Insurrection Act of 1807, as some of his own advisers' favor. With the country in flames, people would welcome martial law. Maybe the military brass would relish the taste of power.

"Never before, never, ever, have we had a chance like this," thundered a gray-whiskered man wearing the black tee shirt and yellow kilt of the Proud Boys. "It is a chance we can't miss. We have no choice but to take it. No choice! Just be ready to go down. But take others down first!"

He was milder than some, and rants finally calmed to the need for a strategy. Most wanted to storm the Capitol, but few believed they could succeed. The Capitol was too symbolic, too iconic for the vast federal security apparatus to let it fall. Other targets ran the gamut: The White House. Congressional office buildings and the high-profile hostages they offered. Other federal buildings. Blowing up railroad cars carrying highly hazardous loads, rumbling a stone's throw south of House office buildings. Contaminating water supplies. Knocking out the electrical grid. Bombing Union Station or beloved monuments on the National Mall.

Opportunities for violence in Washington were endlessly promising. But no single militia was confident of handling a mission by itself. None had been tested on that scale. None was fully prepared; the January 6th Xs on their calendars looming. Gradually they concluded that attacks, envisioned with relish, would soon be contained, then defeated. Taking hostages could only prolong the outcome. Most important, all but two of the targets would not inflame militia across the nation or the President's most die-hard cultists. Likewise, most targets would not inspire ordinary Americans – led by those feeling deserted and insecure, desperate to blame someone for their stagnant lives – to spontaneously join a rebellion. One viable option was the White House, had not its occupant been their President. That only left assaulting the body politic, the lawmakers failing their duty, convened in the United States Capitol. Regardless of its symbolism, its iconic status, there was no better choice. Even if it could not be held long, it could be the launchpad for revolution.

Target agreed to, the debate again went in circles. Did the militias have enough manpower? Enough firepower? Enough time? And an elephant in the room was who should lead or, more precisely, who was willing to yield leadership? None of the likely candidates spoke up – to yield or seize the moment. The anti-government agitators bogged down, as frozen as the polarized Congress they so abhorred.

Finally, Alexander stood and introduced himself, aware he had no following.

"First, let me say that NPM agrees we have a unique opportunity. Our country is faltering, badly, and we need to change that," he said without bluster as the room quieted. "We also believe nothing will change without bloodshed, probably a lot of it.

"We think it's worth trying to take the Capitol, which could save our President and let him go on changing the government we abhor. If assaulting the Capitol fails, then the more widespread disruptions you're talking about could bring martial law. It's hard to know what the generals would do, but a lot of them like our guy so it could work out.

"If you'll pardon my saying so, we are stalled and need to get focused. One way forward may be to narrow who's in the conversation. I suggest asking the leaders of the biggest groups to decide on a leader for all of us. Then, his job would be to rough out a plan to sell it to the rest of us. Thank you."

There was a murmuring of conversation, then support. Eight leaders agreed on, they took their discussion to a corner of the warehouse. Everyone else kicked back, popping beers and renewing grievances about the leftist agenda a new president was sure to pursue.

Night dragged into early morning and finally, the leaders emerged, grim-faced. Egos had not been set aside; no commander picked. A proposal to share command had failed, too. Being brothers in hate was not enough. Silos of extremism proved to be as high and thick as those in the federal bureaucracy or the most entrenched corporations. There would be no strategic marshaling of the angry millions or the violence they could unleash. There would be no coordinated attack.

"Some of us are still trying to get together," insisted an Oath Keeper to scattered boos. "We're still a band of brothers. Hell will be raised, collectively or individually. We will not be going home empty-handed."

His promise sounded hollow, drawing more boos. Alexander left in disgust.

Later, he and Ambrose agreed: The rally remained a powder keg. When tens of thousands wallowing in grievance invest themselves in a cult figure, it is hard, maybe impossible, to admit their mistake. Worked into a frenzy, once they start feeding off each other, anything could happen. They had traveled far. They needed to go home with something, at least bragging rights confirmed by social media posts. Show their kids and the neighbors that their commitment had meaning, by God. The Dancers believed the hunger to take something home, coupled with fear of their country hurtling down a destructive path, remained dry kindling to be ignited. Then the rebellious instincts of neo-Nazis and Oath Keepers, Three Percenters and Proud Boys and lone wolf extremists would kick in. They would pile on.

And NPM, the newbie, had to be primed to capture any moment, to fan the chaos. Step in if others faltered. Take control. Ignite an insurrection. A revolution.

～

As the Richmond confab fell apart – or more precisely, failed to jell – two of the White nationalists found themselves in sync. Barely having met, their eyes locked repeatedly and saw each other asking the same question in disbelief: Are these assholes totally stupid or what?

Driving to his hotel afterward, Jeffrey Lomax thought of those unexpected cross currents. When he saw Seth Baldwin waiting at the elevator, he immediately called out. In Lomax's suite, they talked deep into an expensive brandy.

Lomax was a former Phoenix cop who made sergeant before burning out on city life in the desert. Baldwin had been a Navy Seal. Both had returned home, Lomax to Alabama's Redneck Riviera and a lucrative career developing real estate, Baldwin to his family's ranch in southeast Arizona. Raised conservative, they trod similar paths in their drift to right-wing extremism: Growing displeasure with the country's direction and a government ignoring a populace easing right of center. Friends brought them into casual contact with White nationalist groups. Involvement followed, then leadership roles.

Lomax and Baldwin thought it futile to blather aimlessly about an unfair government in need of change. The paucity of White nationalist strategies soured both men on their local militias. They were disciplined and valued their time; bitch sessions and rallies where militants competed for limited media attention were lost opportunities for decisive action.

Independently, they built their own organizations, growing from handfuls of like-minded patriots to slowly having a multi-state reach. Like the Ambrose brothers' NPM chapters, but bigger. "Today we follow the two Ps – preparedness and patience," Lomax drilled into newcomers. "In due time, my friends, there will be an opening for the two Gs – guts and glory."

Baldwin's message was an echo, without the marketing flourishes that made Lomax wealthy. But Baldwin's weather-lined face and lean frame cast him perfectly as a no-nonsense hero to his followers, and skirmishes with the federal Bureau of Land Management helped seal that status. His family's ranch depended on BLM grazing permits it had held for generations. Baldwin put them at risk every time he challenged – for himself or other ranchers – enforcement actions or occasional fee hikes demanded by environmentalists. Never mind that fees were notoriously low or that he grazed more cattle than the sparse prairie could handle.

He and other ranchers objecting to a regulatory change founded the Freedom Country Coalition in protest. They lost the fight but heightened their standing as victims of a callous bureaucracy. When a rancher crashed his helicopter and died in route to a confrontation, tempers flared. Harsh words were exchanged, and a days-long standoff followed. When relative calm returned, the FCC was tagged anti-government, boosting recruitment of disgruntled ranchers and workers. They branded the government as dominating and intrusive, an easy sale with the feds being the largest landowner in the West.

Many recruits lost interest when Baldwin told them protest and violence were not yet on the militia's agenda. Needless conflict would make the FCC an even bigger target. Best to fight the bureaucracy in court and with constitutionally protected speech.

"What I want doesn't matter if regular folk aren't ready to blow things up," he tried to explain. "Grandma Cohen on my Mama's side was fond of saying, 'Don't bother dropping the bacon 'til the skillet's hot.'"

Like Baldwin, Jeffrey Lomax wasn't put off by violence. In Phoenix, blowing away a serial rapist advanced his career – which he then nearly derailed with a quick-trigger killing of a young Black motorist.

He, too, felt radical change coming with the 2016 presidential election. But – as the name of his right-wing militia made clear – he saw no need to walk the narrow political road Baldwin followed. South Arising gave a public nod to the Confederacy, no detriment in Alabama. His home county voted three-to-one for the GOP nominee whose rule breaking jelled nicely with rednecks looking for Robin Hood. Lomax's high-profile leadership of South Arising snagged more business clients than were lost. Recruiting was equally simple; sign anyone with discipline, extra credit given for a pickup sporting the South's battle flag. The FBI and hate group watchdogs tagged South Arising as anti-government and White supremacist — labels Lomax wore with pride.

As he and Baldwin talked into the night, they found harmony on the January 6th rally: Prepare and if a chance surfaces to reverse the election or, lacking that, inflame the nation, grab it. "If the saddle fits," Baldwin drawled, "tighten the cinch."

Already, militants had worked themselves into a frenzy, legitimized by the President's exhortation: "Be there. Will be wild." For some, those words meant a rally. But others saw them as an undefined but promising call to arms, perhaps a summons to revolution. One offering full justification to bring their weapons.

"He wants wild. Our duty is to get wild. Yes, Sir!" declared one post.

"Man up for the second shot heard round the world — or our Alamo," wrote a Texan.

"Fix the fraud or its bodies and blood. Your choice, Congress."

Lomax called that "the talk of the rabble."

"I will give you this: That rabble is going to be a powder keg, a fricking powder keg," he said. "Add our militias to the rabble, us stirring the proverbial pot and bam! The rabble gets mob fever, fricking mob fever."

"You're talking about ordinary folk, mostly, what you call the rabble," Baldwin said evenly. "They wouldn't like being called rabble, no more than I would. Don't forget, we need them to win."

Lomax took a new measure of Baldwin and decided to ignore the criticism. "Fine, just saying, we have to be ready to stir the pot, stir the pot."

" Do you agree the target is the Capitol and Congress?"

"Absolutely, absolutely. Not monuments like Lincoln or Washington. They're symbolic, just symbolic. Not taking over federal buildings no one gives a fuck about, not a solitary fuck about. Not the White House where we'd be grabbing our own guy's place, for Christ sake. Where, totally without doubt the Secret Service would shoot our balls off, literally shoot them off. That leaves the Capitol, the one thing the pinhead big militias got right tonight."

Lomax, on his feet, walked in circles, slapping his head with his right palm, excitement building. "So, the action starts at the rally, right, with the speeches, topped by our guy's, that is 'our' with a capital O. He's giving everyone a hard-on; a giant hard-on and they want action. They move off, up the hill to the Capitol, the Capitol. He's wrapping up about when the shit Congress, I mean total shit Congress, will be flushing, I mean totally flushing him, flushing the President of the United States of America. But those folks with giant hard-ons want more than another damn speech, even from our guy, or a selfie showing our guy. They came 'cause he got screwed and they want action," he hissed, waving finger quotation marks around "action." "Those people will be hell-bent determined on taking it to the Capitol, to the U.S. fucking Capitol. But here's the deal, the deal: If they don't walk up Constitution on their own, our job will be to lead them, as in leadership. As in get the Capitol surrounded. Then the crowd could turn into a mob, storm it, fucking storm it."

"What if they don't?"

"Then our job will be to create an out-of-control, freaking howling mob that will."

"Sounds like a plan," Baldwin said. "I can see the prez helping out for sure, giving folks a hard-on to march to the Capitol."

They talked on, working through a checklist of rebellion: When their men should join mutineers storming the Capitol. Whether to stow in backpacks or wear or carry guns, ammunition and grenades, bullet proof vests and other gear. Making reservations for hotel rooms, not only for their troops but also to cache handheld rockets and other munitions, and to use as staging areas for diversionary attacks or to join insurrectionists at the Capitol. Working out encrypted communications. Gearing up FCC and South Arising forces back home for days of attacks – against public officials and infrastructure, taking over radio and television stations, fomenting street riots – all crucial to broadening the revolution.

"So, I see this going down one of two ways," Lomax declared. "One, we shut down Congress for a while. Scare the shit out of enough of the other guys that they help throw electoral slates back to key states, key states. New slates are returned for the President. He gets another term. Huge, huge. Wouldn't that make your pecker stand up? There will be a lot of squawking, squawk, squawk, but who cares? Possession is nine-tenths of the law, right? Right? We have the votes on the highest court, right? With our guy in, he'd pardon us for storming the Capitol. We're home free. Heroes even.

"The other way things go down is us occupying the Capitol but the limp dicks in Congress, I'm talking the women, too, getting away. We'd get trapped for sure, at least a lot of us, as in fucking bear trapped. Not what we want, not, but it could happen. We wouldn't hold out long, maybe a few days, few days. Depend on how many good hostages we have, what we do with them. Mostly depend on how much time the feds give us before they say fuck it, just fuck it, and rush us. Lots of stuff beyond me, way beyond. But I do believe we wouldn't last long. They'd send their best, tons of them, tons of their best against us play soldiers. We'd be saved only if there was a ton of shit going on around the country, tons and more tons. In other words, a revolution, revolution with a capital R, huge R. Then, who knows?"

"Either way, either way," Baldwin said, turning away with a smile, "it turns on taking the Capitol. Capitol cops won't like that."

"True, but they may not take us serious enough. Us protesters are not Black Lives Matter or antifa, you know. Those cops see us as harmless old White guys, harmless White guys, and a lot of those cops voted for the President."

CHAPTER 3

The long-barreled .45-caliber Glock pressed through Eldon Weber's backpack to his spine. Probably more gun than I need, maybe kick more than I can handle, he thought, waiting patiently as rally speakers droned on.

He had yet to fire the Glock, bought on impulse as he left North Miami for the rally. Luckily, he held a concealed weapons permit that exempted him from Florida's waiting period when buying a second firearm. Weber got the permit for a stubby .32-caliber revolver. A small man, he felt more secure going armed when picking up cash from his many businesses.

Weber's urge to drive north to protest a stolen election had been building for weeks. Only this President, he sincerely believed, could block White replacement theory from becoming reality. A serious student of demographics, he constantly fretted over whether that time had already passed.

To avoid the magnetometer, he stayed just outside the rally grounds, not with scores or hundreds of other protesters but thousands, Weber guessed. Most, he bet, carried guns; had they wanted to be inside with the President, there was plenty of room.

No matter. He could catch enough of the speakers' familiar

complaints of election fraud and their challenges to step up for America. But with a difference from earlier rallies he had gone to: The speeches, especially the President's, conveyed urgency – January 6th was their last chance.

"I feel like a warrior," Weber said quietly as he turned toward the Capitol. "Kind of scared, actually, but ready to face what comes."

Talking to himself was nothing new. The sound of his voice, like his gun, somehow made him feel more secure, a buffer needed more than ever after two of his businesses had been torched. Single and without family, his little empire was everything to him, built over twenty years of grinding work. First came Web's Landscaping and Web's Car Wash, then four Web's Pizza Parlors, Web's Furniture Delivery, and finally two round-the-clock convenience stores – Web's 1 and Web's 2 – the stores that burned.

Weber liked seeing his name on his businesses, an affinity that may have drawn him to the President. But his politics had several moorings. One was having read Ayn Rand in college, and evermore holding with her views of laissez-faire capitalism and inviolate private property rights. Another was his late grandfather's influence. Having left Germany shortly after Hitler came to power, he was prone to declare, "That was one strong leader, just who the United States needs." Weber was heartened by social media scuttlebutt that the President shared his grandfather's view of Hitler – and disappointed at the lack of clear evidence.

Keeping the President in office would give the country a chance against its gravest threat – Whites losing majority status. Weber saw the flood of illegals crossing the southern border as nothing less than a plot by elitists to allow Black and Brown immigrants to seize political power, forever altering the nation's traditions and culture. His careful research left no doubt: Elitists, led by Jews, can count on the votes of coloreds and mulattoes to support socialist and liberal candidates. Once in office, those so-called progressives will expand welfare and gay marriage, install their henchmen in the Deep State and on the courts, and further open the borders, all at the expense of the White majority. That's why women of color willingly spread their legs to be impregnated by and to dilute the seed of White men.

"We're being fucked out of existence," he fumed, oblivious to the stares of those walking beside him.

For Weber, the high point of immigration restrictions came in the 1920s when Congress passed quotas effectively keeping everyone but Western and Northern Europeans out of the United States. The Immigration and Nationalization Act of 1965 knocked down that racist policy.

"Congress had it right the first time," he groused, startled when a woman wearing red, white and blue from hat to shoes got in his face: "Congress has never got anything right, you rambling dipshit!"

What touched Eldon Weber's ultra-conservative craw most personally was the welfare system. Wasting his tax dollars on food stamps and unemployment payments was bad enough. That immigrants, even legal ones, sucked up more than their share made welfare even worse. His strategy for recovering some of his money was to hire minorities at minimum wage. Then he had the head-spinning thought that it was self-defeating to hire people he didn't want in the country at all. Even part-time, of course, to avoid giving them costly benefits.

Most of those hires couldn't survive on a Weber job, needing second or even third incomes. When they complained, he'd cleverly warn: "The door you came in cost a lot of money. Don't let it hit you in the ass on your way out."

Not surprisingly, his businesses were grossly underinsured. When his convenience stores burned, he found himself financially strapped. An employee he had fired was the culprit, Weber was sure, but police couldn't make a case.

Marchers were splitting up, choosing the closer West Terrace or going on to the East Plaza to demand entry to the Capitol rotunda. When the red, white and blue-clad woman went straight, Weber veered toward the West Terrace, where inauguration construction was underway for him to happily help dismantle.

"Nice talking to you," he shouted at the woman's back.

Two off-duty patrolmen from western South Dakota, Thomas Lowell and Gary Evans, listened to their President only a few minutes before bailing out. They wore heavy work clothes – sans cop insignias – and had duly taken leave to protest on their own time. That fit the values of a small town where secrets lasted as long as cherry blossoms in a hard rain. Likewise, neither had dared join the Proud Boys or another militia.

Jogging away from the Capitol, Lowell spotted a pile of back-packs, then a second and a third. "Hey!" He caught Evans' eye. "What do you make of that? Isn't that fricking blatant."

Evans shook his head in disbelief. Small-town, true, but the cops had no doubt those backpacks concealed handguns, maybe easy-to-break-down rifles and shotguns, too. Maybe grenades or other explosives. Ammo for sure. Lots of ammo.

"Tell me the Park Police haven't noticed the backpacks or kept their dogs from sniffing," Evans said. "Like, they don't know? Give me a break."

They jogged west, reaching the Reflecting Pool and the "Stone of Hope," the Martin Luther King, Jr. Memorial, standing close by the four sprawling outdoor rooms honoring Franklin Delano Roosevelt. Special places for sure, but neither the narrative of King's enduring "I Have a Dream" speech nor FDR's adroit handling of extremist challenges, from the left and the right, intruded on the cops' sensibilities. They didn't know King had thundered his impromptu call for equality from the nearby Lincoln Memorial, didn't care that the red granite for FDR was mined in their home state of South Dakota.

They were focused on quickly retrieving their .357 magnums from the trunk of Evans' car. This was no day to go naked, for sure.

"Rather miss the speech than have some lowlife steal my piece 'cause it's in a pile of backpacks," Evans said as they headed toward Independence Avenue. At the Botanic Garden, Lowell recalled his congressional internship years earlier. To escape the hectic pace, lunchtime might find him with brownbag in hand in the domed garden's quiet cool.

Approaching the Capitol's west grounds, the cops were shocked at the porous security. The flimsy barricade of bicycle racks and wooden street barriers, not lashed together or anchored to anything stable, invited violation. The thin blue line was an apt description – a single strand of Capitol Police, most in street uniforms, manned the barriers. Evans and Lowell had envisioned row upon row of cops in riot gear, with shields, batons and gas masks. Backing them up would be Guard troops with fixed bayonets. Instead, the defenders were already dwarfed by energized marchers, more packing in each minute. Some gripped bottles or bricks. Others hefted flags on staffs easily converted to weapons, or protest signs nailed to club-ready two-by-fours, not the usual lightweight laths. Sharp-edged bulges creased too-tight overalls and down coats. Carrying, no doubt.

Protest chants and catcalls yielded to loud voices arguing about crossing the weak barricades, whether to ignore the yellow police tape flapping impotently in the light breeze.

"No, that would be illegal, totally illegal," lectured a bookish-looking woman wearing round gold-tone glasses.

Several in the thickening crowd came back with variations of "Screw legal." Three young men leaned in concert on the shaky barricade, retreating slightly when glaring officers pushed back.

"A matter of time, Thomas, a short time," Evans allowed with a smile. "When we want to make the Capitol our new home, it will be easy-peasy."

Mama Bones was a New Orleans witch doctor, her cramped quarters off Bourbon Street testament to barely making ends meet by reading fortunes, sticking pins in dolls and, yes, throwing bones. She was a caricature of her profession, tall and strong-featured, mixed race and of dark complexion, gray-streaked hair, ample body filling a flowing patterned dress. Mama's political streak had found attractive the dishonest politics of a man destined to be President. She always was ready to step out for him, happily, in full throat: "He absolutely would have made it big at a young age down in Louisiana."

She had loved the early morning Tweet from the Stop the Steal organizer: "First official day of the rebellion." With her President on the edge of being tossed from office, Mama Bones stood ready to carry the message of rebellion from the rally to the Capitol, to batter down its doors.

Now she roamed the crowd, entertaining, perhaps inspiring. "I have seen the promise of this day," she chanted. "It is ours to grasp."

"My little pins are lethal daggers if a certain VP fails his duty," she said with menace. "I have more than five hundred thirty-five voodoo pins, enough to puncture every scallywag in that bloated Congress."

"Prick those pricks," yelled a white-haired woman brandishing a "Grab My Pussy" sign.

Most important, Mama challenged all: "We must show courage. The cards are perfectly aligned, right down to the deuces. The rightful order of the Republic will be restored. Our children's heritage will be preserved. But we must show courage."

She strategically belted a clear plastic container on her rounded belly, seeded with a ten-dollar bill. She cajoled the protesters, shaking her tambourine, the bill soon joined by others. A lucrative following, noisy and rambunctious, dogged her when she broke from the rally, weaving her way east.

CHAPTER 4

Though slow leaving the rally, the Dancer brothers were confident of their men getting in place. The squads of three or four had not challenged the mags, small price for missing the speech. Instead, they casually walked streets feeding Constitution and Independence, joining a flow of marchers too large for the cops to control, let alone search. Jersey barriers tossed up to control traffic inadvertently gave those on foot a protective funnel. Protesters already had surrounded the historic edifice as the NPMers – weapons concealed in winter garb and backpacks – approached. Alexander's men filtered onto the Capitol's East Plaza, Ambrose's to the Capitol's West Terrace. There, his chief lieutenant in D.C., Willard Hart, checked in on a burner phone bought with cash.

The Harts and Dancers grew up as next door neighbors. When Max Dancer's long-haul truck dropped over a steep embankment one foggy night, Willard, already like a big brother, stepped up as surrogate father, too. He taught the brothers to fish and hunt, winter camping and kayaking. They went head-to-head for joyful hours on courts and fields, giving the Dancers an edge in high school sports Willard had dominated. And they talked, Willard struggling to express the wrongs foisted on his mom and dad, whose long-day labors too often failed to make ends meet. That fellow Reagan busted the unions, putting Michigan in the Rust Belt, Willard said. Little guys have a bleak future. They slip, then slip more, a decent living out of reach.

"Best I can figure," he allowed, "the system, it is totally busted."

After high school, he bounced from job to job until, searching for a better something, he joined the Army and put his bulk to good use in the Military Police. It was a way to live cheaply, what with the commissary and housing and health care paid. But the stripes he desperately wanted evaded him. Even as he served his country, his bitterness toward it grew.

Stranded at corporal, still years from a pension, he was posted at Fort Leavenworth in Kansas when he got a literal and figurative break. Arresting drunk soldiers in a bar, he and another MP went down in a thrashing pile, Willard busting a knee. A year of rehab didn't take, and he was quick to grab an honorable discharge with full disability. Returning home, Ambrose welcomed him with a supervisory job in his trash business. As often happens, Willard's knee eventually healed, and the pension kept coming. Shared concerns about the faltering nation drew him into the newly formed NPM.

"I'm in place, toward the Independence side," Willard said when Ambrose picked up. "I see four, no five of our guys but we haven't hooked up. My best fucking guess, they're all here."

"How long you been there?"

"A few minutes. I hung back to see if more security was coming, the fucking National Guard or whatever. Fuck me with surprise, but it hasn't happened. Saw a couple Metro cops ditch their cars and go in the Capitol. A couple skinny-ass suits running across Constitution Avenue. They could have been FBI or maybe suck-ass-impress-the-boss Senate staff."

"FBI's not gonna leave their lane," said Ambrose. "Likely kiss-ass staff. I'm with the last of the marchers. It could take me twenty minutes to get there, maybe more. What else do you see, Willie?"

Willard pushed out a stream of tobacco juice. "Not much really. A lot of damn hard-jawed people milling around, mad. I'm staying in the open best I can, away from the totally limp dick security line, so our guys will spot me. Better than wandering all over hell. I'll start calling them when we hang up. Now I'm seeing a few of the cops wearing damn helmets and stuff. Most still don't. Not much backup, either. I'm to hell and gone surprised, man. Like they expect a fucking walk in the park with a bunch of old White guys and cock sucking commander in chief groupies? When are they going to figure out shit's coming down?"

"Not until too late, I hope," said Ambrose, smiling at how Hart's years in the military had made profanity another part of speech. "Keep our guys spread out as you make contact. No need to attract attention. I'll huddle with all of you later."

One of Willard's men sidled up. "Keep our guys around here, but just in twos and threes," he told him. "I'll be back."

The trip had taken its toll. Willard needed to step away, even briefly, until Ambrose arrived. He walked to the huge bronze fountain designed by Frederic Auguste Bartholdi, the Italian of Statue of Liberty fame. Constructed to celebrate the U.S. centennial, the fountain's cold base settled his nerves, momentarily breaking the rapid-fire pace of the last few days. Turning on the television in his room that morning, rally news had again bombarded his senses – the tens of thousands gathering, warnings about violence, reports of extremist plans to block certification of a new president.

"You fricking vote stealers are the extremists," he had growled at the TV.

Three rallies the previous day had drawn huge, mostly peaceful, crowds. But several arrests, some on weapons charges, foreshadowed trouble. As did arrests away from the rallies. Park Police were filmed hustling to the protection of the Washington Monument, angry protesters on their heels and a struggling man in tow. Metro Police grabbed an apparent lone wolf, the trunk of his car loaded with guns and ammunition. Speculation swirled over pipe bombs found near Democratic and Republican headquarters, short blocks south of the Capitol. Were the bombs, disabled before they exploded, to kill and maim? Or were they decoys to draw security away from the Capitol when insurgents stormed it? Reporters' questions fueled the tension.

Red flags were everywhere, but top officials – federal and local – played down the threat of violence. Capitol Police can handle whatever comes, they insisted. No need for the National Guard, thank you. Totally fucking fine with me, Willard thought. All the better for us to probe for soft spots if things get wild. Still, why are the in-charge dipshits so complacent? Maybe it does come down to bias. We're whiter than milk. Purer than an unfucked virgin. We're the President's people. We love our country. We're not Black Lives Matter. We're not antifa buttholes. We're not defunding the cops. We love our cops, the right-thinking cops. What the elitist pricks don't get is we goddamn love our country more than they do, Willard told himself. We're the ones who know it is under siege. Know a fricking election was stolen.

Capitol Police numbered two thousand, he remembered from somewhere. Not all would be on duty. More law would be called in. No idea how many or how soon. Given this constipated town – where he once came for training – it will be too slow if hell breaks loose, he laid a mental wager.

But my time here is up, he told himself, heading back to the West Terrace, navigating the crowd. Spotting a few of his men but wanting a better feel for the protesters' mood, he slowly eased toward the barricades. Up close, they looked even more flimsy, defended by a line of cops that looked thinner still.

Most Capitol Police deserve respect, he'd grant. Willard was befriended by a couple of them while assigned to nearby Fort McNair years ago. He found them well-trained and ready to gamely defend their territory, which was nothing less than the heart of democracy. But it still was a job, unlike the protesters who don't have to be here, he thought. Few protesters had police-level training. Life was their training, many living on the edge, one paycheck from another eviction, a car repossessed, and financial collapse. Some lived on society's underbelly, misfits or outcasts, scarred by arrest records and convictions, or avoiding prison by learning to play games with psychiatrists.

Many relished giving a beating and knew how to take one. They were wound tight, primed to strike. Having bought into the President's grievances, they saw themselves his saviors.

A man whose shoulder muscles strained his hunting jacket quit shaking a bike rack. He stepped back in frustration, as if his only option was to club the cops. Willard slipped into the man's spot, and immediately felt the rabble's hunger for battle. On impulse, he pressed juice between his teeth, splattering a young officer's shoes. Staring straight ahead, the cop was unaware of the insult or ignored it. You rosy cheeked dingleberry, you fucking can't handle my people, Willard thought. Their anger, their not giving a rat's ass if they are hurt, you have not a pissant's clue. He read fear in the young man's eyes as more protesters crammed in, their taunts uglier, shaking the barricades more violently. Willard wanted to tell the cop, "Son, please take your sorry ass home to your girlfriend or your mother or your fricking cat. Whoever loves you. But just go home."

He sighed, spat again, this time without insult. Amid the building conflict, he surprised himself by thinking of the NPMers waiting at home. Had they a notion of what could come down, what they could soon be asked to do? How Revolution 2.0 could rest with them? Needing to hook up with his men, he pushed away from the barricade, through the packed bodies, their energy permeating him. It morphed, not smoothly like forms change in movies, but unpredictably. Jagged. Terrifying, but fertile. These folks are on the fucking edge, Willard thought. The boys waiting at home best be ready.

CHAPTER 5

In the days leading up to the rally, NPM squads had fanned out in search of other patriots, their mission to learn if the major militias were ready to lead an insurrection. The Dancer brothers saw storming the Capitol as the starter, national revolution the critical endgame.

Their men hung out with Proud Boys at Hotel Harrington. They found bars – an Irish joint near Union Station, a dive bar on Pennsylvania Avenue, east of the Capitol – where protesters drank. They found Oath Keepers partying in Rosslyn, across the Potomac. Suds loosened tongues. But the NPM squads found no plan beyond disrupting the historically pro forma Electoral College vote. Big-time disruption for sure, with talk of quick reaction forces standing by to turn Washington into a war zone. Munitions stockpiled at area hotels. Plots to spawn riots downtown and fear-inducing violence in the suburbs.

But talk and stockpiling did not a plan make. No coordinated strategy for taking and holding the Capitol was found, only a rampage riding the coattails of rank-and-file insurgents. No indication the self-styled revolutionary leaders would climb from their silos. They remained mired in protecting turf and in their sorry internal conflicts, as they had been in Richmond. Crucially, there was no talk of spreading rebellion across the land. Sure, the rally's timing was bad. Proud Boys was in disarray after its leader got arrested on charges stemming from a Black Lives Matter protest. The Oath Keepers, reputably the most dangerous militia, had debilitating internal conflicts. The Three Percenters were not seen as a serious player, their very name – embracing the falsehood of only a few colonists backing the American Revolution – being ludicrous. Groups carrying explicit banners of hate – neo-Nazi, anti-Israel, anti-Muslim, anti-gender writ large, radical Christian, whatever – were not only too small but hampered by ideological baggage.

But for the Dancer brothers, that disarray only meant the tired old militias were failing to seize a rare opportunity. That disarray did not temper the revolutionary spirit of the President's followers. Polls confirmed their fealty and his grip on the Republican Party. Millions of them justified using violence to right a perceived wrong, to save the democracy they knew. The explosives had been set, awaiting a spark. If the big militias were incapable, NPM could be that spark.

The Michigan chapter's tendrils reached Wisconsin, Ohio, Indiana and Illinois. Alexander's South Carolina branch was in Virginia, West Virginia, North Carolina and dipped into Kentucky, Tennessee and Georgia. In all those states, unlike the Northeast and West Coast, a lot of people had their heads screwed on straight. A good start for rebellion.

Weeks earlier, the brothers alerted their own faithful: Get ready for revolution. January 6th may not bring it but be ready. Gather weapons and ammunition. Quietly talk with people you think will stand up. Gauge their loyalty to the President. If D.C. explodes, be ready; the window of rebellion will not be open long. The establishment cannot let stand the dangerous optic of an uncouth rabble holding the Capitol, of defiance never seen since the Civil War, on a scale to inspire others, a nation. Would the window last a day? Maybe. Maybe more if hostages, the right hostages, were taken. Even when the Capitol could no longer be held, a far rosier picture may unfold in the hinterlands. Festering resentment may be impossible to contain. But that resentment must be nurtured, sustained. Counties and cities seized. New governments installed. Patriots must foment disruption, challenge federal, state and local officials in more places than the bastards can handle. If you hunker down, fortify. Stockpile provisions, fuel for cooking and heating, water and food, of course. Enough to weather a siege lasting as long as there's hope.

If the President's followers go on a senseless rampage in the Capitol, with no chance of success, we may slip away, desert them. But given the chance to take the Capitol, a realistic chance for revolution, we will take it and you must be ready.

Such was the late-night talk of the Dancer brothers and lieutenants like Willard Hart. How a revolution might unfold defies analysis. It was impossible to know what the President's loyalists would do or how the public would react – in support or rejection. The brothers could only have their militias ready, then make a judgment: That the loyalists would ignite rebellion, and the President would urge them on. That he had the stomach to roll the dice.

Ambrose carried a worn 1876 centennial half-dollar, a fifty-dollar impulse buy in a Detroit pawn shop. He liked that it was minted in Philadelphia – America's first capital, a city dripping in revolutionary courage. Over the years, he flipped the coin of Seated Liberty at times of indecision and let the lady's call set his course. Good an answer as any, he figured.

Alone in his room one night, noodling scenarios for how January 6th might go down, he wondered if the President had the balls to go to the mat in his bid for power, whether he truly believed his politics of grievance would hold sway.

"Time for Lady Liberty," he said aloud. He flipped the coin, calling tails. It landed on the bed. Tails.

"And how about regular folks?" He flipped, again winning with tails.

"Ya gotta believe," he said, crawling into bed.

Ambrose didn't need a coin toss to believe in the NPM; it would not fail him, he was certain. Well before the election – as he sniffed opportunity – he stepped up recruiting. As always, he insisted on carefully weighing the commitment of those prospects, National Guardsmen a top priority. If revolution came, the Guard would be called on to smother it in every state. Infiltrating those units carried huge potential. He was encouraged as NPM numbers edged up, but it was a slog.

Even so, he did not see those efforts as paramount, and Alexander had agreed. Not paramount either, was holding the Capitol indefinitely; to the contrary, leading that assault nearly guaranteed an early retirement – being captured or killed. What mattered was that storming the Capitol ignite a spark. A simple spark that brought out not only militias but the millions who had voted to preserve democracy and now felt cheated. The right spark would transform militia groups into a multiplier, amassing a flood of rebels, champions of a righteous cause.

At First St. N.W., Ambrose branched off Constitution in search of his men on the Capitol's West Terrace. Had he been looking, he would have noticed a young Swamp White Oak, planted to honor the nearly three thousand killed in the terrorist attacks of 9/11.

But he was on the phone with former Army corporal Sydney Armor, who he left in charge at home. She was driving with another NPMer in southwest Michigan, where she grew up. After graduating high school, she joined the Army. Assigned to a supply unit, her attention to detail made her a rising star, on the fast track to warrant officer until a private blew her in for harassment.

"I have no clue why Corporal Armor thinks I'm gay," the private told investigators. "When she put a move on me in her cubby-hole office, I fought back. She got pissed and shoved me. That's when I fell and hit my arm on her desk going down. It busted in two places."

In earlier times, Armor might have survived injuring another soldier. But with the military under political pressure to not tolerate sexual abuse, she was sunk. Luckily her enlistment was ending. She was allowed to walk, dodging a dishonorable discharge.

She went to Los Angeles, moved in with a cousin and joined the LAPD. Her bad judgment brought her down there, too. As much a neat-freak as detail-obsessed, Armor detested the large homeless population for living in filthy conditions. Answering a complaint when tents popped up in an urban park, she missed, or more likely ignored, the mental state of a young man who threw feces at her and beat him unconscious. On probation, she was ordered to take an anger management course, but was embroiled in another controversy before her first class. Carrying more baggage than the department deemed she was worth, Armor was gone. Back in Michigan, she snagged a job with a landscaper, feeding tree branches into a chipper. Over drinks with a friend, she complained of being treated unfairly – specious charges, superiors deserting her, tax money spent on homeless shits. Her drinking buddy happened to be in the NPM. He massaged her anger and intro-duced her to Ambrose, who quickly recognized her organizing talents.

"Hey Syd, how's everything?"

"Slower than I'd like. Out here, the rally looks like another one of those Washington deals, all bullshit talk."

"Let me tell you, I just got to the Capitol and this crowd's pretty hot, lots of shouting, some shoving. People really worked up. We'll see. If nothing happens soon, it could end up BS."

"Whatever. The good news is our guys are talkin' to a lot of friends and neighbors. We're askin' 'em like you said to, 'If Congress don't approve a new president and our President needs some help, would you be there for him?' And then, 'What if all hell breaks loose in Washington, do you think we should raise hell out here too, to keep the President in office?' Pretty much everyone we ask is ready to go if things like that happen."

"Good, as much as we can hope for right now," Ambrose said. "What else?"

"Quite a bit coming together. Mike, our guy down at the Guard, he says he asked one of the sergeants about flippin' the Guard and got an affirmative. Mike said the sergeant said, 'We get rid of the top weenies and most of this post will step up.' Mike and the sergeant are workin' on how to kill the weenies."

"Tell Mike beers are on me. What else?"

"Well, our guy Jake has this crazed buddy, not one of us, who's been stalkin' the Democrat governor. The crazy says he knows the gov's movements and can get in sniper range, get her when she leaves the mansion some mornin'."

"Wow. That would send shit flying."

"Indeed it would. And, I think we have pretty good plans for takin' over radio stations in Scranton and Toledo. Those are the only places I've found so far where we have guys who can run a station, but I'm still lookin'."

"Scranton. Right where the president-elect grew up. That I like."

"Indeed. And we're workin' on snatchin' two or three engineers at other TV stations, too, force 'em to put our guys on the air. Nothin' solid yet."

"That's good, but you're getting ahead of me. What would we say on the air? How about coming up with some scenarios and writing some scripts? Maybe that retired PR guy who had his own firm would help. I think he has a consulting gig with the NRA now."

"Yes. I'll talk to him." Then, "Like you told me, I've talked with our vets who did demolition in the Army and two of them work for power companies now, in Ann Arbor and Madison. They're scoutin' the electrical stations, substations, whatever. Hopefully, I'll hear tonight about putting those lib cesspools in the dark."

"That would be sweet. Has any of this slipped out, like someone getting drunk and running their mouth?"

"Far as I know, that is a negative."

"And how are you doing on blowing up a couple reservoirs or putting our boys with drones to work?"

"Still workin' on it."

"How about contaminating the food supply?"

"Still workin' on it. One of our guys, woman actually, drives a food tanker, an eighteen-wheeler. It would be easy for her to poison a load of flour headin' to a cookie factory or whatever. But I'm not sure we want to. Knock out electricity, we say it disrupts the government. Unhappy people will buy that, even if they lose their lights. But contaminatin' food, there's no way to control who gets sick. Old people, kids. Hospitals get swamped. Hard to tie that to disruptin' government. It could look bad."

"You're probably right…Syd, something may be happening, and I see Too Cool and Al. I need to catch them. Quickly, how are you doing on guns, explosives?"

"Explosives, so-so. We've been buyin' dynamite all legal like. And we got a couple boxes when we hit that place that blows up tree stumps, just down the road from you."

"Damn, I know Spiro, sort of a friend. Okay, glad to have it, but don't stash it at my place."

Armor paused. "I'll get it moved right away. Ah, guns, doin' really good. Our guy who works at that gun shop in Kalamazoo managed to shut off the burglar alarm when he and the owner locked up. We cleaned the place out – AKs, large magazines, you name it. Filled the fuckin' van four times. Good thing the shop is really out-of-the-way, or a damn cop would have come by for sure. Too bad I had pretty much drained the bank account makin' buys, legal or not. Anyway, any true believer who needs a piece only has to ask."

CHAPTER 6

Valerie Wells was a Proud Boys queen, a political junkie, and the way things were going, Proud Boys' politics suited her just fine. Call it neo-Nazi if you must, but order was needed. If that meant bashing heads, so be it. As for the boys being misogynistic, they still liked sex. Which suited Valerie just fine.

She and her friend Mildred Fiddle also believed in the core theory of QAnon – how a cabal of satanic child abusers were conspiring against the President. They anxiously awaited "the Storm," when the administration would arrest and execute thousands of the pedophiles, maybe on television.

In most ways, Valerie and Mildred typified followers of the global political movement created by the anonymous Q. The women were conservatives attuned to right-wing media, fearful about the future, and okay with using violence to preserve America's true identity. Education for most followers of Q stopped at high school, but Valerie and Mildred were computer science graduates of the University of Texas.

Because they loved the President and regularly serviced Proud Boys, they knew where they had to be on January 6th. They took vacation from their IT jobs and drove Mildred's car from Austin to D.C.

A Washington Post story tipped them to Proud Boys hanging at Hotel Harrington, near the White House. At Harry's Bar, Valerie and Mildred settled into empty stools by a thirty-something dude who called himself The Baron. He wore a Proud Boys cap and tee-shirt. The women had no doubt he was the real deal, the way he went on about "kicking socialist ass" and "cleaning out the Deep State and draining the swamp."

The Baron was rooming at the hotel with three friends. When they had been serviced, two of them twice, Valerie declared the trip a success, with the rally yet to come. Mildred, in another room, had only two roommates.

The next day the women heard just the first minutes of the President's speech. When several Proud Boys headed for the Capitol, Valerie and Mildred tagged along to the East Plaza to harass the police. As protesters piled in behind them, the women lost track of the Proud Boys. They grew anxious, finding themselves caught too deeply in the crowd. They saw bottles fly and shatter on the expansive marble walkway that covered the underground Visitor Center. Security-driven, it was built after 9/11, forever changing easy public access to the history and traditions and elegance housed beneath the white dome.

"We need to get the hell out of here," Mildred shouted, pushing against the tide of bodies.

"Okay," Valerie shouted back. "Let's find us some Proud Boys."

Laurence Spindale's friend Hasty had been kicked out of the Proud Boys for being too violent. By then, the two had enjoyed the militia life for a couple of years, going to PB rallies but mostly knocking heads at left-wing demonstrations. When called to disrupt an antifa protest in downtown Portland, Hasty was into day two of a drunk. He sucked down more beers on the hour-long drive north. "Commie bastard," he kept yelling at a menacing young man in black who hefted a baseball bat. Hasty jerked the bat from the man's hands and swung with abandon. Four antifa went down before Proud Boys pulled him off. So uncontrolled was his attack that group leaders who routinely ordered violence as a tactic were badly shaken, feeling lucky no one was killed.

Spindale opted to leave the Proud Boys with his friend. He liked the militia's anti-government message, but he wasn't a joiner, anyway. He mostly preferred keeping his own company and was a true son of the Pacific Northwest. Loved the rain. Loved living in hardly more than a shack on the wooded acreage his parents left him. And he had made good money as a logger until work got scarce. In Spindale's embittered view, the damn bureaucrats, federal and state, had already started caving to the tree huggers when his chain saw dropped a Douglas fir at a bad angle. Bouncing off the hillside, the tree kicked back over its own stump, shattering his elbow. Now almost fifty, he made do, cash jobs and hunting and fishing stretching his disability check. Getting welfare while hating government never struck him as a contradiction, even as the elbow pretty much healed.

Unlike Hasty, Spindale had always filed taxes, cheating of course, to avoid attention from the hated IRS. He had licenses to drive, to hunt and fish. His Harley was registered and tagged. Not Hasty. He had no licenses and never filed taxes. Out of nowhere, it seemed, he dropped into Marge's Bar, a wide-spot roadhouse a nice walk from Spindale's shack. The men bonded over beers and whiskey chasers, and Hasty soon moved into the shack. Living rent free, he squeaked by on odd jobs and living off the land. In the fall, he slipped away to remote south- or west-facing ravines to harvest coveted golden chanterelle mushrooms and was briefly flush with cash.

A few years younger than Spindale, Hasty was as mean as he was large, raised poor in a West Virginia mining town. His father and grandfather moonshined to stay above ground. They came to see getting busted and doing time as part of the life cycle. Hasty, then, came by his hatred of revenuers – that is, the government – honestly, giving it no real thought. What he did think seriously about was staying invisible. By age sixteen, his mother long dead, his father was pressuring him to get a driver's license and run moonshine. Hasty found no logic in getting licensed to break the law but did see a problem. If he got a license, the government would have his real name and he couldn't be invisible.

By then Hasty was done with taking the beatings his father enjoyed handing out after over sampling too much shine. One night his father was snoring off a fall-down drunk. Hasty poured high-proof moonshine in the old man's high-top shoes, struck a match and ran to the howls of a world-class hotfoot. Sticking out his thumb got him to Interstate 64, where a long-haul trucker got him to Idaho.

For years, Hasty roamed the state, working when he could without identification. He stumbled across survivalists in the northern bootleg who taught him to trap, without a license of course. He liked the solitude of trapping, not from being anti-social but because trouble found him if he stayed in town for long. After several beers with chasers, his mean streak demanded a brawl. Or he tempted arrest by buying a pickup truck or motorcycle cheap and not getting it registered or tagged. Hauled to jail, he simply refused to give up any information – except the name Hasty. Not an address, not his age, nothing. Eventually, law enforcement around Idaho gathered several mug shots and sets of worthless fingerprints. Only if Hasty did a major crime – robbing a bank or murdering one of the luckless women he hooked up with now and again – would the fingerprints be helpful. Usually, a frustrated sheriff tired of feeding Hasty after a few days and kicked him loose. A couple times a judge held him in contempt, locking him up for a month. Then he'd be free, still the invisible man.

But Idaho winters caught up, tormenting him with arthritis from trapping in frigid waters, living in drafty shacks and tents. Worse, the Legislature decreed that trappers trap responsibly. "Whatever that means," Hasty said with ridicule. "Fuck me if dead critters need carin'." Getting "certified" as a responsible trapper was one too many turns of the government screw. He stuck out a now bulbous thumb and landed in Marge's Bar. When Spindale asked his name, he said,

"Hasty, which I mostly ain't." Years later, Spindale had learned little more.

One thing about the Proud Boys was beyond denial: They gained respectability from none other than the President of the United States during a nationally televised debate: "Proud Boys – stand back and stand by." Immediately, Spindale and Hasty felt a link not just to respectability but power. Now each had a foot in the political mainstream. Hasty almost gave up being invisible in order to vote.

Also beyond denial: Early on election night the President led in enough states to win easily. When the numbers went south, pundits claimed it took a while after polls closed to count absentee votes. Spindale saw no sense in delaying that count until polls closed and was more than curious about the President losing by slim margins in those states. Can't be right. Devious forces must be at work. Spindale knows this stuff, Hasty believed. And he heard questions raised about voting machines being controlled. Questions but no answers. So damn right, the President's win – hell, landslide – was stolen. When he invited them to his rally on January 6th, promising it would be "wild," the former Proud Boys didn't hesitate.

Spindale had enough money for the trip if they slept in his pickup. In D.C., they met protesters who warned that their guns could be taken if they went to the rally. They passed, having been to one of his rallies and really wanting their guns. January 5th was spent riding the Metro, figuring out the time to Capitol South from a Blue Line stop in a gritty neighborhood where Spindale parked his pickup. On January 6th, they wore lined overalls against the cold – bulky enough to conceal their handguns and small tasers. Metro security dogs were their biggest worry.

The commander in chief's speech was heating up when Spindale and Hasty rolled into Capitol South. More riders emptied cars than security could handle, and the only dog they saw was busily sniffing far down the platform. Getting in step with other protesters, they soon reached the East Plaza.

Spindale stared up at the white dome gleaming in the sunlight, topped by the bronze Statue of Freedom. He turned right, looking east at the Supreme Court building. Those damn judges are walking – no sitting, he smiled at his joke – disasters, but he'd heard the President got some good ones approved. He looked back at the dome, unaware of the inscription in its cast-iron pedestal, E Pluribus Unum – Out of Many, One. He gave no thought to how his weapons, to say nothing of his eagerness to use them, starkly contrasted with Freedom's unifying message. Spindale did see the statue wore a helmet, had a shield and a sheathed sword. Then he saw that Freedom – a female figure with flowing hair, clad in a long dress – was a woman.

"Damn it all, but that statue ought to be a man!"

"Come on, come on," Hasty demanded. "Let's get up front. I don't want to miss nothing."

Anthony Larkin Jr. spotted Hasty – his bulk and a beard uncut for months hard to miss – forcing his way through the crowd, a tall wiry man in tow. Anthony – not Tony, if you please – Larkin Jr. was a devotee of the President and, yes, a protester. But in this crowd, he felt out of place: College educated. Verb conjugation not a problem. Profanity not required. Soft hands. Clean shaven.

He looked at the protesters surrounding him, women as well as men, and saw a hard – or was it just rough – edge he wasn't used to. They're mostly blue-collar, good people I seldom mix with unless the plumbing breaks or my car won't run, he reasoned. On average, a generation older, faces carrying experiences I haven't had. He saw well-worn clothes, some greasy or bloodstained. Like they'd been skinning a deer or didn't have time to go to the laundromat before coming East. Anthony Larkin Jr. wore new olive-green overalls and matching field jacket, wool cap with earmuffs wrapping his round face, bulky gloves, heavy lace-up boots. He had paid L.L. Bean more than eight hundred dollars, and now he was threatening to perspire, truth be told.

Wondering if he had gone a smidge overboard, he told himself the investment would prove to be shrewd, for today and an anticipated move. Growing up in Orange County, his Southern California closet hadn't met this need. A degree in religion from UCLA and a year-long internship in his conservative congressman's local office had set him up as a teaching assistant at Liberty University in Lynchburg, Virginia.

At that bastion of Christian thinking – "50 Years of Blessings" graces Liberty's website – he also applied for the strategic communications doctoral program. How better to burnish his religion and political credentials than with a deep dive into mainstream media? And where better to do dissertation research on the irresponsible press than at a rally generating enough energy to rescue the President's unjustly denied re-election?

Anthony Larkin Jr. had followed with dismay media coverage of the campaign and, in its aftermath, dreadfully unfair denials by courts and election officials of ballot box corruption. The "lamestream" media could have exposed those wrongful outcomes. Fox and others tried, but too much of the press was not on – or in – the right. He was determined to write a dissertation that would pour a new foundation for future political reporting.

Sure, Anthony Larkin Jr. admitted, a few in the President's camp had gone a tad far. Like what's his name, the conspiracy guy who said the President's opponent "will be removed one way or another." Or the Oath Keepers' leader who told his troops: "I need you fighting fit by inauguration."

But more often, news got so, so distorted. Interpreted the wrong way. Like the Three Percenters' statement on voter fraud: "We stand ready and are standing by to answer the call from our President should the need arise that We The People are needed to take back our country from the pure evil that is conspiring to steal our country away from the American people...We will not act unless we are told to."

Flatulent verbiage to be sure, but really, Anthony Larkin Jr. asked himself, what is really wrong about backing the President?

Or another Oath Keeper on social media: "It's gonna be wild!!!!!!!!

He wants us to make it WILD ... He called us all to the Capitol and wants us to make it wild!!!! Sir Yes Sir!!!

Or the President telling his new Defense secretary to "do whatever was necessary to protect the demonstrators."

Really, what is wrong with standing by your President? He is the commander in chief, after all, Anthony Larkin Jr. reflected. Wild is not violent. Wild can be fun. What's wrong with a wild old time? What's wrong with following the Boy Scout motto and being prepared to protect demonstrators? Demonstrating is a constitutional right, for sure.

But no, no, no. Most reporters distorted things. Already, they had turned a few arrests into a harbinger of Congress under siege. Thousands of patriotic Americans pouring into Washington dishonestly portrayed as threats to democracy. Sensationalist reporters quoting Deep State officials warning, without evidence, of "a right-wing coup" in the making.

Anthony Larkin Jr. saw no reason, not one iota, to believe coverage of the rally would be any better. But he was determined to chronicle a different story, the true story. He would show patriots standing firmly in the breach, defending liberty and the American way.

It would not be easy. There was this chaotic crowd, terribly hard to navigate. Already he was stressed about removing his gloves in the cold to take notes. An awful prospect. He was game to try, but shouldn't need to, at least not much, having invested in a voice-activated recorder. And his phone had video. He could just imagine the President's loyalists – his fellow loyalists – queueing up to keep the record straight. Honest interviews a long while coming.

Suddenly, there was turmoil, a motion that unsettled him. Then a shrill yell from near the barricades: "You fucking cops are nothing but a bunch of fucking traitors!" Followed by a man with a bullhorn voice: "Stop the steal! Stop the steal!" The shaking of bicycle racks. The bullhorn voice again: "Hey VP, stop the count! Stop the count!"

"Hey VP, stop the count!" the crowd howled. "Hey VP, stop the count!"

Anthony Larkin Jr. saw a bottle fly from the crowd and shatter near the police line. "Oh my!" he said softly. "Oh my!"

He hit speed dial. "Oh Jack, I so wanted to share this with you. It is a bit scary, but there is so much energy here, positive energy, so much power to make things right." He listened. "Yes. You are the adventuresome one. You would love it here." He listened again. "I miss you, too, but I'm fine," he said bravely. "Ready to do my thing."

Another bottle flew, then another that landed inside the police line with a small explosion. Anthony Larkin Jr. saw rising wisps of smoke and his eyes widened. Taunts grew harsher, fiercer, chants more strident. The crowd surged and Anthony Larkin Jr. felt himself squeezed, bound by the crush around him. "Jack, hon, you there? Good, good, LA's a good place to be."

More bottles flew. A woman screamed in pain. The crush tightened. Claustrophobia threatened Anthony Larkin Jr. but he marveled at how accepting everyone else seemed, almost serene. Pressed shoulder-to-shoulder, belly to back and fine with that, just folks forming up to make a constitutionally protected statement. But Anthony Larkin Jr. struggled not to panic. "Jack, whatever happens, I love you."

From the top steps of the Capitol on the House side – popular for photo shoots, like one of new Republicans elected on the Contract with America in 1994 – Darrell Steele's panoramic view captured the agitated crowd. It was growing rapidly, soon to fill the East Plaza. Private First Class Steele could recall when that wide space was a parking lot for lawmakers and staff, even reporters. Big-eyed visitors from Joplin or Peoria wandered across it, passes in hand from their congressman's office, bound for Senate or House galleries to watch democracy in action.

Steele had been no less enthralled as a high school junior, but with the advantage of having impressed his Virginia congressman and snagging a coveted House page slot. That experience stuck and, after flunking out of college, he joined the Capitol Police. Years passed. He saw a lot of history made – legislation of course, national icons lying in state in the domed rotunda, the deaths of colleagues John Gibson and Jacob Chestnut by a delusional shooter in 1998. Most fun were the scandals, the sexual dalliances that doomed the House page program, career-ending revelations that destroyed powerful lawmakers.

An entertaining career, to be sure, but frustrating as a well-deserved promotion to corporal – no big deal – was denied repeatedly. His talents ignored; teeth-grinding disappointments piled up. Private First Class forever, the lowest rank.

Steele's politics veered right, maybe to be contrary to his liberal city and many of his colleagues. Not only did he vote for the brash newcomer in the last two presidential elections, but he also dumped money he couldn't afford into those campaigns – albeit in his wife's name. He embraced tough border enforcement as he saw immigrants drain off the wealth – and promotions – of real Americans. Holding other nations' financial feet to the fire – from NATO to the UN – was long overdue. So was greater isolation, from pulling out of treaties to calling the crock of climate change exactly that – a crock. Most of all, Steele reveled in the President's right-on attacks against the Deep State. Those bureaucratic conspirators – unelected muckety-mucks – ruled with regulations and the twin threats of the federal hammer or inertia, whatever worked in the moment. Steele was convinced the Deep State was a collective gatekeeper admitting few and controlling many. It was frightfully real, right down to his own USCP. He counted himself among the embittered many, not the elite few.

Accumulated bitterness made him opaque to his own shortcomings. Over the years, pounds slowly piled on, threatening diabetes. He failed physical tests but, with retirement near, Steele's superiors winked and signed off. Far from grateful, he took their blind eye as his due, even when his own bad investments delayed retirement, and they kept winking. Now, finally, he needed only three paydays to hang it up.

He watched the teeming crowd with delight. Pumping signs punctuated the throng. "Thou Shall Not Steal – Votes." "Give Us Back Our

President." "Death to Traitors." Chants rang out, "Stop the steal" competing with "Stop the count." Enterprising protesters had hauled in lumber to build a scaffold. From the crossbar, a hangman's noose dangled. What the hell is that about? wondered the chubby officer. A banner hammered in place answered him: "Veep – Do Your Job or Die." He smiled as a young man, muscular arms fully tattooed, adjusted the noose around a white-wigged manikin dressed in suit and tie.

With fascination, Steele watched the unruly find their comfort levels – fist-waving renegades threatening his colleagues, nose-to-nose, more mob-like with each minute; a large bloc holding the middle ground, firing themselves up to join the assault should the blue line fold; the less bold seeking refuge on the Plaza's far side, across the street from the Supreme Court. The cops were getting pelted with more and varied flak – bottles and cans and phones, nails and bolts and fruit and whatever protesters could angrily dig from their pockets. Steele was glad to be on the top steps.

Watching the treasonous conflict unfold, he found himself cheering the crowd on. He wanted to throw something – his badge? – at his colleagues. He wanted to join the chants, wanted a sign to pump. Wanted to be the protesters' inside man, urge them up the steps. Wanted to be their cheerleader, hug them, hold open the door just behind him. He knew he could not, not yet. The ubiquitous security cameras would tattle. And Steele knew that few – none? – of the handful of other officers near him were with him. He had to wait until his colleagues scattered in fear before opening the doors. Before ushering in the righteous crowd. He had to wait until today's work of Congress was in shambles. Wait until the disgraceful rubber stamp of the Electoral College was blotted out.

Knowing all that made it hard to just stand there, to not encourage the crowd. Steele forced himself to wait, to be patient until the barricades fell. Wait for the President's backers to make a heroic charge up the steps. For the virtuous to reach him and he could spread his arms and say, "Welcome to your house. Come on in. Make yourself at home."

A spy had infiltrated the near-riotous throng on the West Terrace. She squatted on the lip of the Bartholdi fountain in a relatively open area, not thirty feet from the NPM's Willard Hart. Like many in the crowd, Amy Bondarenko, a petite brunette of twenty-five who seldom wasn't carded, was taking photos of the escalating conflict. But when the objectors pushed forward or a champion for violence stepped up, she switched to video and audio. Once the moment passed – as several had – Bondarenko emailed the recording to her personal computer across the Potomac, in her modest Rosslyn apartment.

She wore cargo pants and a military field jacket – the smallest she could find. Four more phones were tucked into various pockets, should someone grab the one she held. She wore a red cap shamelessly declaring Make America Great Again. No newcomer to clashes between left-wing protesters and far-right extremists, Bondarenko traveled armed, ready to dig into other pockets for pepper spray and a collapsible baton.

A blurred face suddenly filled her lens, and Bondarenko lowered her phone to confront an old man.

"What you doing?"

"Taking photographs as you can see, sir."

He was unshaven, face lined and darkly tanned, and he cocked his head skeptically beneath a frayed stocking cap. He leaned on a walking stick and Bondarenko saw he was shivering under a soiled brown parka.

"Are you all right, sir? It's cold today."

"Don't you fuss with me, girl. I'm here from Nevada with the Oath Keepers," the old man said, tapping a patch sewn poorly on his coat. "Been a member since near the beginning, and I don't think you're one of us."

"You're right. I'm not an Oath Keeper."

"No, I mean not one of us at all. FBI, fake news, what are you?"

"Don't you see my hat, sir?"

"Anybody can buy a hat. Most folks here just shoot pictures. I see you talking and doing some other stuff on your phone, more than most people," he snarled, leaning closer, his aged breath repulsive. "You're up to something and you need to leave."

She hopped from the fountain, reaching for her pepper spray.

"I saw that, girl. Police know threats, even retired."

"I'm going to walk away, sir. You stay away from me."

She moved toward the Capitol, unsettled that her actions could be so obvious. Never directly challenged before, she shuddered and felt she needed to photograph him. Doubt he can be identified from when he stuck his face in my camera, she thought. She glanced back and saw he was in profile, looking away. Not wanting to be caught aiming her camera at him, she set it at a wide angle. Putting him at the viewfinder's right edge, she shot, shot again as he turned toward her. He glared and Bondarenko retreated, then sought a vantage point closer to the growing bedlam near the inauguration scaffolding.

Though she worked for the Department of Homeland Security, her presence at the Capitol was anything but official, as circuitous as her path to DHS. A journalism major at Virginia Tech's Blacksburg campus, her studies took a visceral turn in 2014 when Russia's Putin seized Crimea in her ancestral Ukraine. Suddenly, journalism looked pale. She wanted the front line, a diplomatic posting, and switched to national security and foreign affairs majors.

The outcome of the 2016 presidential race alarmed her. Not only did the new President cater to Putin, he clearly hungered to be an autocrat. Or more. Bondarenko, camera talents already honed, went on a mission. She tracked the President's rallies, traveling as far as she could afford to photograph and video the far-right's extremism, its threat to democracy. She bought MAGA caps and chanted along with the cult. Disgusting, but spies must blend in, right?

With their President in the White House, extremist groups grew more brazen, more dangerous in Bondarenko's mind. She grew more circumspect, playing the spy from the sidelines – usually as a tourist, innocently in town. She went to the "Unite the Right" rally in Charlottesville and was totally pissed at being in a port-a-potty when a crazy ploughed his car into counter demonstrators. Heather Heyer died just feet from where Bondarenko had been standing.

That was shortly after DHS hired her as a junior analyst of domestic terrorism – clearly not a department priority. After 9/11, international terrorism, particularly radical Muslims, was the focus of every U.S. intelligence agency. When Homeland Security was created, it fell in line. Then came the ugly drumbeat of domestic attacks – terrorist, racist, antisemitic; pick your hate crime of choice. Attacks in churches and synagogues, night clubs and community colleges, from Florida and the Carolinas to Kansas City and Oregon. Congress was forced to grudgingly demand scrutiny of homegrown terrorists. That created a few new jobs. Competition for them was not great, with salaries set low as possible. Bondarenko got hired, shoe-horned into a tiny workspace, working for a political hack whose interest in her work stemmed solely from lust. She played him along, using DHS to enable her personal mission and to shape a resume worthy of a State Department job.

She became an expert in probing the ominous, sometimes illegal, postings on the dark web. Patiently, she created false identities and infiltrated extremist groups online.

After months she finally was communicating with extremists spanning the political spectrum. Some were Muslim, but domestic hate groups dominated – White supremacist and neo-Nazi or others targeting Jews and Muslims, gays and government. She crawled into sites offering weapons and blatantly illegal malware and money laundering. With disgust, she too often found dark web connections to child porn and trafficking. She sent her findings in dull bureaucratese concealing her liberal bent. Nearly all the red flags Bondarenko raised were ignored, predictably, given the administration. Raised in a politically astute D.C. family, she accepted the futility of changing anything from her bottom-rung position. But she was heartened as federal agencies, including the FBI and her own DHS, slowly acknowledged the frightening rise of hate groups and stepped up investigating them.

More threatening to her job were the connections she found

between extremist groups and political appointees in the administration, a few highly placed. Most links involved email exchanges, none clearly treasonous, easy to explain away as informational or evidence of an open-door policy. Still, reporting the links put Bondarenko under suspicion and led to sit-downs with her lecherous boss. Fear of the press unearthing the same connections won out; better to know who an embarrassment might be, the political handlers reasoned. She was allowed to continue, with only a small circle of administration loyalists privy to her findings.

Even more problematic was spying on political rallies. Aware of federal Hatch Act restrictions, Bondarenko wondered exactly what line she was crossing every time she pulled on her MAGA hat or joined a chant. She even sold a few rally photographs – using a willing friend's name in the credit line – she quit that as a frivolous ego trip. She could argue she went undercover to expose right-wing terrorism, and she told herself this administration would overlook, even reward, bad conduct that had a political upside. But not having informed her boss, there was no upside. Her clear intent was to expose the ugly threat the President's extremist supporters pose to democracy. But revealing the emperor wearing filthy clothes was unforgivable. Her only choice was to work in the shadows – collect evidence, build her precious file of videos and photos, and see if they prove of value. In other words, do what she enjoyed most: Play the spy.

A radio bud in one ear, Bondarenko listened to a local reporter for all-news radio WTOP describing the East Plaza's worsening scene. Calmly, she worked in that the President was still speaking, and lawmakers would convene at 1 p.m. in the House of Representatives to certify election results.

But also: "We have a tense situation here with Congress on the cusp of carrying out its duty. More and more, protesters marching up from the rally are threatening Capitol police. It's much worse than half an hour ago – protesters shaking the barricades, spitting on officers, screaming 'traitor'. They're throwing bottles, rocks, whatever. Some of the President's supporters have been in my face, blaming the so-called lamestream press for not condemning what they insist was a stolen election.

"Stop! Stop!" she suddenly screamed. "... Okay, I'm okay. Some jerk who had his bare chest tattooed with – I think I saw this right – 'Dump the Vote or Eat Me Congress', he tried to grab my mic. My! So literary. I hope his mom is proud ..."

There was a pause as the reporter struggled to collect herself. "Sorry to go off that way. Anyway, besides what's happening here, the news is the Vice President has concluded he lacks the unilateral power to overturn state-approved Electoral College votes. In other words, he has refused the President's demand that he, the Vice President, throw the election back to states where the vote was close or into the House where Republicans – who outnumber Democrats in a majority of states – would win. It now appears certain that this country, as it has done for two hundred and thirty-two years, will have another peaceful transfer of power."

Bondarenko questioned how peaceful. Everything unfolding before her, as well as the burgeoning anger the reporter described on the East Plaza, was foreboding. Damn, she thought, looks like I'm going to be in the wrong place again.

Hasty and a gray-haired Capitol policeman stood nose-to-nose, glaring at each other over a wobbly barricade.

"Give it up, man. Just walk away so we can visit our damn house," Hasty yelled, showering spittle. "Look around, man. You are way outnumbered!"

"It ends right here," the officer answered gruffly. "Calm yourself. Calm yourself. It ends right here."

But the cop could see the anger bubbling and knew when it reached critical mass, violence must follow. With every arriving protester, the crowd deepened, and the tension built. The disappointment – the alleged fraud – that had lured them from around the country needed release, like an overheated steam engine. They were jacking each other up, feeding on their own excitement, whetting anger and nurturing courage, finding ugly corners within that they didn't know existed.

The gray-haired officer feared the coming onslaught, and radio traffic portended a more volatile standoff shaping up on the West Terrace. Barring a miracle – or reinforcements – barricades would fall soon, with the East Plaza not far behind.

Behind Hasty, someone yelled, "Give us our house," and a chant was reborn.

"Give us our house! Give us our house! Give us our house!"

CHAPTER 7

Captain Allen Swift scanned the surveillance cameras with frustration bordering on anger. With apprehension, too, knowing many of those nearly ringing the Capitol were right-wing extremists, armed, bent on violence. Swift was privy to intelligence of extremist groups plotting attacks against the federal government. Those threats had grown in tandem with the President's calls for his loyalist to march on the Capitol as lawmakers performed their sacred duty. Pulling together that foreboding intelligence had involved the Protective Service Bureau of the Capitol Police, where Swift was that day's duty officer.

He watched a wall-mounted TV as the commander in chief trotted out his worn complaints of voter fraud. Got one thing right, the veteran officer agreed, allegations of fraud had been ignored or, more accurately, dismissed, because there was none, certainly nothing major. He wanted the President to stay in office, had voted to re-elect him. But Swift did not want the Constitution violated to keep him in office, the beneficiary of an intimidating horde.

His churning innards told him the day would be fateful. Too much intelligence, far too much to be ignored, warned it would turn violent. Incredibly, mounds of evidence painstakingly collected had been ignored, not seen as a serious threat by decision makers at every level. The FBI, Pentagon, D.C. government and, most shocking, Congress itself. The boss of the Capitol Police.

Swift focused laser-like on surveillance camera images, searching for something flagrant, anything he could wave at his bosses, even now, this late. Except for minor infractions, the noisy and rowdy protesters were, dammit, thus far legal. But the human stream tramping up Constitution and Independence put Swift on edge. Make it through this day, he promised himself, then walk. Should have done it long ago, soon as I qualified.

He mentally thumbed through the intelligence – much of it threatening – the FBI and Homeland Security had taken the lead in assessing. "You might have to kill the palace guards," one email read. Someone responded, "Drop a handful, the rest will flee."

Swift did not believe that. The USCP would do its job. Protect the Capitol. As would his son, Nick, a five-year veteran and, on this of all days, assigned to the west steps. Nick's history major at the University of Maryland concentrated on the American Revolution. Great subject matter for grasping why the country's unique history is so worth defending, Captain Swift reflected. But perhaps that immersion also prompted Nick to abandon pursuing a doctorate and join the Capitol Police.

When they talked about it, Nick said simply, "I want to feel the threats and stand up to them." Damn well getting your wish, the father thought. On impulse he called Nick's personal number. No answer. Not surprising. That crowd is a handful.

His gnawing worry kept going back to the intercepted posts, the brutality embraced so casually, the misguided calls to arms that peppered extremist sites. Most recently, the coordination and planning that smacked of military tactics and, potentially, large caches of weapons. Strand upon strand of intelligence that, tied together, exceeded by multiples anything in Swift's experience.

"This is the final stand where we are drawing the red line at Capitol Hill," read another email. "I trust the American people will take back the USA with force and many are ready to die." "There is only one way. It's not signs. It's not rallies. It's fucking bullets."

And, one he took personally: "Be ready to fight. Congress needs to hear glass breaking, doors being kicked in, and blood from their slave soldiers being spilled. Get violent. Stop calling this a march, or rally, or protest. Go there ready for war. We get our President or we die."

Slave soldiers? The Capitol Police? These people have totally lost sight of how democracy works, Swift thought. If they win, the country – our grand experiment –will be lost. Too many of the President's Dick and Jane supporters won't have a clue until it is too late. They've forgotten you can't turn democracy on and off like a water faucet.

He fully credited the FBI and DHS for pulling together the threats and evidence of seditious plotting that went hand in glove. Some days, scores of troublesome posts rolled in. Of extremist militias across the nation coordinating in alarming numbers. Meeting places on the Eastern Seaboard identified. Strategies drawn up to smuggle weapons into D.C. "Ready strike forces" at nearby hotels, on call to assault the Capitol and other targets. Money raised on dark sites to buy weapons, protective gear, phones. Hotels and flights reserved by known militants. Extremist chatter about setting off explosives as a distraction, to draw law enforcement away from the Capitol and make it more vulnerable.

Then came even more shocking reports: Militias had mapped the tunnels connecting the Capitol to House and Senate office buildings. Oath Keepers and Proud Boys were signing on as bodyguards to allies of the President and were in contact with the White House.

"All hell is going to break loose tomorrow...," a former top aide to the President declared on his radio talk show the day before the rally. "Strap in."

Alerts popping up on Swift's computer interrupted his mental review: Buildings evacuated in response to pipe bombs found near Democratic and GOP headquarters, blocks from the Capitol. Weapons and Molotov cocktails found in a car downtown, the driver arrested.

"My god, we're in deep shit," he fumed. "What does it take to convince the powers that be?"

Analyzing threats fell to the FBI, which was dealing with challenges historic and current: Its focus since 9/11 had been international – not domestic – terrorism, and literally days before the rally the agency had replaced its computerized threat alert system with a less vigorous one.

After doing a great job gathering intelligence, Swift found some FBI conclusions bordered on the non-sensical: That a gaggle of middle-aged White guys posed no threat; a clash between the President's protesters and those from Black Lives Matter and antifa posed the greatest threat to the rally.

He also knew – and rejected – the FBI's view that adversarial militia groups were incapable of a coordinated attack, and their threatening talk was not evidence of planned violence. His blood pressure climbed higher still at the contention that the First Amendment protects online posts falling short of a specific plot.

"Does not warrant further investigation at this time," became a favorite FBI summary.

To which Swift muttered, "You cannot ignore an unprecedented level of threats. You cannot use the protection of free speech to shield threats. You are wallowing in irresponsible bullshit."

He could only shake his head as top officials hid behind FBI analyses. D.C.'s mayor resisted using the Guard, worried the President might commandeer those troops to do his bidding. When the mayor finally asked for troops, it was to help with traffic control. The President taking control of troops also worried Pentagon leaders, who fussed, too, over so-called optics – that troops stationed around, and protecting, the Capitol would suggest a military coup.

As for the Capitol Police, Swift knew his office had been lax. Smoke grenades had aged and expired. Riot shields, stored in a mobile unit with no temperature control, had grown brittle, fragile. Certifications had expired for officers authorized to fire rubber bullets and tear gas – a bureaucratic lapse diluting crowd control.

Most important, independent USCP intelligence gathering had

become virtually non-existent, a joke requiring reliance on other agencies. While changing, the new intelligence director was only weeks on the job. When he saw the FBI and DHS evidence of right-wing threats, he sounded an alarm as January 6th neared: "Congress itself is the target."

But those chilling words were buried in a long report. "That should have been the damn lead," Swift had groused.

Calling Congress a target did jolt the Capitol Police chief into finally asking his bosses — the sergeants at arms of the House and Senate – to call in the National Guard. Security for congressional leaders had tightened after a bloody pig's head was left on the doorstep of the House Speaker's residence. But to have the Guard surround the Capitol? Request denied. Bad optics, chief. You can handle a few old White guys.

A surveillance camera trained on the West Terrace caught Swift's eye. He saw protesters pushing hard against the light barricades. Police running down steps to join fellow officers in combat. Watched with dismay as two officers stood immobile, hands-on hips, surveying the nascent melee. The forging mob – my god, it is a mob, Swift realized – ran up the backs of their own people. Several protesters went down, burying cops in their path.

"Officers down," he barked into a shared operations phone. "They need help. Now!"

CHAPTER 8

What Swift saw on his surveillance camera, Amy Bondarenko captured in video for posterity:

Shouts turning into a roar, a flurry of pushing and shoving against the barricade to her right. A bearded man in a sheepskin jacket punching a cop, the man going down under other officers' batons. But his punch was a catalyst, inspiring a rush not to be denied. Those in front slamming forward, desperate to escape being trampled by their own mob. The weak cry of an older man – "You're crushing me, stop dammit!" – unheard or ignored. Insurgents and defenders collapsing in a flailing pile. Two bicycle racks toppling with a clang drowned by guttural shouts. A car-length space opening and filling as quickly with a no-man's land of battle. Cops struggling to stand, to get shoulder-to-shoulder, to plug a breach, failing, dropping back. Wounds opening on both sides.

"Storm the Capitol!" a beefy man yells, pushing into the fray, slashing a long pole at anything blue. Others follow mindlessly. Lemmings captured in the moment. Judgment suspended. Emotion in control. Incited by the repetitive torrent of lies, inflamed by the rally's fresh rhetoric. Frantic to justify heart and gut commitments. Desperate for a victory banner to wave to family, neighbors, the television cameras. The throng surrounding the Capitol, thousands of seemingly ordinary Americans, transformed from angry

believers into an out-of-control rabble, mutineers bent on insurrection. A mob of traitors.

"It's started," Bondarenko said into her phone, glancing at the time. "The first assault on the Capitol in more than two centuries is starting at 12:53 p.m."

For capturing an insurrection, she was not in the wrong place.

A lean man finds space for two quick steps, gaining speed to hurdle a tilting barricade and then two more, barely defended. He charges up the West Terrace steps and, seeing cops trotting down to meet him, runs in circles, grinning broadly, waving his arms, fingers in a V. Cops grab him and he slumps dead-weight, toes of his running shoes bouncing off each step as he is dragged away.

Hard on the lean man's heels comes a whiskered man under a MAGA cap, furiously waving the American flag, followed by a chubby woman carrying a cardboard sign scrawled with "1776 2.0". Turning back toward the crowd, the whiskered man bellows, "This is our day! This is our day! Follow me!" Then he charges into police to be arrested.

The mob does follow him, pouring in, barricades falling like dominos. As they tumble, Bordarenko is exposed to the emboldened horde. Fearful, she spins to one side, jumping atop the large concrete banister on the steps' north border. From her perch, she watches as dozens of officers pile from the Capitol, stalling the onslaught, if just briefly. A few cops now wear helmets or bulletproof vests or carry shields, a sign of reinforcements filtering in. They go toe-to-toe with the throng, wading into the fray with fists, batons and saps – their handguns still holstered.

The specter of political protest deteriorating into an assault on the seat of democracy chills some who, minutes before, were screaming at the barricades. They retreat, resist those forging ahead. Others look around nervously, as if worried about surveillance video capturing them in conduct gone too far.

"Enough!" screams a woman in tears. "This is not who we are. This is not right."

"This ain't why I come here," a jowly man wrapped in a red, white and blue blanket yells into a hand megaphone. "This ain't how we do things in Dubuque."

But they, like the police, are outnumbered times over by those hungry for violence, demanding admittance to the Capitol as their birthright.

"It's there in the Constitution, 'We the People' you fucks," screams a huge man swinging a barricade like a scythe at cops scampering out of reach. "It's in the Constitution, you fucks, 'We the People.'"

Fights break out across the entire West Terrace. Police hold their own — barely. Blood flows, more an issue for police, their ranks thin. Officers separated from their brethren are surrounded, kicked, stomped. From backpacks come brass knuckles, collapsible batons, pepper spray, nasty animal and insect repellents. Fists give way to make-shift weapons — metal thermos bottles hurled viciously, walking sticks wielded as clubs, belts with heavy buckles swung like ball and chain.

Though taking a beating, the cops still don't pull their sidearms. Just as important, insurgents' firearms stay concealed. Both sides are keenly aware of the heavy price of doing otherwise. They endure the pain of hand-to-hand combat to avoid the far bloodier fatal option. But instinctively, the rioters are gauging how far, how fast to go, seeking the moment when their superior numbers cannot be denied, when the time is right to invade the hallowed Capitol.

Bordarenko recognizes extremists from Charlottesville and other rallies. Some have waded deep into the fray to pummel officers, to ensure no letup in the combat. But most militia stay off the front line. They are jacking up others, Bondarenko reasons, keeping the mob mentality at fever pitch. Getting others to do the dirtiest work and avoiding arrest if the assault fails. Or maybe saving themselves for a bigger battle. She wonders when reinforcements — Metro police, military, anyone for Christ's sake — will show up in force, enough to make a difference, to reverse the trajectory of defeat.

Word of the West Terrace breach, immediately relayed to protesters on the east side, sets off victory whoops and, as the news spreads, a wave of cheers. Cameras capture fist pumps and bumps, protesters hugging and jumping with joy, a favored chant.

"Take our house back! Take our house back! Take our house back!"

Laurence Spindale peers at the cell phone of a young man watching coverage of the President wrapping up his speech.

"Did you hear that?" the young man asks. "He said we need to give Republicans up here some guts to take back our country. That's what he said, almost word for word."

"Hasty, mon," Spindale calls over the crowd, "You hear that? Prez said to take our country back."

"What, say again?" shouts Hasty, just three feet away.

"Prez said to take our country back."

Hasty looks around, sees energized protesters getting in the faces of police defending chained-together bicycle racks. "You all supposed to be on the people's side," a heavy southern voice booms. "You all traitors if you ain't."

"Cops are traitors! Cops are traitors!"

The chant grows as fast as flipping a light switch. Barricades fall. Officers resist in a ropeless tug of war, both sides digging in. Stalemate. Then the insurgents slowly take ground, punctuating their case with blows from makeshift clubs, fists reaching in, spit flying in officers' faces. Gaining, but too slowly for Hasty.

"Them boys needs a boost," he yells with a wide-eyed grin at Spindale. Powerful strides launch him above the protesters, his huge body plowing forward, crashing down, smashing two rebels into the bike racks. They scream in pain as he rolls over them, turning sideways to take out three officers. As the racks fall, rabid insurgents seize their chance, and the East Plaza is breached.

Cops at nearby barricades rush to help – weakening the lines they were defending and offering the mutineers new openings. More police confront them, but too few to halt the onslaught. Breaches pop up across the entire plaza. Militia extremists who held back switch gears, from extolling the mob to joining the fray, then leading it. They spawn running battles like those that minutes earlier broke police lines on the west side. Assailants and defenders battle at ground level, above the cavernous Visitor Center. Hollowed out to ensure security, a mob is now fighting police, both sides drawing blood above the very space where Americans queue up to witness democracy in action.

Alexander Dancer stayed on Constitution Avenue with marchers crowding the sidewalk beneath elms, lindens and maples – some of the one hundred forty species on the Capitol grounds. Hearing the clamor of the spreading conflict, he joined others circling the Capitol at a safe distance. They wandered near the crabapple trees honoring the Sullivan Brothers of Waterloo, Iowa – George, Madison, Albert, Francis and Joseph – who asked to "stick together" when they enlisted in World War II. All died when a Japanese torpedo sunk the U.S.S. Juneau.

Alexander heard his phone on the first ring. It was Ambrose.

"I was just told the lines broke on your side."

"Yup. Pretty wild over here, as advertised."

"Our guys staying out of it?"

Alexander paused. "I think so. A couple of them called me and I talked them down. They wanted to lead the charge."

"I can't believe we're not seeing a big honking line of Guard or Army personnel carriers, even Strykers, rolling up Independence. When that happens, whoever is in the middle of things is gonna get busted. We need to keep hanging back, see if others make it in the Capitol before we commit."

"Right. I do see more cops in protective gear, so they're getting some reinforcements. But we still have the numbers, easy."

"Same on this side ... Best entertainment here is guys scaling the walls and the inauguration scaffolding and running up and down the bannisters like wild monkeys."

"Best I have is the scaffold for a hanging. If the assholes in Congress don't do what's right, it could get a lot of use."

Seth Baldwin, the Arizona rancher, had his own talking down to do, not of over-zealous foot soldiers but of his new-found partner in insurrection, Jeffrey Lomax.

"Here's the deal, the real deal," Lomax said loudly from the noisy crowd. "Here on the east side, the rabble, they are ready, ready as a bitch dog in heat. And I'm ready to turn my boys loose to lead them, lead them right up those steps and into the Capitol! Are you ready on your side?"

Baldwin took a deep breath, holding the phone tight to his ear. He imagined Lomax struggling to walk in circles through the churning protesters, slapping his forehead.

"You there, Seth? Seth?"

"I'm here. Listen a minute. Your so-called rabble may be ready, but it's too early. People are still coming up from the rally. We need to let the crowd build."

"Not many more showing up here that I can see," Lomax interrupted.

"Look, if we charge and the cops start shooting, we'll get tagged as the bad guys, even if it's us who gets killed. Plus, the National Guard or the Marines could roar in any minute. I have my men looking for unlocked doors and windows. That would be a better way, Jeffrey. My Grampa Cohen always said, 'The bestest tomato is the just-ripe tomato.' This tomato ain't just-ripe yet."

There was a long silence, unusual for Lomax. "Okay. I'll call you back, call you back."

Walking yet another circle, head down, Lomax bounced off a hard body, landing squarely on his ass. He looked up into the bemused eyes of Alexander Dancer.

"I know you ...you," he faltered.

"Yes," Alexander said slowly. "Richmond."

"You were the guy who tried to talk sense to those idiots, fucking idiots. I am Jeff Lomax. No thanks to you I got stuck in that room with the so-called leaders for like long hours, real fucking long hours."

"Alexander Dancer." He gave Lomax a hand up.

In an awkward silence surrounded by noise, Lomax seemed ready to walk away. Then, "How do I know you're not undercover?"

"I could ask the same."

"Could, could. But I am known. Like, those do-gooders who track us have my picture on their sites. Far as I know, you got your picture nowhere, totally nowhere."

"I hope not. But I am here. If it helps, I'll tell you this much: I'm not alone."

Another silence. Then, "Since you're just standing there, standing there like there's nothing better to do than chat, I'd guess you all are waiting to see if things heat up pretty much on their own."

Alexander said nothing.

"I recall now, recall your group in the Carolinas is hooked to one in the Midwest, led by your uncle or brother or such."

"My brother Ambrose. He's here, too."

"Really? Okay," Lomax decided. "Let us roll the dice, really roll, roll, roll the dice and talk. If things heat up big-time, I mean really big-time, are the Dancer brothers geared up to, ah, pardon the pun, cut a rug, so to speak?"

Now Alexander gave pause to where the conversation was heading. "Yes, we are."

"Okay, okay. I have got the South, right? You sort of build on my territory. Ambrose has the Midwest. A buddy of mine has the West. All together, we cover a lot of ground, a lot of ground. I think we have something to talk about, without much time for talking?"

"I agree." Alexander said, feeling like a groom marrying after a one-night stand.

CHAPTER 9

Alexander called Ambrose to say he and Lomax were coming to the West Terrace and suggested checking out Freedom Country Coalition and South Arising on the Southern Poverty Law Center's registry of militias. It took Ambrose only a few minutes on his cell phone to confirm the two were there.

Joined by Seth Baldwin, the four exchanged information – about troop strength in D.C., what might trigger an assault on the Capitol, how their militias at home could create national mayhem. Though short of time pursue many details, they agreed to join forces.

The Dancers saw no real downside. Now, when the right time came – if it came – they had allies. If Lomax or Baldwin failed to step up, the Dancers were ready to act alone, anyway.

As their new partners walked away, Ambrose told his brother, "If I were them, I'm not sure I'd trust us, but that's their call."

"They saw me in Richmond, and no one there got ratted out," Alexander said. "Or maybe it's my winning smile."

Ambrose waved him off, saying he had to call his lead in Michigan.

"I'm listening," said former Army corporal Sydney Armor.

"No, Syd, you need to talk," Ambrose said. "If you haven't heard, the barricades have fallen. This could be the real deal, not D.C. BS. So what's happening?"

"I do know and am shocked at the great shit I'm watchin' on Fox. Bottom line, we're in better shape than I expected. Good news first. We got a lot of guns and ammo stockpiled – and any real patriot already had a closet full.

"I'll spare you details, but we picked up more explosives, mostly dynamite, enough to keep our demolition boys happy. They can take out a bunch of electrical lines and substations, mostly substations. We're still tryin' to figure out if we want to take out major grids. That could fuck up power for millions."

"Probably more than we want," Ambrose said. "Disrupt government and not people as much as we can, so we're seen as better than the shits running things now."

"We have teams ready to blow up a couple reservoir dams. These are not huge ones with tons of people livin' downstream. Like you say, mostly disruption. "Now, some good and bad. We're set to take over radio stations in Scranton, Toledo and Madison."

"Nice but holding anything in socialist Madison could be hard. Better add some extra people if you can. And the bad?"

"Our guy who works PR has backed out of writin' what we want to say on the radio. He doesn't think a revolt will fly. He's damn gutless, worried about losin' his freelance gig with the NRA."

"He know the NRA is on our side, probably?"

"He doesn't think so. Says they're part of the D.C. crowd."

"Keep trying him. Don't know when I can do it, but I'll try to write some messages. Or we'll have to wing it."

"Now, a couple crap shoots. Our guy Mike says he and the sergeant can take over the National Guard here. They believe most of the guys – including women, too – will follow. Second, remember the crazy who claims to know the gov's routine? He says a vacant building within easy range of his sniper rifle will give him a clear shot. I have no idea how either of those deals will come down."

"Don't sweat it. It's Mike's dick on the block. Losing Mike is worth trying to turn a bunch of guardsmen. And if the crazy doesn't get the governor, nothing lost but the crazy... A question: What about cops? Many of them turning?"

"Not many, and I don't know if we can count on the ones who say they will."

Alexander, Lomax and Baldwin talked to their lieutenants at home, too, getting encouraging reports of strong support for the protesters and seeing the President as the victim of a rigged election. Many at home wished they were at the rally, to march and help right a terrible wrong – one to be salved only by keeping the President in office.

That's great, thought Alexander, before his training as an intelligence analyst kicked in. It's great when sitting comfortably many states away. But will they leave their easy chairs if rebels pound on their doors, ask them to put their jobs, families, their very lives on the line? And on that point, what if the chief narcissist fails to step up? That's the bottom line, most likely, Alexander believed. Without him, how much stomach will folks back home have?

Lomax's lieutenant predicted better than even odds for seriously disrupting Guard units in several states but warned it would be messy. In Oklahoma, which South Arising barely reached, the Guard strongly backed the President. Lomax's smattering of members in Texas said grumbling about succession was getting louder. At the least, the Lone Star state would be a boiler pot, likely going its own way, and too big for the feds to control. Promising reports were coming out of Michigan and several western states, too.

Also encouraging: South Arising and Baldwin's FCC had identified at least fifteen radio stations and a handful of television outlets, mostly in the remote West, that they could commandeer. As important, they had lined up troops with the expertise to broadcast.

"We'll take a bunch of hostages," Baldwin said. "Besides helping broadcast, they'll be insurance against power getting cut off. From those stations we can deal in information or misinformation – whatever suits us – to reach a hell of a lot of people. We can cause a boatload of confusion for the feds while they're trying to hold down the revolution."

Alexander knew such intelligence was always hit or miss, only as good as the source, and that public resentment or anger or appetite for change – let alone dramatic change – was hard if not impossible to gauge. In other words, there was no way to know if revolution would succeed.

He pondered that, then thought, the Founding Fathers had no certainty, either. They skated on the edge of disaster through most of the war. Might as well flip Ambrose's 1876 half-dollar. Or go with, "Ya gotta believe."

CHAPTER 10

Theodore Wormsley's first reaction had been to go to the rally. After all, ever since he lost faith in the government years ago, only this President had given him hope – and pause about the lone wolf terrorism that had consumed more than half his life. He imagined stepping away from his solitary campaign and joining an angry throng to loudly demand that a stolen election be reversed. He grew excited about a pilgrimage to a rally repeatedly billed as "wild," being ready to do whatever the President ordered to fulfill that vague promise. Then Wormsley regained his senses.

It wasn't that he lacked commitment. He fully appreciated how the President had reordered the way the country did business, at home and abroad. How he ignored traditions of the office, threw out niceties and shocked the Washington elite. How he had diminished the liberal media and declared courts and federal agencies his own. The President knew how to deflect controversy by creating new chaos. His enemies and the media could not keep pace with this china shop bull. His loyalists didn't care about the scandals and most people didn't know who to believe. The President had taken demagoguery to new heights, and Wormsley loved it.

Most important, the President had bestowed respectability on right-wing militant groups — which Wormsley aligned with, in his own solitary way. While still on the political fringe, they were no longer universally detested piranhas. They were players in waiting.

But to really change things, truly reshape the country, Wormsley recognized, the President needed another term. Four more years would tighten his hold on the courts, perhaps give him Congress. He could gather enough power to replace a stumbling democracy with a firm-handed autocracy that would protect the American way for generations. Unfortunately, Wormsley couldn't see the rally reversing the election. All the President's grievance-driven gyrations – fully justified – had failed to change election results obviously laced with fraud. Now, to overturn a presidential transition so far along would be akin to turning a battleship. There was no way to wrest control from a vengeful Congress, still smarting from a failed impeachment conviction. Forcing Congress to send slates of electors back to several states? Wormsley couldn't imagine a bunch of middle-aged zealots making that happen. Finally, expecting an eleventh-hour reprieve from the Vice President, a man dragged down by Christian values and lacking the President's unquenchable thirst for power, bordered on silly.

That said, most crucial for Wormsley, personally, was staying off the government's radar. Attend the rally and he would almost certainly fall victim to the ubiquitous security and media cameras and protesters clicking selfies to prove "I was there." If wild meant a riot or marching on Congress, as the media were warning, mass arrests and investigations would follow. A military veteran and law-abiding citizen, he was in the system, sure to be tracked down. Go to the rally and the crux of his life, his anonymity, his precious cover, safeguarded for years, would be destroyed. No way could he still operate in the shadows, a faceless lone wolf.

Growing up in central Arkansas, he was imbued with the South's ingrained racial bias. An early memory was his grandfather's demented, deathbed boast of his role at the Tulsa race massacre in 1921. "I'd been deputized by the sheriff, but when the shooting started, I knew my true duty," he said over and over. "The flames, they did their job."

During the Dust Bowl, the old man moved his family back to Arkansas, a less demanding migration than to California. Ozark land was cheap enough to afford eighty acres. Hunting and fishing, barnyard critters and a garden hacked out of rocky soil augmented town jobs for a meager lifestyle.

Theodore Wormsley remembered his folks finding reason for hope in Ronald Reagan's election. "Better than the peanut farmer," his mother liked to say. But that paled next to the statement his father made by tacking a Confederate flag on the front of their frame house. It sat close to the gravel road, an easy target for any passerby choosing to object, but no one ever did.

Like many of their neighbors, Wormsleys fought for the South, proudly wore the Klan's hood and robe, and passed down family lore about lynchings. They raged against school desegregation and the Civil Rights Act, cheered the killing of Martin Luther King, Jr., and complained about immigrants stealing American jobs.

Raised in that culture, Wormsley joined the Army just out of high school, with postings that broadened his horizons only as far as adjoining Missouri and Oklahoma. The Army did train him as an electrician, adding to mechanic, carpentry and other skills common to growing up rural. The military did one other thing: Profanity was so pervasive that Wormsley's clumsy attempts at creative execration made him feel inferior. His solution was to quit cussing except in extreme situations.

He made corporal and chose friends who shared his hatred of Blacks. With the Army largely integrated, he came to resent, first, military authority, and then government in general. Honorably discharged, he was hired by an electrical contractor in Little Rock. After making unwelcome advances toward a receptionist and racist comments to another electrician, both Black, Wormsley was fired. Workplace anger joined his growing catalog of grievances. He found that piecework suited him, paying enough without the restrictions of steady employment.

He drifted into a circle of drinking buddies active in an anti-government militia. For a while, the militia gave him a way to vent.

Weekends often found him on a remote property, honing martial arts and firing weapons – what he called "my vigilante skills." But a few years passed without training turning into action. Never-ending rhetoric about "snuffing the Jew and Black commie bastards" grew stale.

"Why don't we blow up City Hall or something?" Wormsley asked one of the militia's leaders. "Sort of let the word get out who did it and see if it gets us some new recruits."

"You clowns can barely blow your nose," he was told. "When you're ready, I'll let you know."

Wormsley seethed but was unsure of himself. He sought out other militia foot soldiers and, finding echoes of his exasperation, toyed with forming his own militia. Having no idea how, he turned inward, replacing the militia with a gym, taking martial arts classes, and seeking his own way. He developed a passion for reading military and political history that broadened his knowledge of autocrats. He slowly assembled a small arsenal – weapons and explosives and poisons, drones and other lethal tools – and taught himself to employ them with expertise. His targets were enemies of American values as he perceived them. Wanting neither applause nor support, he found security and satisfaction in operating as a lone wolf.

CHAPTER 11

At noon on January 6th, the House chaplain offered a prescient prayer, saying in part: "Defend us from those adversaries, both foreign and domestic, outside these walls and perhaps within these chambers, who sow seeds of acrimony to undermine trust in Your divine authority over all things."

Within the hour, the battle for the Capitol would be joined, scant minutes before the Vice President gaveled to order a joint session of Congress meeting in the House. He declared he did not have constitutional authority over Electoral College votes submitted by the states or to throw the election into the House of Representatives, where the President's party controlled a slim majority of states. With that, he shot down the President's last best hope of derailing the election.

But election deniers were not done. When votes of the third state – Arizona – were called for, a representative and a senator objected, suspending the roll call. Lawmakers adjourned to their respective chambers to debate the objection.

Republicans insisted the Constitution gave state legislatures the power to change slates of electors, a move justified by election fraud. No way could the President's leads early in the vote count conveniently shrink to slim losses in several battleground states. No way, they charged, fraud is the only answer.

No, leads often change as votes are counted, Democrats countered. Article II of the Constitution created the Electoral College and gave state election officials – not legislatures – authority to certify electoral votes. Congress's job is simply to count those votes. As for fraud? Those allegations were slapped down in sixty court cases, many by judges the President appointed.

Lawmakers' attention waned as the conflict outside mushroomed. Some members tuned in news radio for information. Others called family, assuring them the chambers were safe. Calls to law enforcement brought the alarming news that Capitol Police had asked the city for help. A few dialed an unresponsive White House, seldom getting past the voice message machine. No one knew more than the media were ominously reporting:

Horrible images of police battling fellow Americans who looked like friends and neighbors – against the backdrop of a Capitol besieged by its own citizens. The unprecedented sedition created optics worse than timid security officials could have imagined.

Reporters learned little from lawmakers but got good soundbites.

Democrats emphasized that protesters had marched from the President's incendiary rally to assault police – and sometimes the press. "This is the President's crowd, clear and simple," asserted a California House member. "Whatever happens is on him."

Most Republicans voiced confidence that the bulk of marchers were loyal Americans, incapable of betraying the country or their government. Some speculated that troublemakers were antifa or connected with Black Lives Matter.

Observed a radio talk show host: "Even with their lives threatened, democracy itself threatened, this Capitol Hill crowd remains all-in partisan."

CHAPTER 12

Herbert Squelch stared out his window on the fourth floor of the Rayburn House Office Building, fascinated by the conflict below. Through trees bare for winter, he saw angry protesters shaking their fists, throwing bottles at dodging cops. A woman hit a helmeted police officer over the head with a child's wooden baseball bat. Two cops reached out, grabbed her arms, and jerked her over a barricade. She landed on her stomach, was quickly cuffed and led away.

"Did you see that?" Squelch snapped at an aide. "Those cops slammed her down and are dragging her off! For protesting! That's her constitutional right!"

As usual, the second-term Florida congressman saw what he wanted, which gave him a thirst for conspiracy theories. A favorite was Hillary Clinton leading a pedophilic ring operating out of a pizza restaurant in Northwest Washington. Ten years after Sandy Hook, Squelch still bellowed at rallies that the horrendous elementary school shootings were staged. He justified carrying a handgun into the Capitol, arguing the Second Amendment negated House rules. And he staunchly backed the President, embracing every wacky court case alleging election fraud. "Another judge to impeach!" he insisted whenever a specious case was lost.

The previous night, Squelch had been in a well-appointed suite at a landmark hotel near the White House. He rubbed shoulders with the President's lawyers and a young woman who was White House liaison to the Defense Department. A House colleague nodded at two men wearing military fatigues. "Oath Keepers," she said quietly.

The two men tried to be inconspicuous in a corner of the room. Only the taller of the two would speak and only when called upon. Once. Very briefly.

One of the President's lawyers, a balding stereotype of a mob mouthpiece, outlined what he saw happening if the Vice President failed his duty: Rally protesters would march on the Capitol, outcome unpredictable. If possible, he said drily, protesters' actions should be guided. He turned to the men in fatigues.

"What is your status?"

"Standing by, sir," the tall man said.

"I thought that's what another group is doing," the lawyer quipped, bringing a smile from the tall man.

"Besides standing by," the lawyer said, "you must be ready if the President invokes the Insurrection Act. The military may need help to keep order. Please let the other militias know."

Both men nodded.

Squelch left the meeting feeling depressed. He had no faith in the Vice President. The man had no stomach for tossing the rule book. And relying on a mob was no plan. Walking up Constitution Avenue, enjoying the frigid evening, he pulled a burner phone from his topcoat pocket. It was given to him weeks earlier by a Proud Boy at a rally for the President. On stage, Squelch had passionately condemned a stolen election. Afterwards, the Proud Boy had approached.

"I can have two guys – more if you want – watching your back twenty-four/seven," he said. "Until someone takes a shot at you, the Capitol Police won't protect you. They lack bandwidth and besides, you are in the minority. But you're out there all the time, working for our guy. Believe me, antifa or some other nutcase will come for you."

Squelch was tempted but declined. No one had raised a finger against him so far. Besides, having Proud Boys as wingmen would really screw his carefree sex life. But having been urged to "call any time," he was.

"You know who this is?"

"Yes sir. Calling to accept my offer?"

"No, thank you. But I wonder if you're ready for tomorrow."

"We are. The boys really turned out."

"I just came from an important meeting. Tomorrow, unless the VP comes through, you need to press every chance – stir the pot, get inside. Understand?"

"I understand."

"The train needs to come off the track. If it does, who knows what will happen. Our side still has a lot of people in important places. And I just heard the President is thinking about using the Insurrection Act. If that happens, militias will be deputized."

Glad I made that call, Squelch thought, still glued to the growing violence below. He glanced at the muted TVs behind him, saw the House debate droning on and decided to go watch it. As he left his office, a dated crawl about the VP crossed the screen.

"Man couldn't find his balls," Squelch exploded at the aide. "Fuck the Constitution. Just fuck it."

"Damn me, I was too damn honest," the Senate Minority Leader said aloud. He stood on his balcony, oblivious to perhaps the most arresting view of D.C., stretching west from the Capitol's high ground: The National Mall, accentuated by the Washington monument and the Lincoln Memorial, pieces of the White House grounds, federal and Smithsonian buildings along Independence and Constitution avenues, the city's skyline on the right, high-rises across the Potomac filling in the panorama. He watched an arriving flight weave its artful way down the river, then turned away from the tragedy unfolding just below him and went inside.

Minutes earlier, the Minority Leader held the floor, explaining what he called his most important vote, of thousands spanning decades. Most important speech, too, he could have said. He believed and had approved all his speechwriter had served up. The problem, he knew as he yielded the floor, was having said too much, too definitively. Speaking honestly, cementing his view for prosperity, had shortchanged the day's politics.

The President had every right to claim election fraud in court, he intoned, then needlessly added: *But no claim of election fraud – massive enough to change the outcome – had been proven.*

For Congress to set itself up as a national election board, *would unconstitutionally disenfranchise the nation's voters and would overrule the courts and the states who send forth Electoral College slates.*

Voting to overturn the election would put democracy in a death spiral.

All true, all his words, the Minority Leader thought. And all politically foolish.

The President's base – my base, too – believes election fraud was massive, enough so to easily change the outcome. The base believes their votes were disenfranchised and judges were blind to evidence of fraud. Believes corrupt election officials in key states submitted illegitimate slates of electors.

Driving all that, the base believes, is the need to overturn a crooked election if democracy is to be pulled out of its death spiral.

He could have – should have – played to the base, the Minority Leader thought.

He could have suggested that reversing the Electoral College would set a bad precedent. Words like precedent get no attention. Or he could have joined colleagues demanding a commission to quickly investigate fraud allegations. That may have delayed certifying the vote. Dragged things out. Let passions cool. That would have been political, for heaven's sake.

Isn't political how he always had been? Does a bear shit in the woods? Does a coal miner have black lungs? His career was built on finding the best political solution, then selling the best justification he could conjure up. Sometimes he wallowed through hypocrisy to accomplish his political goal, his role in stacking the Supreme Court a prime example.

And that is fine, the Minority Leader told himself. That is called winning. But uttering soundbites that later will bite him? Preaching truth that will anger and erode his base? Antagonizing a President whose public criticism alienates senators who are my lifeline to power? Doing all those things, that is called losing.

Somehow his political instincts fell prey to his outrage at seeing the Capitol under siege. It was a weak moment. He had failed to hold his political prism up to that damn speech. Unforgivable. For the first time, after decades surviving political battles, the Minority Leader suddenly feared he had lost a step. Maybe more. He felt like an old man.

Senator Theodore Control of Oklahoma beat himself up, too. In the privacy of his Dirksen office, he nursed a large tumbler of single malt, neat. He propped his alligator boots on his mahogany desk and mentally rewound his performance on the Senate floor, calling for a commission to investigate voter fraud. Talk about making chicken shit from chicken salad. With a sigh, he imagined how a less than friendly historian – writing about the day's departure from pro forma approval of electoral votes – would chronicle his speech:

Giving Senator Control five minutes to rant about election fraud was not a reflection of his reputation in that august body, the historian would write. Arguably, no senator was more disliked by colleagues. Neither did he take the floor through seniority. He was a junior senator and younger than most – his longish jet-black hair holding more oil than a stripper well. No, he held the floor because he loved center stage. A House member, a rabid backer of the President, needed a senator to join in objecting to Arizona's slate of electors. Offered the role, Control pounced. Other GOP senators were primed to support the objection as a partisan duty, but not do the dirty work of sponsoring it. Enter "Cruise" Control, seeking the limelight.

Surprisingly, he did not open with his usual rant, the historian would go on. He clearly was determined to keep himself in check, to talk reason to the nervous chamber, to appease.

"Those folks outside are harmless as newborn babies," he soothed in his prairie twang. "They feel a sacred right and duty to defend the commander in chief. Nothing less than the Constitution guarantees lawful assembly. Let us agree on this, too: Those folks are as American as the boys who run up that humongous stars and stripes flag at Sooner football games. Main Street through and through. Exactly like most of us here on this hallowed floor, as American as apple pie and fried chicken, finger lickin' good.

"Now, I know a bit of pushin' and shovin' is going on, even a few bottles throwed. But we don't know who's infiltratin' a good crowd. We've been warned of troublemakers heading our way, to throw bottles or worse. Maybe from the crowd that messed up Portland, out in Oregon. They and others maybe want to defund our outstanding police. I swear, those boys in blue don't get paid 'nuf at all. But the main point is a good crowd has been infiltrated. Safe bet, I rise on this floor to say, the President's people are peaceably, peaceably now, supporting their commander in chief. They see it as their duty.

"We have a duty here today, too. Not a pro forma one, like is usual every four years. This year is special, with questions – legitimate and serious questions – about how some votes got cast. Not just a couple votes in one state or two states but a bunch of votes in enough states that maybe a mistake happened. As in a serious, serious mistake."

C-SPAN tapes show Cruise Control searching the chamber for affirmation, the historian observed. His colleagues wait patiently, ready to vote. Some doodle or read or study their shoes. A sound like thunder creeps into the chamber. Angry protesters outside? Senator Control cocks his head as if to listen, then hurries on.

"Mistakes cannot stand in a presidential election. Stakes too big. We're not only talking outcome here. We're talking national integrity," he declared, voice ratcheting up. "We're talking people's confidence in our system. If folks don't have confidence, how will those on the losing team ever accept a new president?

"If we don't get confidence back, we will never heal the divisions of recent years – divisions the radical left caused. Never! Today's protest will look like a Sunday school picnic, dwarfed by huge unrest after elections stretching well into the future! Unrest that will sit squarely on the heads of the radical left perpetrators of election fraud! Perpetrators this Senate must bring to justice!"

By then, Cruise Control was in high dudgeon. When his eyes got wider, the historian speculated, he realized his ears were booming with the sound of his own voice. Slipping into rally mode, he had discarded his unfamiliar appeal to reason in favor of a rant. Like peeing in a blue serge suit, he got a warm feeling without having it show. He sensed more than heard the disapproving stir in the chamber, the grumbling of Democrats mixed with the despondent muttering of fellow Republicans.

He must have sworn at himself, the historian would write, knowing he had flushed what scant chance he had to sway votes crucial to the President's survival.

Defeated, he quickly ran through his proposal for a bipartisan commission to investigate allegations of voter fraud in key states and quickly report back to the Senate. He called for a vote that failed miserably, even losing some in his own party.

Yep, Senator Control told himself, draining the scotch, when the history books are written, that's what I expect.

Madam Speaker slipped off dress heels and settled into her desk chair, taking in her own stupendous view of the National Mall. She sat far enough from the window to not see the crowd below, but could not escape the alarming clamor, filtering in.

How could I have let this happen? She wondered. How could I have been so naive? No. More than that. So stupid.

We were warned bad things could happen. Fully warned. All the chatter picked up by security, not just predictable chest thumping but stuff about preparations the damn militants were making. Sure, the FBI played down the talk as falling within constitutional speech, the preparations as not necessarily illegal. So what? They were giant red flags. Sure, no one wanted to throw god-awful fences up or have guardsmen with guns and bayonets every ten feet. How many times did I hear how bad those optics would be?

"Fuck the optics!" Startled by how old her voice sounded, she said, "That's what I should have told everybody."

She remembered looking in the eyes of security officials as they reassured her and seeing their uncertainty. She sensed – no, she knew – their call was mostly political, to avoid terrible PR, a huge black eye. After all, we are talking about the President's rally no less. His people, All-American patriotic Whites from the hinterlands, exercising their constitutional rights of assembly and speech. Not antifa. Not Blacks. No, the President's people. If we had put a chain link fence with razor wire around the Capitol, he'd have climbed on his bully pulpit and ripped us a new one. Demagogued us to death.

Doesn't matter. I should have done it, Madam Speaker told herself. That is what my gut said. If not the fence, at least the National Guard or tons more cops. If I had, this shit would not be going down. My gut tells me this day will end up bad. The President's damn rabble is getting here faster than reinforcements. Where the hell are the reinforcements?

She sighed deeply and walked to the window, her posture sagging. She looked down, saw those fine Americans in nose-to-nose battle with her Capitol Police, pumping their fists, screaming, spitting, drawing blood. Fine Americans, deranged, patriots gone asunder.

"I should have listened to my gut, taken the unfair hit," she said. "That's what leaders do."

Quick knocks and her chief of staff opened the door. "Your security chief wants to see you, Madam Speaker. Now."

CHAPTER 13

Moments after the first barricades fell on the West Terrace, Captain Allen Swift's boss, the chief of Capitol Police, asked the Senate and House sergeants at arms to declare an emergency and, again, to call in the National Guard.

"Approve it, dammit. This time, approve it," Swift said aloud.

In that first hour of full-blown insurrection, the chief repeated his request four times. He got no response. The situation deteriorated. Other precautions were taken, other pleas went out, but no significant help arrived.

Ignoring his congressional chain of command, the police chief appealed directly to the commander of the D.C. National Guard. The commander readied guardsmen, but insisted on first being authorized by his boss, the secretary of the Army.

The D.C. mayor also appealed directly to the Army secretary, to no avail.

Capitol Police ordered the evacuation of the Cannon House Office Building and the Madison Building, an arm of the Library of Congress.

A Metro Police commander formally declared violence at the Capitol a riot.

"My god, what does it take?" Swift asked as he again checked surveillance cameras, hoping to see help on the way. Except for a small unit of Metro Police – and a few Metro officers joining the fray without orders – none was.

Swift groaned as he watched his officers retreating from the mob on the East Plaza. Slowly they backed their way up the Capitol steps, pelted at every step with bottles and cans, stones, ball bearings. Lone operators tormented them, attacking on a flank, swinging a club or squirting bear spray, shouting obscenities before darting away. Cops separated from colleagues fell prey to small packs of rebels, as vicious as hyenas. A downed cop, head bleeding, was half-dragged, half-carried from the mob's reach. Beleaguered officers gripped their handguns, stifling the urge to pull them as their ranks were thinned.

"I want you to, come on, pull that piece, pull it," Swift raged at the monitor. "Those assholes would turn and run. Pull it, use it."

But he knew the word was out: Defend the Capitol. Do not provoke. Do not turn a brawl into a gunfight. Hell, he thought, we can't even fire stun grenades.

"Pardon me, folks, but fuck those so-called optics. How much of our blood must be shed? Just bite me. These mutinous assholes haven't even cleared their throats and we're playing footsie."

Then, an alert: Rioters were battering doors and windows. Swift imagined the scramble inside the Capitol. Too few officers to cover every door, hundreds of windows, and, at the same time, protect lawmakers, staff, even the damn press.

He shook his head as a slice of the raging mob overran the last now worthless barrier protecting the East Plaza. The clock showed exactly 2 p.m.

Within minutes, the last barricade on the West Terrace fell, too. Like the rerun of a bad movie, Swift watched the spectacle of the horde driving battered officers up the west steps. They fought to hold their ground, a beachhead protecting a tunnel leading into the Capitol. Shoulder-to-shoulder, they traded blows with club and fist, footing sometimes slippery with blood in a near-Medieval scene. Badly outnumbered cops stood against a traitorous scrum bent on storming not just a building but an iconic symbol of democracy. More seditionists poured in against the blue cork plugging the tunnel beneath the Senate chamber.

"My god. How can this be happening?"

Swift wondered if his son, Nick, was in the tunnel, part of the cork. Sweat trickled down his spine.

Another alert: One of the sergeants at arms had finally approved calling in the National Guard.

"Really? You tardy prick."

Yet another alert, this one caught on surveillance cameras. Swift watched in horror and anger as a rioter on the Capitol's northwest side hammered at a window with a plastic police shield. He saw the window break and the insurrectionist gingerly crawl past broken glass and drop into an unguarded hallway. Other marauders followed.

The Capitol of the United States had been violated.

Swift looked at the clock: 2:12.

CHAPTER 14

When the first traitor slipped through the shattered window and perched on the sill, he quickly glanced left and right, half expecting a barrage of gunfire. He hopped to the floor, moved to an outside door and opened it to a handful of intruders. They entered cautiously, momentarily distracted by the Capitol's classic splendor, its ornate beauty. They gazed around in awe, like uninvited guests at a fancy house party.

Remembering the reason for their intrusion, one invader shouted, "We got our house back!"

"People rule," yelled another.

And a third, with frightening intent, demanded, "Find the traitors!"

They fanned out, not knowing where they were going or what would come next. But the marauders were jubilant in their occupation, believing their presence alone would bring Congress to a halt, derail the ouster of their President. At least they had succeeded in interrupting the nation's business more severely than since the British burned the Capitol in the War of 1812.

The first window shattered was one of six hundred fifty-eight in the Capitol, which stretches seven hundred fifty-one feet and four inches north to south, three hundred fifty feet east to west. With so much real estate to cover, the insurrectionists spread out, throwing open or kicking in doors as their ranks grew. Slowly they penetrated the seat of government – one million, five hundred thousand square feet, spread over five levels soaring to the Statue of Freedom atop the dome, two hundred eighty-eight feet high.

Traitors at the fore marched proudly with flags – American, Confederate, political – unfurled and waved madly or donned like capes. They traded backslaps, high fives and hugs. Joyful yells echoed off the lofty ceilings. With little sense of direction, the invaders moved instinctively toward the centers of power, the Senate and House chambers and the rotunda. By the minute, their numbers swelled, from a handful to scores to hundreds, roaming at will, boisterous but still largely peaceful. Shouts of "Stop the steal" and "We've taken our house back!" setting the tone of their exploration.

They almost immediately confronted Capitol Police, who backed off or stood aside, badly outnumbered, not wanting a blowup. Mostly, the cops were alone or in twos or threes, isolated, wearing the uniforms of a routine day with no protective gear. Handguns stayed holstered. The day's marching orders anticipated standard crowd control, a lawful protest by the President's White disciples.

Some officers tried to reverse the intruders: "This is not right, guys. Let's end it right here." Now and again an officer offered a smile or friendly gesture, whether to placate or welcome being uncertain. They were rebuffed, ignored and, increasingly, faced hostility. Harassed officers quietly radioed their command post, seeking guidance. "Don't provoke. Stay calm." As the crowd grew larger and more aggressive, officers wondered why their Civil Disturbance Unit hadn't shown up, in full gear, ready to impose control. Maybe this mutiny can still be ended before it gets out of control, they whispered into their radios. But time had slipped away.

Ambrose hung back as the mob invaded the Capitol. He waited to hear shots, expecting to see the President's people pouring out in chaotic retreat. When that didn't happen, he called Willard Hart. "I'm going in," he told his lieutenant. "Tell our guys to catch up with me."

Three of his militia joined him as he reached the vanguard of the President's people. Those in the lead moved slowly, checking unlocked rooms, forcing open others. Ambrose stepped into an ornate hideaway office where three men stood over two others, one of them old.

"Hey, bro, looksee what we got," one of the invaders told Ambrose. "He says he's a senator and this here'n his assistant."

The man pulled from a pint of whiskey and passed the bottle to a tall man with one arm.

Ambrose recognized the old man, a senator from the Midwest. Ohio? Iowa? A pretty big deal, he recalled, maybe a committee chairman who hit the news a lot when a Supreme Court nominee was being confirmed.

Might as well get things rolling, he thought.

"Great work, men. I'm Ambrose, head of the NPM. I'm making the good senator and his aide my hostages."

He was greeted with protests from the senator as well as his captors.

"You will not," said the one-armed man. "He's our prisoner, dammit. We caught him fair and square."

"Hostage? I am not," shouted the senator. "I'm a good backer of the President."

"It will be one cold day when we give him up," said the third man. He was short and compact and slowly pulled a small caliber handgun from his coat pocket. Ambrose's men stepped away from him, showing the guns at their sides.

"We're working with other militias to keep the President in office," Ambrose said calmly. "We need hostages for negotiating. Does not matter if they are for the President or not. They will all be valuable."

Addressing the compact man, he asked, "Are you militia?"

"No. We drove up from North Carolina to help the President."

"My brother heads the NPM in the Carolinas. You're welcome to join us or tag along to keep track of the good senator."

The compact man tossed a disgusted glance at his unsteady friends and pocketed his gun. "Okay, we'll tag along. Maybe join later."

"Thank you," Ambrose told him. "If you and your friends would lead the way with the senator and his guy, we'll follow. Go toward the rotunda, the center of the Capitol."

As more people invaded, hallways grew crowded, noisier and unruly. A skinny man kicked frantically at a heavy wooden door. Someone had spray painted "Close Our Poorous Border" on another door. Fine work by an intellectual brother, Ambrose thought, walking on.

His entourage grew with the arrival of four Seth Baldwin men and five more of his own. Their destination was across the rotunda. Having studied options for where to best hold hostages, the Dancer brothers chose the House Dining Room. It was easier to defend than most large rooms and offered food, water and toilets.

Ahead, a man in a pirate costume, black patch covering one eye, looked down at a small woman, bellowing, "What's the Senate going to do about the vote count? You gonna quit on the count?"

The woman, a well-known West Coast senator, held her ground. "What I hear is," she said calmly, "we are going to finish our business as soon as you traitors are arrested."

Gutsy, but not smart, Ambrose thought as he approached.

"Bullshit, you bitch," insisted pirate man, tobacco juice dripping to stain an NRA patch crudely sewn on his shirt pocket. "You gotta hear things. What?"

"String the bitch up," a woman shouted to howls of support from the surrounding crowd.

"I'm having us a trial right here, Missy Senator," yelled pirate man, grabbing her arm. "How your jury look to you?"

"Hold it," Ambrose shouted. "There'll be no trial."

"Fuck you!"

"I'm Ambrose Dancer with the NPM in Michigan. We're one of the militias backing the President and we're rounding up hostages. Right here I have a senator and his aide. I'll be taking the lady senator, too."

"Bullshit. We're having a trial by her peers, like the law says to. Any patriot who wants to hang her, step right up."

Before anyone moved, Ambrose nodded to one of his men, who swung an old-fashioned blackjack. Pirate man crumpled, unconscious if not dead. Stepping over him, Ambrose told the woman senator, "You come with me." She was more than ready.

They moved along, a disciplined knot amid helter-skelter.

Valerie Wells, the Proud Boys queen, stood mouth agape in the doorway of a hideaway office. Mickey, one of the men she had happily serviced the night before, nudged her inside. She could hear glass breaking, the screams of battle – noise almost blocked out when Mickey closed the solid oak door behind her.

"I just stumbled in here, must be the hideout for someone high up," Mickey said. "When I saw you in the rotunda, I knew we had to do it. Holy moly, we can tell our grandkids we screwed in the Capitol of the United States of America."

He stepped behind her, cupped her breasts, but Valerie took his hands. "Look at this place for a minute." The damn textured wallpaper must cost more than I make in a year, she thought. The embroidered sofa and chairs, too. The heavy damask drapes were open to a spectacular view of the city, the avenues that had brought them here, the National Mall with the memorial to Lincoln peeking around the monument to Washington.

"This has to be a quickie," Mickey said, slipping off her coat. This time she did not slow him as he stripped her below the waist. Dropping his trousers, he tipped her back on the sofa, maneuvered between her legs, their shoes marking the sofa.

"Oh yeah," he said, leaning in, breath quickening, "this will be something to tell the grandkids.

Mutineers reaching the Capitol's epicenter – the rotunda – cavorted beneath the cast iron dome painted the color of marble in classic designs. It soared above a circular space of unparalleled honor. Only presidents and a few revered shapers of the nation had lain in state there, eulogized as democracy's finest. Now, the rotunda echoed with seditious calls to dismantle the republic.

"Finish the revolution."

"Tea Party 2021!"

"Find the traitors. Death to the traitors!"

The cavernous room offered the rebels ample space to celebrate disrupting Congress and to declare victory over perceived political corruption. With gleeful abandon they wallowed in the delusion that their cause justified violence and arbitrarily reversing the election.

Mama Bones swirled wildly, voodoo dolls in hand. "My pins are hard at work, my good friends," she chanted. "Pricking the big-D pricks in Congress will give the President his due."

A QAnon believer was on a tear about pedophiles running and ruining the country. Competing nearby, a man balanced precariously on the base of a statue, demanding the Second Amendment be tightened to ensure limitless gun buys without annoying background checks. People took selfies, toasting with small bottles of airline liquor.

"I'm here, Osage City, I'm really here," squealed a thirty-something woman doing FaceTime with someone in Kansas.

The woman senator in Ambrose's tow tried to charge a man gouging an historically themed oil painting with a screwdriver. Ambrose roughly jerked her back, keeping his group moving toward Statuary Hall and the House Dining Room.

Inside the rotunda, several people struggled to force open the massive Columbus Doors and allow insurrectionists on the East Plaza to enter. "Damn electronics," one man screamed repeatedly. Outside, at the top of the steps, mutineers battered the twenty-thousand-pound doors with all manner of clubs.

Their efforts proved futile until electronic deadbolts inexplicably triggered, and the seventeen-foot-tall bronze doors swung open on their recessed tracks. The mob swarmed in.

Private First Class Darrell Steele of the United States Capitol Police was there to greet them. He knew the certification of electoral votes had been halted. He knew the Vice President and members of Congress were in hiding. In the turmoil, he had talked briefly with protesters arriving from the Senate side. *We are seizing the moment,* they told him with confidence. *We will reverse the theft of our President's election.* And Steele had picked up scuttlebutt that special militia units were waiting to back the military when the President imposed the Insurrection Act.

"Everything is falling into place, exactly as it should," he assured himself. "It's my time to step up."

Only a few officers remained in the rotunda, standing defensively near the curved wall in a benign charade of protecting the Capitol. They wanted to run the rabble out, bash heads, reclaim the building they had sworn to protect. But they knew the mob would tolerate them only if they posed no threat. So, they didn't, and felt safe enough, like would-be prey in the company of well-fed predators.

Those officers had watched with suspicion as Steele seemed to befriend one rioter, then another. Encouraged a fat woman wearing a People Power sweatshirt to snuggle in for a selfie, parting with a fist bump. Still, when the door swung open to the mob, they were startled when he stepped forward with a broad smile.

He spread his arms to warmly greet the President's people, his people, to congratulate them for reaching the cusp of fulfilling their mission. Steele's colleagues strained to hear his words, breaking up in the din. They thought he said, "Welcome to your house, my friends.

Welcome to your..." before a large man swung a metal pipe. Steele went down, blood spurting from above his ear as he disappeared beneath the traitorous surge, the large man roaring, "Don't stand the fuck in Hasty's way."

CHAPTER 15

Recalling maps of the Capitol, Ambrose knew the hallway to the Speaker's office was near. Suddenly, just yards ahead, a party of about a dozen crossed their path, moving quickly.

My god, Ambrose asked himself, could it be? The decisive pace of half a dozen well-conditioned suits, with ear buds and dark glasses, shouted out: security detail. At their center was a woman, her hair escaping a head covering. She wore a dark suit and moved smoothly on spike heels, all saying power and class, money no object. My god, Ambrose thought, that's Madam Speaker.

He had talked with his men about the off-chance of such good fortune, snaring a game-changing hostage. Talked about the time that could buy to foment national unrest leading to revolution. Talked about the challenge of bringing down chest-protected guards with head shots. Could his men be that disciplined? What if the Speaker was killed? Not the worst thing; sow more confusion.

Bottom line: Opportunity. Strike.

"That's Madam Speaker," he said, plenty loud for his men to hear. "Queen bee in the middle. Don't shoot her. Wait 'til I fire, then take head shots."

He caught the stunned looks of his men, saw fear strike the man who had passed the whiskey bottle. "Don't you dare," the woman senator shouted in his ear, struggling against his grip. He swung the butt of his Glock square to her forehead. She went down hard.

The protective detail's lead agent had left the Speaker's office too late. Rounding a corner, they ran into frenzied traitors. With Ambrose coming from the rotunda, they were blocked in. Retreating to the Speaker's office was still an option, but once there, they would be trapped. The lead agent, choosing to confront the rioters, drew his handgun.

"We're coming through. Everyone down," he ordered. "Faces on the floor. Now!"

Some in the mob did. Others hesitated, confused at suddenly having a man waving a large gun screaming at them. A rioter pulled his revolver. With no hesitation, the agent fired three rapid shots. The man sprawled backwards, red drenching his shirt front.

It's now, Ambrose told himself. He stepped into a clear spot, aiming his Glock two-handed. The lead agent faced away, focused on moving Madam Speaker through the crowd. Ambrose involuntarily caught his breath and squeezed twice. The agent's head splattered like a cantaloupe, hollow points doing their grisly work.

The other agents turned to face an unexpected shooter. Ambrose fired twice more, dropping one of them, a woman he thought. His men opened fire, trying to pick targets but quickly stunned by the volley the highly trained detail put down. Ambrose slid behind a statuary base as bullets rained in, ricochets following. He saw whiskey man, one from the NPM and the old senator's aide go down, almost certainly dead. At the first pause in firing, he peeked out, saw a third agent lying still. Madam Speaker was on her knees, bent low, an agent on either side. More shots were exchanged. One of his men screamed. He reached around the marble base, aimed above Madam Speaker, hoped she didn't take a ricochet, and fired several times.

As Ambrose expected, an agent jumped protectively on the Speaker, momentarily taking himself out of the fire fight. Ambrose saw another agent thrashing in pain, and knew he had the upper hand. "Stop firing! Everyone stop firing," he screamed.

The mob went silent, guns lowered, as if seeking escape from the sudden bloodshed. One agent remaining defiant, balanced on a knee, arcing his gun back and forth. Defiant, yes, but uncertain, weighing the impossible odds, how to best protect the Speaker.

"Put it down easy," Ambrose told him. "You, on the Speaker, up easy, without your weapon. We go again and we will kill her."

The agents hesitated only a moment, knowing the insurgents reviled the Speaker; without a doubt, they would wait in line for the chance to execute her. Maybe this unknown assassin giving orders offered life.

One of Ambrose's men, Lawrence, moaned loudly, gripping a shin cocked at an ugly angle.

"Get their weapons, Hank," Ambrose said. Getting no response, he glanced around. On his back, arms by his sides and eyes closed, Hank was coffin-ready but for the blood running from his throat.

"Someone else," Ambrose said, struggling to speak with authority. Hank had been a friend, a reliable hand. "Someone get their guns, dammit."

He knew he had little time to gather the new hostages and get to the dining room. His force was barely enough to control Madam Speaker and her aides, but two of the men who grabbed the old senator had survived and seemed on board. Insurrectionists who had blocked the Speaker's path were still stunned. But others were arriving, eager to bask in the gore of the missed firefight. They would soon find their courage.

"That's the Speaker, damned if it ain't," a middle-aged bantam rooster of a man allowed. "Damned if it ain't. We need a rope. Where's a rope?"

"Now listen up, all of you. I'm Ambrose with the militias. We were taking prisoners to our headquarters in the House Dining Room when we came across this outfit. Now they're prisoners, too, all of them."

There was grumbling. "Who's this Ambrose?" "We need a people's court."

"Joe," Ambrose told one of his men. "Zip tie the agents, hands behind their backs. Mark, get a couple hostages to carry Lawrence. You all in the crowd, someone call 911 for that wounded agent."

"Maybe we'll just put him out of his misery," said bantam rooster man.

"Maybe you will," Ambrose said coldly, ready to make that deal if it meant moving on. "You can have the other agents, too."

"We'll carry him," said the agent who had protected the speaker. "We won't be a threat. Promise."

"No way in hell would you keep that promise," Ambrose answered.

"Please," said Madam Speaker. "I will order them not to be a problem. They do what I say."

Her voice was steady, but as she looked directly into Ambrose's eyes, he knew she would not argue. He was her best hope for surviving.

"Not going to happen, ma'am." She set her face, saying nothing more. "We're going now, ma'am. As you know, it's not far."

Ambrose took her firmly by the arm and, gun at his side, started easing through the ugly crowd. Demands to "String her up" and obscenities matched every step. For all of them, the walk was long.

CHAPTER 16

A short time earlier, House debate had entered predictable point and counterpoint – Republicans trotting out theories of a stolen election, Democrats noting court opinions knocking them down. When Madam Speaker needed a break, she had turned her gavel over to a fellow-Democrat from California.

"What is there to hide?" an Arizona Republican had asked solemnly when he was distracted by an alarming clamor outside the double doors where Americans watch the sergeant at arms announce: "Madam Speaker, the President of the United States."

The state of the union that day was tense. The clamor triggered anxious conversations among the eleven lawmakers from each party allowed on the floor during Electoral College debate. Other members and staff watching from the visitors' gallery were keenly aware that protesters roamed the building. Suddenly, gunfire echoed into the chamber. Lawmakers leaped to their feet, alarm washing their faces.

"Order! Order!" demanded the Speaker's stand-in, pounding the gavel as an aide whispered urgently.

"Of course, of course we must. Right now," he told the aide, the open microphone capturing his panic. Then: "I declare the House in recess subject to the call of the chair."

As if a starting gun had fired, a score of suit-clad Capitol Police rushed onto the floor. One officer opened, then quickly slammed closed the double doors. "They're coming, hallway's full of them!" he yelled.

As that alarm was raised, a text from the Capitol Police warned of a "security threat inside the building." Fear multiplied as members and staff read: Get in offices. Take visitors and emergency equipment with you. Lock doors. Stay away from windows. If in a public area, hide. Remain quiet. Silence electronics. Await further instructions.

And an order dripping with irony: No one will be permitted to enter or exit the building until directed by the USCP.

The order had somehow missed the horde of protesters-turned-mob, rattling the doors of the chamber.

"Barricade the doors," an officer commanded. "All of them!"

Desks were pushed into place, chairs added for weight. The makeshift restraints shook in defiance as insurgents threw themselves against doors, shouting to be let in. Officers drew their guns.

"Don't fire," the officer in charge said.

Throughout the Capitol and in nearby buildings, doors were locked and barricaded, drapes drawn. Members' families and hapless tourists, visiting to witness a congressional ritual, found themselves trapped.

Hundreds made calls – seeking information, pleading for help – but none with more urgency than from the House chamber. Lawmakers of standing – in reality or their own minds – pleaded with Capitol Police and Defense officials: Where the hell are our vaunted SWAT teams? Get the Army, the National Guard, someone, anyone, in here.

They called the White House with the same demand, to plead for the President to go on TV or tweet his loyalists into halting the violence. Few calls got through. Most messages went unanswered.

"I've supported you through thick and thin and you turn your crowd loose on us," complained one Republican congressman. "You narcissistic coward!"

"My death will be on your hands," said another. "Not that you give a shit."

Calls were made to loved ones, most to say, "I love you." Or goodbye. Or to lie, insisting everything was fine, not to worry.

Capitol Police interrupted callers, urging them to be ready should rioters get in the chamber. Put on your gas masks, they were told, but many couldn't find their masks, let alone knew how to put them on. Get under your chairs. Remember, chair backs are bulletproof. Always keep them pointed at your attacker. Seriously?

Remove lapel pins identifying you as a member. A lawmaker of color thought: That may help you White folks but not me, not when a mob led by racists busts in here.

Several lawmakers and staff readied for a fight. They broke the legs off chairs and tables to use as clubs. A gentlelady from the Northeast hefted her walking stick, pulling the rubber tip off its steel point. Some read directions for using their mace or small stun guns.

Over and over, everyone was told, "Stay calm." Yeah. Right.

An insurgent broke a vertical window lining the double doors, demanding to be let in. A plain clothes officer fired once. There was a scream. "They shot her, the fuckers shot her dead," a traitor shouted.

"Don't shoot. No more shooting," ordered the officer in command.

More windows were broken. Doors shuddered under the weight of insurrectionists' shoulders.

A chant went up: "Let us in! Let us in!"

Scoping out hallways, police found a route still free of the mob. Word spread: "We're going to move."

Guns ready, officers led an exodus joined by a few reporters, other officers bringing up the rear. The frightened procession rushed down the back stairs and hallways to safety.

A handful of members and their aides watching the debate from the visitors' gallery were left behind.

Freshman Rep. Meshio Gonzalez stifled the urge to cry out when she heard the window break and the shot fired. She swore her chief of staff, Marie Wilton – her first day on the job – turned white.

They had watched in alarm as uniformed police moved through the gallery above the House floor, urging observers to crouch in front of their seats. Gonzalez went to her knees, squeezing her petite frame in front of her second-row seat. Wilton did the same, making herself as small as possible.

Gonzalez peeked over a seat to watch chamber doors being barricaded as her colleagues wrestled with gas masks. She quietly cheered those making ready for battle. Could hear an officer tell a frightened member over and over, "Stay calm, stay calm." She took out her phone but didn't call, knowing her daughter in Oakland would insist on a full report.

A plain-clothes cop on the floor whispered loudly to a uniformed one in the gallery. He and another uniform started moving through the seats, moving people toward the press room door reporters use to access their balcony working space.

The mob's pounding and shouting got louder. "Let us in! Let us in!" Gonzalez tasted the bile of fear and swallowed. Her alarm grew as her last colleague exited the press door. The cops stopped and looked around. They will come this way, looking for others, for me, she thought. They must. They didn't. Gonzalez rose to her knees. "Don't go. I'm here. Don't go," she yelled into the clamor.

The cops didn't hear her. They left.

"Shut up, Sheri, shut up!" someone ordered. Fearful eyes met hers as Herbie Squelch snaked himself ridiculously down the steep aisle, headfirst. "Just shut up. I think they're already on the floor, but I've got this."

She looked in disbelief at Herbert Squelch, his thick brown hair matted with perspiration, corners of his mouth white with spittle. He's scared more shitless than I am, Gonzalez thought. But he's got this? What the hell?

"Hey, Herbie," she said, surprised with her familiarity. They had met once at a members-only reception, a brief throwback to a time of bipartisanship. His far-right politics and her own were total opposites. She didn't recall introducing herself as Sheri, the anglicized name used by liberal friends, but maybe she did. "You must have been behind me," she whispered. "I didn't see you."

"Yeah." He was feeling lightheaded, maybe from excitement, maybe from having his head down. "I'm going to move." He wiggled farther down the aisle like a caterpillar, then backed into the row of seats across from Gonzalez.

"We need to leave," she said.

"No. They're down there, on the floor."

But the mob wasn't. This was their chance. They would be on their own, but it was a chance. The chamber had quieted. They heard scraping.

"They're forcing the doors, pushing back the desks," Gonzalez whispered. "Let's go."

"No, they're already on the floor," Squelch insisted.

He was wrong. Had he looked, he would have seen the doors opening enough for a skinny man to slip in, glance around nervously. No shots greeted him and in seconds he pushed the desk and chairs aside. A handful of insurrectionists entered, also cautiously, two with handguns. Betting the chamber was theirs, a bearded man, wearing red cargo pants and a leather jacket with a Confederate flag on the back, skipped down the center aisle and up the short steps to the Speaker's chair.

He plopped down in the plush leather, loudly declaring, "Ladies and gents, welcome to your house! Yahoo!"

The mob charged in, scurrying like investigating ants. The traitors peered under desks, opening doors where someone might hide. They searched for historical plunder, for bragging rights or to sell. A few paused in awe to take in the chamber's subdued elegance, startled to find themselves at the source of so much history. Selfies were taken, the Speaker's chair a favorite prop. Furniture was broken and carpet slashed, just for the hell of it. One man grabbed an antique brass spittoon and walked to a wall to relieve himself, the model of discretion.

"Shit. We're stuck," Gonzalez said. She kicked herself for listening to Squelch.

Stuck was an understatement. The press gallery doors offering refuge minutes earlier opened and three invaders stepped inside.

"Let's check it out," said a short man with a slight accent, turning left, toward them. "You guys take that side."

He moved quickly through the aisles, needlessly squatting at each row, moving toward them.

"Someone distract him. Make him go back," Gonzalez mouthed the words, almost in prayer. No such luck.

"Hey guys, work this way," shouted the short man, excited. "I got paydirt."

Gonzalez looked up and Squelch struggled to roll over. Eldon Weber smiled down at them, cruelly, hefting the .45 he had never fired. The other men sidled into the row behind Gonzalez.

"That one," said Weber, pointing his gun at Squelch's head in a two-handed grip. "He's got a Congress pin, I think. What's your name, sonny?"

"Herbert Squelch. And I am a congressman. So is she. I don't know about the other one, probably her aide."

"Yes, I am a member," said Gonzalez, voice quavering. "And this is my chief of staff. And what is wrong with you people, assaulting our Capitol like this?"

"We were invited here by the President to save a stolen election," said Weber. "Now we going to take you downstairs to be tried."

"Wait!" screamed Squelch. "I'm one of the President's strongest backers. I go with him to rallies, even introduced him once."

Weber shifted his sweaty grip to keep the .45 steady and forced a smile. "Bullshit. You bastards all lie like rugs."

"No, I was with people from the White House last night, at the hotel, doing strategy for the rally. The President's lawyers were there, too," he gushed. "I talked to a Proud Boy later. Really. I'll give you his number. Check me out."

One of the other invaders waved a small congressional handbook.

"I found Herbert Squelch and his picture," said Willard Hart, of Ambrose Dancer's crew. "That's him. He's in the right party, at least."

Weber glanced up, disappointed. "I don't know about turning him loose... I sure don't want to turn the spic loose."

"Here's Gonzalez, too. Wrong party. From communist Oakland in the great socialist state of California."

"That's good," said Weber. "At least we can haul her Hispanic ass down for trial, right there on the floor of the United States House of Representatives. Sweet!"

"Not going to happen, my friend."

Weber glanced sharply at the two men.

"We haven't done introductions but I'm Willie with the NPM militia headquartered in Michigan. My friend here is NPM, too. Our orders are to take hostage any members of Congress we find. Thanks for your help – and you're welcome to come along."

"If I do, where are we going?" asked Weber, knowing he wasn't going to challenge the militiamen.

"Not sure. Our leader Ambrose is around here somewhere. I'll give him a call."

CHAPTER 17

Anthony — not Tony, if you please — Larkin Jr. waited cautiously halfway up the east steps. Already, some protesters were exiting the Columbus Doors. That worried him. Maybe they just wanted to say they got inside the Capitol, or maybe they have another reason for leaving, a scary one.

The invasion of the rotunda had diluted the crowd on the steps, now occupied only by protesters. Arrivals from the rally were at a trickle. Anthony Larkin Jr. could imagine a noose slowly closing around the Capitol grounds as reinforcements arrived. He must take care not to get trapped. I could not bear, just could not bear, the humility of being arrested, he thought.

Already, the afternoon had turned ugly once. A terribly unfair incident since, besides supporting the President, he was there to interview lawful protesters. To show them exercising their constitutional rights and gather evidence of the media's biased coverage.

A young woman, ignoring the turmoil, had stood quietly, holding a neatly lettered small sign: Votes Were Stolen and I Can Prove It. Anthony Larkin Jr. approached and asked what proof she had. She stared intently through owlish glasses and said earnestly, "I'm the daughter-in-law of a janitor in the Georgia Secretary of State's office, and I know what my father-in-law found."

Anthony Larkin Jr. quickly hit video on his phone. "Please repeat that, speaking very clearly."

She only got to "janitor" when a flying Bud Light bottle shattered the bridge of her nose, knocking her unconscious. Not trained in first aid, Anthony Larkin Jr. was frozen by the blood, then relieved when an older woman knelt to help. He backed off, turning toward the Columbus Doors. Enough time has passed without explosions or anything else scary that it's probably safe to enter, he thought.

He met two women coming out, lugging an aluminum coatrack. Smiling broadly under their MAGA caps, one also had a splintered Members Only sign tucked beneath her arm. The other carried a blue bag stamped POLICE.

"Excuse me, ladies…," Anthony Larkin Jr. began, but they swept past. Looking to his right, he saw two men destroying a large window, one swinging a baseball bat, the other wielding a flagstick with the campaign banner of the President. He held up his phone to video.

"What you doin' man?" demanded a gruff voice. "You a CNN piece of shit?"

Anthony turned and looked directly into hostile eyes, though the young man stood three steps down.

"No, sir. I'm with the campaign," he said, certain his benevolent President would excuse a minor white lie. "When the lamestream media broadcast lies I'm going to have proof of what really happened."

The young man thought about that, baffled at how filming vandalism could be helpful. He shook his head and trotted away.

Stepping through the mammoth doors, Anthony Larkin Jr. felt he was in a time-warped movie, an Animal House reprise improbably set in the rotunda's high-domed classical elegance. A bare-chested man wearing buckskin breeches and buffalo horns danced with a middle-aged woman in gypsy attire. She waved a voodoo doll punctured with pins. At his feet he saw "Stop the Count" spray-painted on the floor. A man in a gray uniform and sporting a neatly groomed gray beard strode by, waving a Confederate battle flag from an Alabama regiment. Two young men leaned against the curved wall, sharing a bottle of wine. They passively watched a man with a machete hack at a huge colonial era oil painting. Two cops studiously ignored him. Broken furniture, glass and statuary littered the sandstone and marble floor. Anthony Larkin Jr. was still taking in the bizarre spectacle when his eyes started burning. Remnants of pepper spray?

He dampened his handkerchief from his water bottle. As he dabbed his eyes, a young man with a pasted-on toothbrush mustache grabbed his shoulder and read from a small book, *Quotes of Mein Kampf*: "He who would live must fight. He who doesn't wish to fight in this world, where permanent struggle is the law of life, has not the right to exist."

"Adolf got that right, bro," the mustached man said. "That's why we're here, bro. Right?"

"Let me ask you why...," Anthony Larkin Jr. began, reaching for his phone.

"No time, bro. Gotta spread Adolf's word: 'Sooner will a camel pass through the eye of a needle, than a great man be found by an election.' Boy, did he get that right. Why we're here, right bro?"

The mustache man spun away. The noise worsened. Anthony Larkin Jr. felt confused, light-headed. His stomach churned. Who are these people? Why isn't someone stopping this desecration? This mindless destruction? Where are the President's people? He needs to know how badly his followers have been infiltrated, how his rally has been captured by — by whom? Right-wing extremists? More likely antifa, their black garb swapped out to look like working Americans, blending in with legit protesters like me. Or maybe I am witnessing how far the Deep State will go, polluting the rally with bureaucrats in disguise, or FBI, carrying out a public relations nightmare the President cannot escape.

He glanced up and recognized the John Trumbull painting of Washington resigning his commission as commander of the Continental Army. Anthony Larkin Jr. knew that was Washington's choice;

he could have declared himself president or king with little opposition. But he deferred in the nation's first peaceful transfer of power to elected lawmakers. It gave Anthony Larkin Jr. pause.

He saw a man wearing tan overalls, sweeping the room with his cell phone. Nearby, a woman wearing jeans and a plaid coat did the same. They could be the infiltrators, getting video, filming the destruction to feed the media. He raised his own camera, hit zoom to make sure he captured their faces. Then he swept the broad rotunda, slowly, feeling good to be capturing what surely would be evidence of antifa or Deep State trickery.

As he stepped deeper into the room, adrenaline pumping with his expanded mission, a man shouted at him, "Are you okay, son? You are sweating like a stuck hog."

Anthony Larkin Jr. didn't know any stuck hogs, but suddenly felt perspiration streaming down his face. His questioner wore a gray uniform and had a gray beard. He carried a Confederate flag and slung over one shoulder was an assault rifle, like one from news clips of school shootings.

"Get that damn hat off, son, and loosen up your coat. With all these folks, those heavy clothes make it hotter than a deprived nymph in here."

Anthony Larkin Jr. complied but had to ask, "That gun, sir, how did you get it in here? If you don't mind the question, sir."

"Not at all. It breaks down real nice, fits in my backpack. Do not think I'm the only one carrying more than handguns. Most don't want to be captured on security cameras. I want to be. I'm hoping the Capitol Police make shots of me public, and it inspires other folks."

"Inspires folks to do what?"

"Whatever we need to keep the President in office. He is our only hope for saving America."

Anthony Larkin Jr. was startled. "But he just wants an honest vote count. You make 'whatever' sound like a revolution or civil war or something."

"Hell yes, son. He can't say it, but that's what he wants us to do, if my shirttail cousin Jeffrey Lomax knows from Shinola."

"Jeffrey?"

"Damn, forget that name. Trouble for him if things go bad. He's a militia hotshot. Me, I don't give a shit, what with cancer hard on my tail. You stay cool now," he laughed, walking away.

Anthony Larkin Jr. again felt sweat running, even with the wool cap in his pocket and his coat open. The visual bombardment was too much: The Confederate uniform walking away, assault rifle dangling; a couple singing Glory Hallelujah in off-key harmony; a man emptying a fire extinguisher on a painting; the witch doctor spinning by again.

Mama Bones danced to the QAnon theme song, playing loudly on a phone held high by a prancing young man with facial tattoos and spiked hair. He punctuated the music – "Wwg1wga... Where we go one, we go all" – with an index finger. They sang along joyfully, attracting others who raised a finger – for the "1" – in the Q salute.

The young man's sweatshirt was emblazoned with the QAnon symbol, its bold colors circled by a large "Q." A sash draping Mama Bones' bare shoulder was covered with QAnon lapel buttons. Crossing the sash was another declaring "The Storm is Coming" – the Q prediction of the President's minions executing his enemies, perhaps on TV.

The witch doctor twirled directly in front of Anthony Larkin Jr. and their eyes locked. Her cougar-like grin made him feel stalked, as did the young man jostling him as they danced away. The incessant beat of the Q song. Lingering pepper spray. It was all too much. Too much. He wanted to run back to California and Jack.

"Get ahold of yourself," he muttered. "Work to do."

He trudged across the rotunda, down a hallway littered with glass. "If you see the Speaker, send her our regards," beamed an older man, in step with another carrying a polished wooden sign labeled "Speaker of the House." Looking up, Anthony Larkin Jr. saw it had been ripped from above a door.

Following the hallway, he glanced out a window and down at the battle on the west steps – the crowd surging, falling back, two burly men dragging a police officer by his heels. Others stepped to kick the cop, curled in a fetal position, hands over his head. A man slapped him with a police shield. A woman jabbed him with a flagpole. When Anthony Larkin Jr. saw blood, he turned away to watch a man reach down and pull another to the top of an exterior wall. That's sure to make the news, he thought, relieved to not be watching the combat.

He struggled to understand the conflict and damage. He wondered if protesters like himself – or imposters from the Deep State – had mutated into common vandals. He saw men smashing two coffin-size lanterns designed by famed landscape architect Frederick Law Olmsted in the 1870s. Scaffolding erected for the inauguration was in shambles, television and sound equipment busted and strewn about. Blue paint discolored the balustrade at the top of the west wall.

Disconnected thoughts cluttered Anthony Larkin Jr.'s mind: blue is a good color for street art; my taxes will pay to repair this mess; it's better to look at vandalism than blood, but why am I making such choices?

Momentarily lightheaded, he backed away from the window and was caught in the flow of the crowd. Shoulder to shoulder, he sensed caution, anxiety in some people, concerned about security cameras. Worrying about arrest and knowing pleas of being curious or dispatched by their President were not likely to save them from jail.

But most were raucous, declaring, "We're in charge now." They burst wild-eyed into rooms in search of lawmakers, demanding "Hang the bastards." Anthony Larkin Jr. wanted to interview them, make sense of their rampage. Why are you attacking Capitol Police? Why move from lawful protest to unbridled sedition? Why are you plundering the Capitol? Two older women wearing red MAGA hats walked toward him, arm in arm. One carried a large metal pipe, the other a crowbar. He turned to a wall until they passed. I shouldn't be afraid of my own people, he told himself.

He came to Statuary Hall, where each state honors two historic figures – Virginia has George Washington and, until 2020, Robert E. Lee. Spray paint was still wet on some statues. He saw a man wearing pilfered police gear – a cap, bulletproof vest, duty belt with only handcuffs still attached. What had happened to the officer, or officers? Glancing between two statues, he saw a man relieving himself. Condoms adorned the bronze fingers of Mississippi's Jefferson Davis. He stopped, idly pondering whether the vandal might hail from the North or the South. An insistent voice interrupted.

"Damnit, I seen the tweets my own self, just not long ago," a beer-bellied man wearing a "1776 Again" sweatshirt declared to whoever would listen. He waved his phone. "See this here, the President says, if you know how to read between his words, the VP didn't have the guts to do right... And in this'n he says to support the Capitol cops. He doesn't say leave the Capitol. 'Til I hear that, brother, I'm taking it as an order from on high to stay put right here in our house."

Anthony reached hesitantly for his own phone, wanting to restart his mission, even in this baffling turmoil. At least, the beer-bellied man was making decisions.

"Excuse me, sir, I'm doing interviews for the President so we'll have evidence of what happened today if the media fails to tell the truth."

"How do I know you ain't a damn reporter? Or under the cover FBI? You got some credentials or something from the campaign?"

"I assure you, sir. I am not the press. I am a divinity student who loves the President."

"Talk is cheap. In Missouri we say show me." The man stalked off.

Dejected, Anthony Larkin Jr. made his way back through the rotunda and to the Senate side. He saw a door ajar, the lock broken, and stepped into one of the hideaway offices assigned to senators for work or more intimate pleasures. Four men helped themselves to liquor from an art deco cabinet. Broken bottles littered the floor, their contents soaking the heavy wool rug. Lamps were overturned and drawers pulled from cabinets and dumped. The canvas of a slashed wall painting drooped to the floor and a large mirror, smashed, cast strange reflections.

The men celebrating their vandalism wore work clothes and sweat-stained baseball caps. They glared at Anthony Larkin Jr. in his city slicker gear. "You lost, boy?" The question threatened. He left, fearful, the men's laughter trailing him.

Unhinged, he stumbled back into the rotunda, barely missing a smear of feces as he leaned against a wall. He moved away, seeking relief as he looked up at the beautiful dome. Everything swirling about him was contrary to – no, that is wrong, he said quietly – all of this is a perversion of what the dome embodies: The likeness of George Washington, ascending to heaven, flanked by female figures of Liberty and Victory, who symbolized confidence in the Union when painted by Constantino Brumidi as the Civil War ended. Where is the liberty in anarchy? Anthony Larkin Jr. asked himself. Where is the victory in treason? How can a riot inspire confidence?

He walked toward the Columbus Doors, his mind searching for a connection between those who invaded the Capitol and the President, his President. The beer-bellied man flashed back – the tweets he read aloud about a gutless VP, but none telling those storming the Capitol to leave. Not telling them to leave had inspired the beer-bellied man to stay.

Unexpectedly, he was hit by recollections of the weeks of rallies and tweets that sold the grievance of a stolen election, of nothing less than a landslide being pulled away. The President telling his followers to come to Washington to take back their country. Like the beer-bellied man, thousands had been inspired to march on the Capitol for this, a treasonous riot.

The thousands surrounding the Capitol and the hundreds invading and desecrating it, the extremist militias? Those legions cannot be antifa or the Deep State. By the hundreds? Thousands? No way, Anthony Larkin Jr. admitted sadly. No, these are the President's people. This is the President's mob.

"I'm coming home, Jack," he said loudly to his lover, unsteady as he stepped outside, fishing for the phone that was to have captured truth. He threw it as high and far as he could, worried briefly it might hit someone, smiled when it struck the bottom step and shattered into pieces.

CHAPTER 18

On the West Terrace the battle line shrunk as the mob squeezed in, piling up all the way back to the Peace Circle, egged on by militia in its midst, and an insurgent on a bullhorn.

The bullhorn man stood on a platform erected for the inauguration. He was clean shaven with a blond flattop, khaki jumpsuit and paratrooper boots. An American flag draped his shoulders.

"This is our house, the people's house, and the time is now," he bellowed with a DJ's cadence. "Our founding fathers acted in '76. We will act today. The time was right in '76. The time is right today. Take back your house! Take back your house!"

"Take back our house! Take back our house!" the conspirators screamed, pushing on the backs of those in front of them, a ripple carrying to those directly challenging the police line.

Most police still had no armor or shields as they were pummeled with fists and clubs of all description. Combatants reeled from tear gas released on both sides, coughing, eyes aflame. A few cops had gas masks. Some insurgents wore off-the-shelf models, but most settled for the minimal protection of bandanas.

Subversives scaling the walls turned the wild scene surreal, harkening to a feudal siege as they dismantled scaffolding and fashioned makeshift ladders, struggling for handholds until other rioters pulled them over the top, to join the main battle.

The flag-draped flattop loudly relayed news of the President's blameful tweet that the VP had failed him.

"String him up!" the West Terrace insurgents chanted, not aware the VP had been spirited from the Senate chamber and through still-clear hallways only seconds ahead of rabid mutineers, clamoring to hang him. He hunkered down in a parking garage, waiting for the rabble to be cleared, refusing to give traitors the satisfaction of driving him from the Capitol grounds. Refusing to allow the Vice President of the world's only democratic superpower to be seen fleeing from a mob in globally broadcast images.

The blue line got shorter as officers went down faster than reinforcements arrived. Some fell into the peril of the mob. A cop fighting next to Corporal Nick Swift cried out when a makeshift spear probed beneath his shield, finding his groin. Falling in pain, he was hammered with clubs, kicked with steel-toed boots. "Man down," Swift yelled, swinging his baton across a rioter's nose, seeing bone shatter, blood spurt. He stepped in protectively, slashing madly as other officers grabbed his colleague's ankles, pulling him to safety.

Swift moved back into the contested line, wishing for the riot gear of the man he had rescued. He actually laughed when he heard his sergeant, blood streaming from a nasty cut to her cheek, radio for help with unblemished irony: "I think we're going to need a few more men."

As her blood mixed with others, footing grew treacherous. Swift slipped, fell and took a painful blow to the crown of his head. Cops on either side helped hold his ground until a woman built like a linebacker muscled in and fired bear spray. Gaps opened in the police line. Rioters surged. The cops could regroup only by pulling back.

The battle line tightened, then more, until it was short steps from the tunnel a president-elect was to soon exit and swear "to preserve, protect and defend the Constitution ..."

More officers went down, carnage casting doubt on that peaceful transfer of power happening. Defending those short steps was no longer worth the blood police were shedding.

"Fall back to the tunnel!" a lieutenant ordered. "Back to the tunnel! You with shields, to the front. Shoulder to shoulder. Shield to shield. Build a wall!"

CHAPTER 19

Tablecloths covered the tall windows, blocking the National Mall landscape that, since pre-Civil War, had been far more impressive than any offering of the House Dining Room. Diners had long suffered heartburn and worse, but their survival carried greater certainty than that of the Republic on January 6th.

Madam Speaker and most of the hostages sat on cushioned chairs, their backs to the windows. Other hostages stood beside them – human shields at the windows, dissuading snipers.

As soon as the entourage had reached the deserted dining room, Ambrose ordered the hostages' phones and tablets seized. And to ensure control of militia messaging, he collected his troops' devices. The feds had weighed jamming phone service in the Capitol, but didn't, knowing their only link to the hostages was through the militias.

In a quick call to Sydney Armor, Ambrose used a simple, prearranged code to confirm his troops in Michigan were eager for rebellion, hungry for a green light. Worried that his phone service could be cut off, Ambrose inhaled deeply and – confident his militia partners agreed – gave the go-ahead.

Revolution 2.0 – or a fall into a very deep rabbit hole – was underway.

Besides having cell service, the extremists could tune in radio and television. They learned the mob had released Madam Speaker's security officers, but only after heated debate over executing them. The wounded agent was hospitalized in a serious condition.

Physically, most of the hostages were fine. One aide suffered a panic attack, curling into the fetal position and sobbing incessantly. The aging senator was sporadically confused. He stood regally every few hours as if on the Senate floor, cleared his throat and declared: "In responding to the gentlelady's question, 'Do you agree that farming is lucrative because Congress wrapped agriculture in protective cocoons of subsidies and disaster relief?' I swear, as a farmer, that if I fall out of bed the government will catch me before I hit the floor." Hearing no response, he would make a self-satisfying nod and sit down.

With the battle for the Capitol still raging, the militia leaders summoned their men. They were scattered around the building and, except for one Baldwin man seen being arrested, and several warring at the tunnel, the rest made it to the House Dining Room.

As for Lomax, Alexander called repeatedly before the South Arising leader finally picked up.

"Where are you?"

"In the rotunda, the rotunda. Where are you?"

"The House Dining Room, with Ambrose and Baldwin. We've got hostages and we've pulled everyone in to make a stand here if it comes to that."

"I heard on the news. You got the Speaker and others. My god, the fat is frying, frying. What's the plan now?"

"Same as we talked about, turn our troops loose in the hinterlands, get a civil war going, get the President to order martial law. Exactly what we talked about."

"Wow. No backing out now. We've rolled the dice, rolled the dice. Gotta win or we're totally down the tubes, totally, totally."

"You have that straight, Jeffrey, like we talked about, with no room for weak knees. Your folks ready to stir things up?"

A pause. "Of course, course. They're waiting for the word."

"We've given our folks the word. Will you?"

"Of course, of course."

"Where are you?"

"Like I said, the rotunda, rotunda, calling in my troops."

"Isn't it crazy there?"

"Yes, yes, Alexander, crazy crazy, but I found a quiet spot to talk."

"Got very lucky, very lucky, Jeffrey," Alexander said, looking at Ambrose, listening on speaker. "You know how to get to the dining room?"

"Can get close, close enough to find it, once the boys all get here."

"Are you going to disappoint me, Jeffrey?"

"Disappoint? Oh, disappoint. No, course not, course not," Lomax said and hung up.

Alexander looked at his brother across the dining room table they had moved into the kitchen, their makeshift command post away from the hostages.

"Quiet spot to talk, my ass. There's no quiet spot in the rotunda."

"Most likely his quiet spot is at an interstate rest stop," said Ambrose. "Already chicken shit fleeing back to Alabama."

His phone rang and after listening, introduced himself and said, "I'm putting you on speaker for my brother Alexander and our other militia leader, Seth Baldwin.

"So Agent-in-Charge Little of the FBI," Ambrose continued, "I expected a call right after you IDed my phone, when I called Ms. Armor. It took you a while."

"Before you took the hostages' phones, one of the aides managed to get a call out to say they were more or less okay. And since you obviously don't know, sir, we work at our own pace."

Ambrose didn't respond. It was Little's call. Finally, "You know the smart thing would be to release the hostages and work with us to clear people out of the Capitol. That would really help you down the road."

"I don't know if that would be the smart thing," Ambrose said. "Maybe the President's people will end up holding the Capitol."

"The Capitol Police have a lot of help on the way, son. You and your boys are already in a load of trouble."

"I am not a son, pops. And my men are not boys. Quit patronizing me. Just tell me what you want."

The pause was long. "We want to talk to the Speaker, to make sure she's all right."

"First, let me share a little information with you. We have fourteen hostages — five members of Congress, eight staff and a reporter. We have plenty of men to handle them, I'm not saying how many. But don't even think about having snipers shoot through the windows. They'd hit the hostages. And since we're in the dining room, there's plenty of food and water and a pot to piss in, thank you.

"As for Madam Speaker, we may be okay with a Zoom call, maybe soon, probably using a TV network. Madam Speaker, someone from the FBI, and us as hosts would probably be on it. Maybe a moderator to introduce everyone. We would do this just to show the public the hostages are okay, so there would be no questions about what's happening in the Capitol, and no negotiating. You break the rules, we would shut the Zoom down. Any questions?"

Little thought for a minute. "You've obviously thought about communicating to a wide audience. Why do you want to do that? More specifically, exactly why have you taken hostages and holed up in the dining room?"

"When the time is right, the answers to your questions will become clear."

"Mr. Dancer, I can't be of help if I don't know what you want."

"As I said, you'll get answers when the time is right."

"Okay. But it's important to show hostages besides the Speaker, to show they are all right."

"Off hand, I don't see a need for that. Madam Speaker can let people know how everyone is doing."

"What if she wants to introduce someone or say something to her family or the country? Something that's not political or gets into negotiations. Like asking people to pray for her and the others? Personal stuff."

"We're getting way ahead of ourselves."

After a long silence, Ambrose asked, "You still there?"

"All this will never fly. My people will never go for it. Neither will the Speaker. We're not going to negotiate people's lives on TV."

"Of course not; that's one of the ground rules. And if you don't want a Zoom call, fine."

"You need to understand, sir, we control your communications, the electricity, the heat. We can leave you shivering in the dark until you get reasonable."

"But there is this, sir: Whatever you do to us you will be doing to the hostages. Don't squeeze us, Agent Little. Lives are in your hands." After letting that sink in, Ambrose added, "I assume I can call you back on this line whenever I want."

"You can."

"Good. Keeping it that way will be best for everyone. Again, don't squeeze us too hard. I will tell you this, the old senator's not doing great. Neither is one of the aides."

"What's wrong with them?"

"The senator is kind of confused. Probably from stress. The aide is in a fetal position, probably from stress, too."

"Then you should release them. It would show good faith on your part."

"I'm not in the good faith business, Agent Little. Tell your people we may be able to do a Zoom call as soon as tonight. And again, don't squeeze us. We can roll out a body a day right through the inauguration."

CHAPTER 20

The battle for the tunnel had raged all afternoon – while rioters flooded the rotunda, Madam Speaker was captured, the House gallery yielded more hostages, and militias opened talks with the FBI.

Not surprisingly, confusion marred the Capitol Police retreat. In the tunnel, too many bodies crammed tightly made it hard to stay shoulder-to-shoulder and to swap out protective gear for the cops at the front, all while under assault.

Predictably, the cops' slow retreat aroused the mob anew – resolve stiffened, blows were delivered more viciously, those not at the front pushed harder, seeing victory a single push away.

"Take the tunnel! Take the tunnel!" shouted the flag-draped flat top, and the crowd echoed, "Take the tunnel! Take the tunnel!"

They would press into it a couple of feet, a couple more, self-seen patriots elated to be in the Capitol, if barely. Then the cops would hold, their training and discipline kicking in, drawing on a previously untapped oath to protect a sacred place and its inhabitants. Time and again, they clawed back precious ground, streamlining the technique of moving from backup into a frontline gap left by an exhausted or injured colleague.

Police used their long batons against the clubs and makeshift spears probing armor for vulnerable spots. Trading mace, cops with superior gas masks got the better of that. Enough blood still flowed to make footing slippery.

As a corporal, Nick Swift was in the thick of battle, often stepping into a vacant space. Twice he took punishing head blows and took himself out of the line, dazed.

Gary Evans, one of the South Dakota cops, backed away from the combat. "This ain't working," he told Thomas Lowell, gently touching a cheekbone showing white before blood coagulated, a nasty cut from a shield.

"Let's stun the assholes," Evans said angrily. "Get this show moving."

"I was thinking about that, too," said Lowell. "The canisters have markings. I bet they can be traced."

"Maybe, but if you haven't noticed, this place is loaded with security cameras, plus people taking pictures. You may be okay, hanging back like you have, but I'm probably screwed anyway. Turn around."

Grudgingly, Lowell did, staring right into a phone. Now I'm screwed, too, he thought.

Evans dug in the backpack and pulled out a stun grenade. As duty officer the night before they left, he was able to slip into the munitions room to steal two grenades their chief bragged were military grade.

He did a few windmills to loosen his right arm. "I think I can put it at the top of the tunnel, above everyone, unless a cop sticks up his shield."

"You want to get people's attention first?"

"Nah, it's way too noisy ... Wait, tell the megaphone man. Maybe he can jack the crowd up."

Lowell returned in a minute, as the flag-draped flattop shouted: "Stun grenade going in. Stun grenade going in. Be ready to charge!"

Evans threw a strike. There was a slight pause, then an explosion, and a cacophony of screams and shouts.

"Now!" yelled flattop. "Charge now!"

Attackers met defenders in a tunnel-wide struggle, bodies hurled against each other, clubs and batons nearly worthless in a space too tight to swing, neither side gaining purchase.

Evans' throw had been too good, the stun grenade spinning deep into the tunnel, dropping beyond cops waiting to step up. The blast did take a toll. Cops farther back went to their knees, holding their ears in pain, crying out. But those on the front line barely felt the impact.

Figuring that out, Evans and Lowell debated whether a sweet spot could be found, just deep enough to clear out cops and aid their own forces. Doubtful another throw would be that precise, they decided to save the remaining grenade for a better opportunity.

"Time to work off being pissed," Evans said. An empty fire extinguisher lay nearby, a large one. "This should crack some damn shields."

He looked at Lowell expectantly but got no response. Watching fellow officers get battered had worn on Lowell. I came for a rally, to pressure the limp dicks in Congress, he told himself, not to assault my own kind. Brought my gun for antifa, not a mutiny.

"I'm not feeling so good," he told Evans, knowing how lame that sounded. "I'll see you back at the car."

Evans said nothing, turning away, toward the battle. It continued, ebb and flow, flow and ebb, with the mutineers' vigor starting to wane. The tunnel had truncated the battlefield, making it hard to pull a forward-leaning cop into the open to be pummeled. Wounds were inflicted less often, bloody footing soaked away, becoming less treacherous.

Nick Swift eased toward the front rank, his fourth trip – fifth? He waited for a well-placed blow or exhaustion – insurgents' constant pressure soon turning arms and legs to jelly – to force an officer to step back, no longer a reliable cork. Swift shook his head to clear fatigue. Or was it the reckoning of too many blows?

But we're winning, wearing the bastards down, he muttered. Nearly all cops were now in full riot gear, supplied by the steady dribble of reinforcements. Promising reports filtered in: SWAT teams were on the way. Most important for morale, they had held the tunnel and the corner of the building it served, unlike the rest of the overrun Capitol. By god, they would not fold now.

The officer in front of Swift dropped to his knee, dazed, face dripping blood. Swift stepped over him, leading with his shield, a short slashing motion that gashed a turncoat's forehead. His downed colleague pulled from danger; Swift aligned his shield with those on either side.

A length of chain flicked behind Swift's shield, bouncing off his helmet. He parried clubs and spears, thankful for a facemask, even one dripping spittle.

"Why ain't you on our side?" he heard a young man scream. "We're in the right."

Swift wanted to say, "You know, or should know, you lost the election. You don't save democracy by destroying it." But talk rang surreal, without purpose.

Sweat trickled from his helmet into his eyes, beneath his vest. The adrenaline of combat slowed, fatigue burrowing in again. He was jostled to his left, exposing a gap between his shield and the one to his right. Swinging his baton, his left foot slipped.

"Damn blood," he thought, lurching into a rioter who tumbled backward, creating a space Swift fell into as Evans stepped forward. Gripping the large fire extinguisher at its circular crown, he swung it in a full arc over his head. When Swift's head hit the tunnel floor, his chin strap popped loose and his helmet rolled away, leaving him exposed.

The crunch of breaking bone vibrated up the extinguisher and into Evans' arms. The extinguisher from his hands as if molten hot. Horrified, he softly cried, "No. My god, no. No."

As fighting in the tunnel hit its peak, Bondarenko climbed a surviving television scaffold in time to film an officer dropping to his knee, another stepping in to help. Minutes passed and the ugly exchange of blows grew repetitious. Lowering her phone, she found it hard to fathom how she became calloused to violence so quickly.

Reluctantly, she turned it back on in time to capture a cop – the rescuer she had filmed? – falling as a rioter swung a large tube, hammering a single blow to the downed officer's head. He never moved as others in blue rushed forward in rage, batons hacking savagely, holding their ground as he was dragged from the mob's reach.

Shaking, Bondarenko forced herself to keep filming until the fray again became repetitive. She fought to control her wildly beating heart – fearing she had witnessed a killing – and messaged her ugly evidence to its safe repository. She knew it must be turned over to someone, and she would face consequences at Homeland Security. Any chance of remaining anonymous was gone, as if the day's hideous record of traitors' faces was not already enough.

Dipping through the scaffold railing, she monkied down the metal arms to the balustrade of the west steps, welcoming its hard succor as she sat down hard. With mutiny raging steps away, Bondarenko leaned back and let her eyes close, craving sleep, exhausted. The searing pain in her side was brief, as was seeing the grimace of an old man, the one at the fountain.

Kneeling before her, his soiled parka flared, he expertly withdrew the long-handled switchblade and glanced about. No one appeared to have noticed.

"Better safe than sorry," he mumbled, sidling away.

CHAPTER 21

I n the House Dining Room, militia leaders chewed over uncertain paths their hinterland troops – labeled the "Confederated Militias, the Confederated Militias" by the still-absent Jeffrey Lomax – could follow to spark what he branded the "New Revolution, New Revolution."

Before the rally, the Dancer brothers roughed out a three-part strategy that turned on occupying and holding the Capitol. Absent that, they reasoned, there would not be time to tip the nation into revolt. But a standoff in the Capitol would reorder the battlefield. Add the right level of terrorism – enough to alarm the public without boxing governors into calling up their National Guards. That was step one.

Step two was heightening people's fear by creating mayhem so widespread that Guard units and law enforcement were overwhelmed. If forced to choose, most cops and guardsmen would side with the President. Other militias would finally engage. With his cult pitted against leftist foes, those still in the middle would be forced to choose sides, fueling civil war.

With the nation ruptured, the brothers would deem their job, their duty, accomplished.

Step three was beyond their control, resting with the President and the military. He could invoke the Insurrection Act and order the military to stifle the revolution, then use the pretext of continuing violence to stay in office. Or the generals could opt for a coup in the name of national security.

Ambrose and Alexander wanted the President to survive but would be fine with military rule that ensured traditional values for true Americans. That said, the Dancers did harbor a gnawing worry that some generals were unreliable, unwilling to abandon the principle of civilian control over the military.

For all their late-night plotting, no one was more shocked than Ambrose when the Capitol actually was occupied. He scarcely believed the good fortune of taking the Speaker hostage, with the prospect of a standoff blossoming into nothing less than the New Revolution – probably without Lomax's Rising South.

The last thing Ambrose did the night before the rally was write scripts for the militias to broadcast. If radio and TV stations were commandeered, a coherent message would be crucial, both for committed rebels and the average citizens he hoped would flood the streets.

At a small desk in his cheap room, he laboriously chased the right words and tone. Finally, in the early morning, he sent an email to Sydney Armor, his top lieutenant, with copies to Alexander, Lomax and Baldwin. "Revolution – Tweak as Needed" the subject line read. The need to adapt to uncertainty was a given.

CHAPTER 22

"Allen, it's Mike."

"You're with Nick, aren't you?"

"Yes, Allen. He's been injured, badly."

Dr. Michael Burns waited to be sure Captain Swift had composed himself. Their friendship covered thirty years, to when Burns led a team of doctors that inserted multiple rods in Swift's legs after a motorcycle accident. "Uncle" to each other's kids, now Burns' "nephew" lay unconscious on a cot, unfolded at the interior end of the West Terrace tunnel, where a triage center was busy.

"What happened?"

"He was hit on the front-left side of his head with something blunt and heavy, above his ear. I'll let you know which hospital as soon as I learn."

"How bad is it?"

"I'll have someone call you as soon as possible."

"No!" the father barked. "Tell me what you see, dammit, what you think, so I know how much to tell Mary and the other kids."

Burns took a deep breath. "There's a lot of bone damage. The operation will be tricky. I think there will be serious swelling."

"Is he going to make it?"

"Probably."

But Swift could hear Burns faltering. "What, Mike? Just tell me what you think."

"Okay, Allen ... If he makes it, I will be surprised if he's the Nick you know."

CHAPTER 23

By late afternoon, after fits and starts, the traitors were driven from the Capitol. Getting reinforcements to turn back the mob had been as problematic as a breech birth.

The first federal SWAT teams didn't join defenders until a full hour after a rioter shattered the northwest window – then in numbers barely slowing the assault.

The first National Guard troops weren't activated for another hour – with orders to handle traffic.

Police from nearby counties and D.C. drifted in, some on their own, but were far outnumbered by rioters still eager for a fight.

The President issued a tepid, thirty-six-word tweet in mid-afternoon, urging respect for "our great men and women in blue." It had no impact.

Blood was still flowing, particularly in the tunnel. Invaders still vandalized offices and desecrated historic artifacts, buoyed by the news that militias held hostages – the hated Speaker of the House among them.

"Folks, 'til the cops quit swinging, we gotta defend ourselves," yelled the flag-draped flattop. "Bottom line, folks, our President said nothing about not killing the pissants in Congress. Until we hear that, stop the steal is alive and well! Stop the steal is alive and well!"

On went the battle.

Not until 4:17 p.m., more than three hours after traitors brought down the barricades, unleashing wholesale assaults on police, did the President upload a video on Twitter asking his people to stand down.

"We love you," he told them in closing. "You're very special...I know how you feel, but go home, and go home in peace."

By then, several hundred riot-trained feds had joined the Capitol Police, to start sweeping the Capitol of renegades. More reinforcements were arriving. Hallway by hallway and room by room control was regained. Facing heavily armed officers in full riot gear, insurgents turned docile and quietly headed for the exits. Few arrests were made. No more shots were fired.

The outnumbered defenders in the tunnel could claim a small victory – holding a cavity of purely functional masonry on an otherwise lawless day.

With that 4:17 video, momentum for insurrection dissipated, like fog burned off by morning sun. Granted permission to halt their attack on democracy, weary rioters dropped their weapons.

Outside the tunnel, the flag-draped flattop changed his tune. "Folks, the President says it's time to go," he intoned with devoted acceptance. "He got us this far. He knows what he's doing, I'm sure. Soon enough, he'll make his plan clear. It's time to declare victory and go home. Declare victory and go home, folks. We took the Capitol! We stopped the count. We stopped the steal! And as long as we've got the Speaker – hear that now, we've still got the Speaker – the steal will stay stopped!"

CHAPTER 24

Details had been worked out for a Zoom call with Madam Speaker at 9 p.m. With the clock ticking – and a national audience waiting – Ambrose called Agent Little.

"We're delaying the call."

"Why?" Little demanded. "Everything is set up. Families of hostages need to know how they are doing. The nation must know how the Speaker is doing. She is second in succession, you remember?"

"Of course, I remember. For now, people will have to take our word for it that our prisoners are all doing as advertised. There's been no change. We'll have the call in the morning. I'll get back to you later with a time."

He hung up, wondering what spin the media would put on delaying the call scant minutes before attacks would begin across the country. "I'm getting as damn bad as the feds, worrying about fucking optics," Ambrose murmured to himself.

He settled in an armchair, dragged into the kitchen from the dining room, and tuned into Fox News. Alexander, Baldwin and a couple others joined him, their conversation interrupted by a speculative report suggesting a violent incident had overtones of terrorism. Soon, denying terrorists were not at work would be preposterous.

The NPM's attacks on Chamber of Commerce offices in several cities – Myrtle Beach and Columbia in South Carolina and Athens, Georgia and Akron, Ohio and Detroit in the Upper Midwest – quickly dominated the airwaves.

Demolition teams had set small bundles of dynamite in window wells, all timed to explode within an hour of each other, well after closing time to lessen the risk of casualties. Even so, a passerby in Detroit and a security officer in Athens were killed; wrong place, wrong time.

A Black Lives Matter yard sign was left behind to cast blame in Detroit. In Myrtle Beach, pages downloaded from a rambling anarchist manifest were printed and scattered about, implicating antifa.

Alexander also sent a team to Richmond to spray paint surviving statues of the Confederacy with "We Shall Overcome" and "BLM." There too, incriminating yard signs were found.

Evidence clearly shows leftist retaliation against rally goers who stormed the Capitol, reporters dutifully intoned. Flipping channels, Ambrose found some commentators asking if the evidence could have been planted – a question drowned out by the obvious.

In the West, at sundown, a dozen barns and other old buildings burned mysteriously – yielding stunning footage against the setting sun. To be sure he was counted among the victims, Baldwin torched one of his own line shacks – a weathered remnant from when cowboys rode fence. To underline the potential for more serious attacks, his men firebombed an historic mansion in Astoria. From the bluffs above Oregon's first settlement, flames engulfing the unoccupied house were visible for miles.

But everything was quiet in the Gulf states, Lomax territory. In their last conversation, Alexander felt certain, Lomax was anxious, starting to unravel at the enormity of their undertaking. Storming the Capitol, even with people killed, was one thing. Taking hostages, and killing people to do it, rose to another magnitude.

"If that don't get you shot, shot, you sure as hell will rot, rot in the slammer." Alexander could almost see Lomax walking in circles, slapping his forehead with his palm. "Gotta win or you're totally down the tubes, totally, totally," Alexander remembered Lomax exclaiming – "us" and "we" suspiciously missing. Going all in is not your style, is it Jeffrey? Alexander reflected. Too chancy. And no, you were not in the rotunda, gathering up your men. You were already on the run. Totally, totally.

"Goooood morning, Vietnam," fairly shouted an insurgent identifying himself only as Lark. "It's hot. Damn hot! Real hot! Hottest thing is my shorts. I could cook things in it. A little crotch pot cooking."

Lark was doing his best impersonation of Robin Williams impersonating DJ Adrian Cronauer. Lark and three other Baldwin men had burst into a small radio station near Washington state's Tri-Cities on the Columbia River, taking the DJ and an engineer hostage. Other Baldwin teams commandeered stations near Moab, Utah and Philmont Scout Ranch in New Mexico. Ambrose men had similarly grabbed stations in Scranton and Toledo, and Alexander's troops occupied one near Raleigh in North Carolina.

Now, Lark and insurgents at the other pirated stations were delivering the message Ambrose crafted before the rally and Sydney Armor updated:

"I'm with Freedom Country Coalition, one of the militias that has knocked Congress to its knees. We are answering our President's call, our honestly elected President's call. Elected in a landslide, a big landslide, maybe the biggest in history if all the votes got counted. And as everyone now knows, we have stopped the steal. Stopped the steal! The patriots of the FCC and the National Patriot Movement are holding hostage the dishonest Speaker of the House and other dishonest Congress members. We believe where there was voter fraud, dishonest electoral votes will be reversed. We believe on Inauguration Day, it is our great President who will swear the oath for a second time. He will keep making America great. Again.

"But that's not for sure yet. Holding control of the Capitol is not for sure. The weaselers in Congress want up off their knees for sure. They want your Capitol back – your house, yes, it's your house – and they're getting ready to send in all the federal agents of the Deep State. All of them against our few. We must make sure they don't take your house back. It can't happen.

"By holding the hostages in the House Dining Room, our militias are preventing that. This is our Alamo, our Custer, our Normandy. We will never surrender, and the best way to make sure the steal is stopped forever is to rise up in every state. Take over control of every state. Only then can we know every vote will be fairly counted, without dead people voting or voting machines being rigged using computers in Italy or somewhere.

"So, join us! Join us and tomorrow fill up the streets. Let your governors and mayors, your city councils and county sheriffs, let them know this election can have but one honest outcome. Really let the sheriffs know. The Second Amendment is really important, truly very important, to every one of them. They won't let you down. They really know how to count votes, particularly fraudulent ones. And call your friends and neighbors in the National Guard. America's finest. None finer.

"Already the leftist extremists from coast to coast and in between those places are pushing us into civil war. They want to block the true election, the landslide election of an honestly elected President. Already, they are firebombing and setting fires. Can you believe it? But we know who they are. It's not hard. They are leaving their calling cards. Unashamed. They are unashamed. They must be stopped by any way we know or can think of or have never thought of before. We must be strong, so strong, and they must be stopped by any way we know how.

"To ensure the real story, the only true story reaches you, we are broadcasting from this and other stations, stations broadcasting in support of an honest election. Beware the lamestream media. The media are protecting the elitist establishment and the Deep State. The crooked media. They want to take your freedoms, would take them, too, if they could. So, turn to and tune in the media you trust most and know. You know who they are.

"And turn out, in your streets, ready to fight the election frauds. Frauds are everywhere. That's where you must fight them. Everywhere. Turn out and fight for our landslide President, elected with honesty. Completely honest honesty. Fight for our very democracy itself. Know that we and our President love you. Until later, God bless America."

In the House Dining Room, the Dancer brothers and Baldwin listened with satisfaction. Knowing the broadcasts were coming, they had delayed setting up another Zoom call. Agent Little would be furious. Better to let him cool down a bit. They also had called the Associated Press and other media to ensure coverage of the broadcasts.

"Good job," Baldwin told Ambrose. "The message was good, maybe a touch overdone but you pretty much caught the voice of the great man."

"Thanks. I tried. For someone plainspoken, talking stilted, or whatever he does, ain't easy."

CHAPTER 25

People rushed into the streets at news of the fires and explosions, the desecrated Civil War statues.

Oath Keepers and Proud Boys led those on the extreme right, believing seeds of national rebellion were sprouting from the Washington standoff. Across the country, other hate groups and anti-government zealots, long thirsting for action, poured out, too, fixed on destruction; no formal invitation needed.

On their heels came devoted followers of the President as well as combatant leftists raging against pamphlets and other planted evidence. Some lefties carried hastily scrawled protest signs. Loosely knit anarchists – demanding social services delivered by the very public agencies they would dismantle – infiltrated leftist ranks, armed with more than signs, courting violence.

Antagonists quickly clashed. Tension stoked by watching D.C.'s long day of rioting sought release. Shouting turned to shoving. Fists and boots inspired clubs and knives and guns. Casualties were inevitable. Police weighed in, some to temper conflict, others taking a side under cover of their badge, usually on the right. Ambulances wailed, and not just in cities inflamed by Dancer and Baldwin militias. Tinderboxes with a track record for unrest – Portland, Seattle, Detroit, L.A. – did not disappoint.

Street battles hardened into riots. Looters vandalized businesses in L.A., Newark, Oakland and elsewhere, then set them ablaze. Firefighters struggled to keep up. Police moved to the sidelines until angry combatants exhausted themselves, then dispersed them. If arrested, troublemakers made low bail and were back on the street within hours. Emergency rooms overflowed. Panicky parents risked supermarket trips to forage for baby formula. Workers called in sick, desperate for the protection of their home.

Across the land, public officials pleaded for calm. The politicians among them took a broader look, weighing the end game. Would violence be short-lived or mirror the race riots and war protests of a half-century ago that throttled the nation for years? Or could this be worse, as dark as the firing on Fort Sumter? Were deeply festered sores bursting with unexpected force, rocking the foundation of democracy? Or toppling it?

All had a stake in the outcome, but politicians also had a unique opportunity to lead. Being more visible, they had more at stake. When scores finally got settled, their survival – political and personal – could turn on which side they picked. Not necessarily the high ground but the winning ground. That's how tin-horn republics work, and America was looking like a tin-horn republic.

The militia leaders, glued to a television in the kitchen, were fascinated as they watched spider veins of violence pop up across the nation. Though still too few to be called a civil war, those fractures were of their making, and satisfying.

Reflecting, Baldwin said, "My Uncle Jacob always cautioned, really solemn of course, against taking pleasure from the misfortune of others. He always said that right before he said, 'Damn, I'm enjoying this.'"

Drawing chuckles, he went on, "Not to be critical, Ambrose, but I think you did get one thing wrong in the script for the stations. You were behind the curve, way behind the curve, as that prick Lomax would say, when you told people to hit the streets tomorrow. I think we picked up a day."

With the promise of a tumultuous next day making sleep impossible, Baldwin poured each of them another finger of whiskey.

CHAPTER 26

Theodore Wormsley, like millions of Americans, had turned on his television to watch the President's rally, clicking on Fox News, of course.

Coverage began predictably: The President's catalog of grievances. The faithful's clamorous support. Inane interviews with rabid loyalists and a nearby protester. Wormsley's spine stiffened when his commander in chief allowed, "I'll be there with you" walking up Pennsylvania Avenue. But it was no surprise to see him step into his White House-bound SUV.

As the thickening crowd surrounding the Capitol grew more restive, shaking barricades and confronting police, Wormsley's interest shot up. With the first brawls, the first shattered window, then reports of protesters invading the Capitol, he was mesmerized, captured between fascination and disbelief. He flipped channels, searching for nuggets that might suggest the depth of the emerging insurrection. Commentators noting the presidential silence – as the Vice President and Congress fled and angry partisans turned into a mob – made Wormsley think the President was encouraging insurrection. And when word leaked out that a militia had taken hostages, the Speaker of the House among them, he quietly swore at missing a chance to make history.

"I should be there," he said aloud.

He channel-surfed for hours, until the President finally urged the mob to go home and order in the Capitol was slowly restored. But the hostage standoff could last days, Wormsley reasoned, and must be part of a grander strategy. Already, militias were on the attack, commandeering airwaves, and citizens – for and against the President – were at each other's throats.

Wormsley's mind swirled, both with questions and possibilities. Would street battles worsen? Would the President take his call to "fight like hell" beyond the rally? Were his legions across the land truly ready for revolution or even civil war? Which militias were involved? Were they committed or still playing toy soldier? How about the military? And how many lone wolves, like me, would jump in?

Excitement kept him from sleep as he grappled to figure out an attack far more lethal than any in his past. Not a blip in the news, one to lead the news. One sending out shock waves of fear at a magnitude dreamed of by every thinking terrorist. One worthy of revolution – if it came.

Wormsley thought of himself as a thinking terrorist. Early on, he saw that most terrorists – or at least mass killers – lacked discipline, too often acting on impulse. Attacks in public places like bars put them at risk, particularly in open-carry states where people were apt to shoot back. Driven by emotion, they were incapable of aborting a mission going sour. They did stupid things that drew attention from neighbors or employers or, worse, the police. They did not make escape plans.

To further his terrorist ambitions, Wormsley had saved to buy a small house on a remote acreage in Conway County, the second-most rural in Arkansas. It was an hour northwest of Little Rock, where he most often found work as a handyman. Should flight be necessary, he could flee to the nearby Boston Mountains or navigate twisting state highways and county roads to Interstate 40. He lived simply, seldom socializing with his few friends. Being of medium size and having no distinctive features or body art, most neighbors would struggle to identify him. He varied where he shopped and paid his bills and taxes on time. Rarely did anyone enter his house. When his libido called, he saw a prostitute in Little Rock whose only interest was the money.

It was a monkish life, made worthwhile by exhilarating missions. He found his targets through media stories: A government official or politician advancing a policy damaging to the country, in his view. School board members or teachers or the gay community writ large leading children astray. Wealthy benefactors of liberal causes that eroded traditional values.

He was patient, usually waiting for local controversies to cool down before striking. Letting months pass before making a late-night call to reignite a victim's earlier horror. Instilling fear kept destructive individuals on the defensive, more vulnerable, less apt to advocate again. So Wormsley believed.

He also had his so-called "safety buffer." Miscreants in any state touching Arkansas were spared. That meant no missions in Missouri, going at least to Iowa. Kansas and Illinois were off-limits, too; though not adjoining, they were too close. Juvenile? Perhaps. Why not right a wrong across Texas in El Paso, half-way to the West Coast? Wormsley, after avoiding detection for nearly two decades, trusted his safety buffer.

He judiciously took other precautions, too. Never using the same weapon in more than one attack. Often using disguises. He was thankful when burner phones came along. Wearing at least two pairs of medical gloves made fingerprints a non-issue. If concerned about having left tire tracks, he bought a new set.

He could look back on his missions with satisfaction. There was the county commissioner in Virginia who spearheaded removing a statue of Robert E. Lee, years before that was a popular leftist cause. Worse, the commissioner lamented Confederate statues when he ran for governor. He lost the primary, but Wormsley was certain he would someday target another hero of the commonwealth. The commissioner's wife found him, peaceful in bed except for the deep gash under his chin. Weeks later, calls from a heavy breather so upset the grieving widow that she moved out of state.

In a Seattle suburb, the school board resisted parents demanding the removal of library books they condemned as pornographic. With the debate simmering, a board member was killed by a shot fired from long range. Re-election campaigns of the other incumbents were so demoralized that a new right-thinking board swept into office.

Parents of a trans child were battling over toilet rights in school when an explosion destroyed their mountain home near Asheville, North Carolina. Only the father was home. He lingered near death for days but survived. Months later the mother answered the phone at sundown and heard a muffled voice say, "Look out your window, at the next ridge." Seeing an explosion rip through the tree line, she screamed uncontrollably as a vehicle's lights flashed repeatedly before driving slowly away. The family soon moved.

Wormsley's stories could easily fill a book, which he believed he should write, both as a guide to others and to chronicle missions that, in recent years, he took more frequently. Why, he wasn't sure. Maybe he was more confident in his abilities, or a badly divided nation offered more targets. But many law enforcement agencies had spent – no, were spending – huge amounts of time chasing him, as they had the Unabomber. Sharing a first name was pure coincidence, of course, but federal investigators hadn't caught up with Theodore "Ted" Kaczynski until his published manifest caught the eye of his brother. Wormsley had yet to write anything, had no brother, and was near certain the FBI had not found threads tying his attacks together, let alone to him.

As years slipped by and successes piled up, his sense of self-worth mushroomed. No longer did he think of himself as a lone wolf, part of a cadre of anonymous operators. He thought of himself as The Lone Wolf.

But the President's insurrection, Wormsley realized, would not allow his usual planning. Even his safety buffer was impractical. If insurrection blossoms into revolution, he must act quickly. Wormsley was determined to inflict destruction with a frightening death toll – driving home that true Americans have an unyielding commitment to this President. But where was his target?

CHAPTER 27
JANUARY 7TH

Congressional leaders enlisted a retired television anchor to moderate the Zoom call with the Speaker. Eduardo Hammond, a tall Black man, hair gone white, sat at his old desk in his former network's main studio. He was no Walter Cronkite, as there hadn't been for a long time. But Hammond was highly respected, his authoritative baritone filled with gravitas, appropriate for the moment.

Across from him sat Percy Wood, the FBI's deputy director. His portfolio included managing agents like Brian Little, who actually knew something about crisis negotiation. While Wood didn't, his reliable ticket for promotion had been handling unsavory chores. The running joke was, "I know Percy would." Now, Percy Wood could hand off most of those chores – but not the Zoom call.

Going national with Madam Speaker was a hot potato his boss, the FBI director, happily tossed to Wood, who saw a chance to further burnish his political credentials. Helping rescue the Speaker could prove golden when the aging director retired. If Wood did well but she didn't make it, that surely wouldn't be held against him. Blessed with a carnival barker's tongue, he always excelled on TV.

Ambrose had ordered two tables to be squared up in the dining room, he and the Speaker facing one another. Extra tablets were handy should other speakers be called in. Every national network had looped in for what promised to be the mother of all Zoom calls.

"All right, as a reminder: This is an opportunity for Madam Speaker to let people know how she and our other hostages are doing, no more no less," said Ambrose. "No speeches, Madam Speaker, Mr. Wood, and no negotiations. Breaking rules carry consequences. My colleague, Mr. Baldwin, is sitting off-camera, controlling a sophisticated mechanism needed for the broadcast. It's called a plug. He jerks it from the wall socket and our tablets are dead. Any questions?"

Greeted with silence, Ambrose sat back to watch a clock's second hand near 10 a.m. He said, "Mr. Hammond, you may set the stage."

A red light went on and Hammond intoned, "Good morning, ladies and gentlemen. I sit safely in my old studio with Percy Wood, deputy director of the FBI."

Ambrose's eyebrows lifted as Hammond continued, "In quite different circumstances, you see two other people – the Speaker of the House, of course, and one of her captors, Ambrose Dancer, leader of the National Patriot Movement, a militia based in Michigan. The insurrectionists took Madam Speaker and others hostage yesterday afternoon and are holding them in the House Dining room."

Insurrectionists? Not patriots or even protesters? Too inflammatory, dammit, not the stage setting I expected. Ambrose cleared his throat and his image briefly filled viewers' screens, his jaw clenched, eyes angry.

"As you surely know," an unruffled Hammond continued, "other insurrectionists were driven from the Capitol but not before they stopped Congress from counting the Electoral College votes for president. The militias, now confined to the dining room, are in a standoff with law enforcement."

Ambrose cleared his throat again, more loudly, his piercing eyes seen by millions of viewers as Hammond pressed ahead.

"Mr. Dancer has set certain rules for this broadcast – no speeches about democracy and no hostage negotiations. Mr. Wood can ask the Speaker only about her welfare and that of other hostages. Mr. Dancer asked me to explain that militia leaders allowed this Zoom call to ensure Madam Speaker's report on the hostages is transparent and so she can assure everyone they are not being mistreated. With that, Mr. Wood, you may interview the Speaker."

Percy Wood cleared his throat loudly in obvious response to Ambrose and said, "Thank you, Mr. Hammond. Madam Speaker, our previous meetings were under better circumstances, so I need to first ask how you are."

"Thank you, Mr. Wood. Given the circumstances, I'm all right, and looking forward to being better."

"I'm sure you are, Madam Speaker, as we all want you to be."

"Mr. Wood," interrupted Ambrose, "editorializing is not part of the program."

As Wood put on an innocent look, Ambrose said, "Don't play games with me."

"My apologies, Mr. Dancer. Please tell us, Madam Speaker, how are the other hostages?"

"Our captors didn't take anyone hostage who was wounded so we're all right physically. Stress is taking its emotional toll, particularly with the senator and one of my aides."

"How serious are their conditions? Do they need a doctor?"

"I can't say, really, and don't want to discuss their conditions publicly beyond expressing my concern that prolonged confusion or stress may cause long-lasting medical problems. It would be helpful if a doctor could examine them, even virtually."

"Perhaps we can talk with Mr. Ambrose later, off-line."

"Sure, later," Ambrose said, trying to sound sympathetic.

"Are you okay with food and water, the basics?" Wood continued.

"Yes, Mr. Wood. This is a dining room, after all," said the Speaker, flashing a smile for the first time.

"Anything else you need, other than being released?"

Ambrose looked at Wood as if to say you're crowding the line again.

"One of the staff has a son getting married tomorrow. Naturally, she wants to be there."

"Of course she does," said Wood. "We'll talk about that off-line, too, if Mr. Dancer agrees... Please confirm for us, Madam Speaker, how many hostages there are."

"Fourteen, Mr. Wood. Two senators, two House members besides me, eight staff and a reporter – patriots all."

"Madam Speaker...," Ambrose said, his voice sending a warning. Her spine stiffened and her face assumed its leadership mask. She was not about to apologize.

"That matches our count of missing persons, Madam Speaker. Thank you," said Wood. "Is there anything else our viewers should know?"

"Yes, if Mr. Dancer will indulge one of my summer interns, Brent Wilfrid, who has an unusual diabetic condition. Just before coming on, Brent told me he was experiencing heart palpitations and a severe flushed sensation. You surely have a doctor standing by to monitor this broadcast. Brent would like to talk with a doctor. He's on his college debate team and said he doesn't mind being on national TV."

Ambrose paused, then said, "Let me think a moment," creating the kind of awkward silence television abhors. He couldn't immediately find a downside. Maybe appearing sympathetic will get more people to our side, he thought. "Okay. Why not?"

Madam Speaker turned and nodded to a young man. Ambrose had noticed him before. He was hard to miss at six feet four and two hundred sixty pounds, the extra weight making him look soft. Rosy cheeks could still place him in high school. He moved forward with a clumsy gait that smoothed out as he reached Seth Baldwin and grabbed a leg of his chair, jerking it up. Baldwin sprawled, his head hitting the floor. Wilfrid swiftly stepped past him, shouting, "Rotten damn traitor!"

Ambrose fumbled for the gun in his back waistband as Wilfrid plowed into him, pulling the Glock free as he landed painfully beneath the intern.

The tablet tumbled with them. Millions got a glimpse of

Ambrose's startled look, a flash of his hand and the gun's rough contours as the tablet spun away and landed upright against a table leg. Startled viewers heard two loud gunshots, then Wilfrid's anguished cries and Ambrose screaming, all giving his tablet dominance over the Zoom call. Loud pounding and another gunshot horrified the national audience.

"Get him off me! Fat motherfucker, bloody fucking brains! Get him the fuck off! Kill the fucking Zoom! Jesus!"

After the chilling glimpse of the gun, the Zoom showed only a tilted portrait of the dining room from ground level. But the audio was beyond sensational, capturing for history a sickening murder in the aftermath of an unthinkable day. The intertwined screams of Ambrose and Wilfrid and the delay between the second and third shots triggered unbridled speculation.

"It is all too clear that we witnessed nothing less than a deliberate execution," declared one commentator. "It's also hard to believe young Wilfrid hadn't at least briefly considered the consequences of attacking the 'rotten damn traitor,' as he called Ambrose Dancer."

And: "Perhaps Brent Wilfrid hoped his attack on Dancer would cause other hostages to mutiny, but probably not; the hostages are unarmed and badly outnumbered. More likely, he simply felt their situation was so perilous – in fact, it remains so perilous – that he might as well roll the dice. In any case, Brent Wilfrid committed an act of pure heroism in resisting treason."

"In the seconds between the second and third shots, we heard pounding, almost certainly young Wilfrid kicking in agony as his life drained away," yet another commentator declared. "Ambrose Dancer couldn't take a few extra seconds to get out from under Brent Wilfrid, let alone call medics who may have saved the young man's life. No. Dancer had to immediately free himself from the gore he triggered. So he pulled the trigger a third time, executing a teenager."

"That pounding we heard – let's play it again to remind us...," said an analyst who took the same tact. "That was Wilfrid kicking madly as his life ended. Then the traitor Dancer fired again, killing the young hero to free himself as quickly as possible.

"To underline how cold-blooded Ambrose Dancer is," that analyst added, "he still had the presence of mind to order the Zoom unplugged."

Minutes after the shooting, Alexander called the FBI to say two hostages would be dragging Wilfrid's body into the hallway. With confirmation he was shot twice in the side and once in the head, media analysts concluded the third shot was to the head, confirming Wilfrid was executed and prompting self-congratulations for being right all along.

CHAPTER 28

The slaying of the rosy-cheeked intern, broadcast over and over, dampened insurrectionists' public support. How much was uncertain, akin to proving a negative. By early afternoon, Brent Wilfrid's parents, O.J. and Connie, were on the news and social media everywhere, though they made only one public appearance, that from the front porch of their modest home in Boise. The media had been told the Wilfrids would not take questions.

O.J., burly as the son he had barely raised, tried to speak but gave up after breaking down repeatedly. Connie, not so. Voice strong, eyes flashing, she bluntly condemned Dancer and all the President's followers who invaded the Capitol:

"He slaughtered my son, then bitched about being awash in his blood. Somehow, with God's help, O.J. and I will live without him. But all of us have been denied his promise, the good I know he would have achieved. I have opposed the death penalty but have worried it could be needed at times. This is one of those rare times. Ambrose Dancer deserves to die a terrible death. I would have him drawn and quartered in a public square. That murderer is also a traitor. Like-minded traitors deserve to be locked up forever. They are a threat to our country and our way of life. I voted to reelect the President.

Within days after the election, when he continued the stolen vote nonsense, I knew I had made a mistake. He has manipulated his followers and brought them to Washington to commit treason and is the greatest traitor of all."

When she finished, she and O.J. turned and walked the few steps into their house. Remarkably, no reporter shouted a question.

Predictably, civic leaders and politicians of all stripe offered sympathy to the Wilfrids and condemned the attack on the Capitol. Some of the President's faithful stopped short of the latter. They framed the insurrection as a well-intentioned defense of election integrity, or the right to assemble somehow going tragically wrong, perhaps manipulated by ill-defined leftist agitators.

No such hedging larded the statement from the Office of the Speaker. In a press release, her long-time chief of staff said:

"I issue this statement with trepidation, not knowing if it puts the Speaker and other hostages at greater risk, but believing it is what she would say:

"I extend my deepest sympathy to the family of Brent Wilfrid and trust they will find respite in their faith. In his brief time in my office, he showed himself to be hardworking, eager to take on difficult challenges, and empathetic. Most impressive for someone so young, he understood that government service is not about individual profit or personal aggrandizement, but a commitment to improve society and, especially, address the needs of our most vulnerable citizens.

"Regardless of personal cost, I must say this: Yesterday's assault was traitorous and cannot be allowed to stand if our democracy is to survive."

From a comfortable chair pulled into the kitchen, Ambrose Dancer, feet propped high on a chopping table, listened as a television anchor read the prepared statement. On balance, news reports reflected little public stomach for revolution. Ambrose wondered how much leftie bias influenced those reports but knew he had overreacted; his men would have quickly pulled Brent Wilfrid off. Showing restraint could have attracted supporters. Instead, many people – millions? – who might have joined the cause were now fence sitters. Or worse.

Being pissed at himself didn't mean he also wasn't pissed at Wilfrid. Or felt remorse. The devious shit used a phony heart complaint to hustle the Speaker to get at me, Ambrose thought, gnawing a fingernail. Or maybe Madam Speaker knowingly let herself get hustled. Either way, rosy cheeks got what he deserved.

Regardless of the public denunciation, Ambrose believed his violent reaction had bolstered his position when he told Agent Little that negotiations were suspended for the time being and declared: "By now I think you know better than to mess with us." Then he hung up.

Later in the day, Ambrose questioned briefly whether his bluster had worked to his advantage.

"I want to go on national television, by myself," he said when Little picked up on the first ring.

"Not going to happen."

"I can start rolling out dead hostages."

"And I can promise you an excruciating death when we immediately bust in, unless you blow off your cowardly head," Little rejoined. "But to your point, we've talked with the hostage's families about various scenarios. There's too much shit happening around the country. On TV you could issue a call to arms and make it worse. The families agree we can't let that happen. And if you start killing hostages, they support having us move in to save whoever we can. We've checked you out. We know you and your brother are highly trained, but most of your men aren't. Against our finest they won't last a minute."

Ambrose couldn't argue: Against their best, a minute may be generous.

But getting on TV in a bid to sway public opinion wasn't the only reason he called. He let the silence drag out, as if thinking. "Okay.

We're fine with playing the waiting game for a while. But I must talk to my number two in Michigan, check on my troops."

"That's not going to happen, either."

"I'm talking about a quick call, like you wanted to check on Madam Speaker and the others."

"Look how that turned out. Not going to happen, not after you killed that kid. That dining room is your jail until we put you in a real one or put you down. Period."

"No, sir. You are wrong. Precisely because I killed that kid, it is going to happen. Otherwise, I roll the reporter out, dead. Just to get your attention. Are you going kill that reporter to keep me from making a short call? I don't think so. Plus, I have two men on every hostage. Your men attack and we'll decorate this place with the brains of every damn hostage including the Speaker."

Ambrose heard the agent inhale and gave Alexander a smile. Five minutes later, Little called back.

"All right, but just a welfare call. You'll be on a brief delay. We hear anything that signals an order, we cut you off."

"Of course."

Ambrose hung up and eyed another fingernail, thinking he shouldn't have second-guessed himself earlier.

CHAPTER 29

Reports of violence peppering the country continued to dominate the news. The paucity of attacks in Gulf Coast states left little doubt Lomax was missing in action.

More encouraging were scattered cases of other militias — mainly hate and White supremacist – claiming credit for attacks. But they fell far short of being game changers, if only because most people held supremacists in such low regard. Ambrose had never understood why. Whites as a class clearly are superior, just look at who holds wealth and power, he reasoned; nothing racist, a fact of life.

As for people taking to the streets, they mostly boiled down to right-wing militias squaring off against antifa or others on the far left. Committed liberals and most of the President's supporters had quickly had their fill.

Ambrose was dismayed to not see reports of ordinary citizens – blue-collar workers, small business owners, students, cops and firemen – stepping up against the steal and the tentacles of government that condoned it – judges, election officials, Deep State bureaucrats.

He called Alexander and Baldwin over.

"We absolutely gotta grow this revolution," Baldwin agreed. "Get more militias involved, sure, but mostly get beyond militias, pull in the man on the street. It would help a bunch if the President invoked the Insurrection Act, too."

"Maybe we should help him do just that," Alexander said.

They looked at him, waiting for details.

"Well first, Ambrose calls Sydney, tells her in code to pull out the stops, stage two of our plan. But not just our troops. We need to get the rank and file of other militia in the game, even if their leaders aren't. When things get ugly, we put out a statement saying it's time to end the violence, that we want to release the hostages..."

"Where the hell is that coming from?" Baldwin interrupted.

"I think I know," snapped Ambrose. "Let him finish."

"Coming from what you just said, Seth, the Insurrection Act," Alexander went on. "With violence continuing, it helps the President's case that only the military can restore peace. Not what he wants, but the only way to save the country."

"Do you think the generals would obey his order?" Ambrose asked.

"I do," said Alexander. "He is the President, the commander in chief, which means a lot to those guys. With America burning and Inauguration Day less than two weeks away, the military chiefs aren't going to sit on their hands, ignoring an order to restore order.

"I think you'll agree, the other militias are pissing themselves for a chance to be legitimate security forces. Given the nod, they'll step up, far more than they would for us."

"I want him to send in the military, of course," Baldwin said. "Having lost his plays with the VP and Congress, the military is his best shot – maybe only shot – for staying in office. In that scenario, the inauguration could be delayed. Or the brass could find power mighty tasty."

A call to Ambrose interrupted them. Hanging up, he said, "That was the good Agent Little. I can call Syd in an hour."

"Okay then, if we have time, there's something we've never talked through – how all this plays out for us," said Baldwin. "Sure, we were ready to roll the dice. But I never expected to be in a starring role. I thought we'd get in the Capitol and hoot and holler and then go home. But Ambrose grabbed Madam Speaker and here we are. So, are we screwed, any way we cut it?"

"Alexander and I have talked about all that," Ambrose answered. "We did wait until the mob took the Capitol. When other militias didn't lead, we stepped in and – with the leverage of the hostages – put a rebellion in play. But now, the best scenario of revolution with folks in the streets is not happening. Still could, but next best is forcing the President to call up the military."

"I know all that," injected Baldwin. "But how does it play for us, Ambrose?"

"If he holds onto the presidency, he'll need scapegoats. Being an ungrateful bastard, we'll be the scapegoats. Later, maybe he gets himself elected president for life and feels he can pardon us. But short term, like the next few days, if he doesn't go with the Insurrection Act, we keep playing the hostage card until we give up or a SWAT team dials our number, lights out."

"In a word," said Baldwin, "we're screwed."

CHAPTER 30

On January 6th, after Ambrose marched the hostages to the House Dining Room, he had called Sydney Armor.

"Hey Syd, this is the call I never expected to make."

"What's happening?"

"I've got the Speaker and other hostages."

"Holy shit. Are you real?"

"I am. It'll be all over the news before long. By then we'll be hunkered down."

"Holy shit."

"You're repeating yourself, my friend, but that's fine. As planned, you be in Flint tomorrow morning and I'll try to call you, using our little code. Then toss the burner and shag ass. I doubt I get more than that one call."

"Holy shit. Do you think we can pull this off?"

"Ya gotta believe, Syd."

"Yeah... Ambrose, be careful."

He couldn't hold back a chuckle. "I will. You, too."

As planned, Armor was sitting in her pickup on a residential street, going over plans for the NPM and its allied militias, when her burner rang. She was not far from Interstates 75 and 69, ready to flee in any direction.

"Dolly Parton here."

"Hi Dolly. Ambrose."

"Of course. How are you?"

"Okay," he said, guessing the FBI already had her phone's GPS coordinates.

"I insisted on calling you, briefly of course, to find out if everyone is all right."

"We are."

"I'm betting on it. You need money, have Randy open the safe-deposit box ..."

The line went dead. Apparently, someone suspected Ambrose was using code. Someone was right, but too late. Messages had been sent.

Sydney Armor rolled down her window as she slowly crossed the deserted street, tires crunching on packed snow. She tossed the burner, watching it bounce into a storm sewer, and drove away. Minutes later she merged into I69 traffic, knowing the GPS coordinates were in her rearview mirror, literally and figuratively.

When Ambrose said he was "okay," rather than "all right," it was a green light to use the radio scripts he had written before the rally. One urged the President to invoke the Insurrection Act, used only thirty times since 1794 – in recent decades to enforce desegregation laws or put down urban riots. If used now, the military, for the first time, would be turned loose on citizens it had sworn to protect.

It would fall to Armor to edit the scripts, blend in developments, and decide when to send them to mutineers commandeering the stations. So far, the feds hadn't silenced devices at the stations, wanting to keep communications open. That could change in a hurry when the scripts were read and picked up by AP and other media outlets.

The second code involved money. No mention signaled the revolution was off. But any mention of money ordered full-throated disruption and destruction. Ambrose ordered that by saying "betting" – and the FBI ended the call.

Very simple codes, thought Armor, for launching a revolution.

~

Agent Brian Little snapped off the recording of the call, angry that Dancer won that round.

"We shouldn't have allowed it," he told Elizabeth Bly, his young assistant. "I warned them but got overruled. Hard to do but we should have sacrificed the reporter. But no. Damn optics again."

He perched on the arm of a sofa in a House hideaway, his temporary office, and idly wondered whose it was. Probably a pompous assistant leader or committee chairman, he speculated, noting photos signed by presidents of both parties, standing with a White man he didn't recognize. Didn't care, either.

Little had been pulled in from Philadelphia to negotiate the release of the hostages. Negotiation was his forte, a skill needed infrequently. He also was the FBI's field director for surveillance and investigations of domestic terrorism, which belatedly was deemed a more serious threat than international terrorism. That shift was mostly a public relations ploy, Little suspected – until now. No longer would showing the flag against domestic extremism be a PR job.

"To play devil's advocate, I never heard anything suspicious on the call," said Agent Bly. "I thought we should have let them talk longer. Might have learned something."

"Finances for that bunch can't be complicated and were worked out before they came to D.C.," Little explained. "When Dancer said, 'betting,' then followed up with 'safe-deposit box,' I'll bet that told her something. So did talking about their health, somehow."

Agent Bly's large but trim frame filled a wing chair. She had a lot to learn, but Little found her a great sounding board, right down to asking so-called dumb questions.

"I've listened to your phone calls with Dancer and watched the crazy murder on TV, and I've been through the brothers' military records," she said. "I don't know if they're good or lucky."

"Both, I think. Lucky to snatch the Speaker. She should already have been tucked away somewhere safe. I'll cut her detail slack, in the confusion, for not knowing how deep the shit was until too late. But Ambrose is good, too. When he saw his chance to grab her, he didn't hesitate, and he knew a good place to take her. Someone had scouted the Capitol."

"Ambrose seems to be the leader."

"I agree. While you were flying in last night, I went to the hospital and talked to the Speaker's security guard, the one who was wounded. He heard the guy who led the attack call himself Ambrose, when he was talking down the mob. And he's gone public more and is older than his brother, for what that's worth. From reading their military records, what do you think?"

Bly looked at him. "To imitate your eloquence, we may have no idea how deep the shit is. These guys could be very dangerous."

Alexander's record in the Rangers showed him consistently scoring above average on written tests and in the field. Promotions were regular. In Afghanistan he fulfilled his missions, and his men's safety was paramount. He was a problem-solver and team player.

Though Ambrose offered more, he left the Army's Delta Force with checkered reviews. Brilliant or nearly so, he knocked the top out of IQ tests, and no one doubted his courage or ability. Most impressive, he was a strategist who could reorder tactics on the fly.

But he couldn't resist tempting the flame. He garnered praise for always stepping into harm's way to protect his squad, more praise for volunteering for risky one-man missions. But comrades who depended on him started to question the risks he seemed to crave. Some felt jeopardized. Then, during his second tour in Afghanistan, villagers reported finding bodies in shallow graves, in remote areas where Ambrose had conducted solitary missions. The bodies were Taliban, which was fine, but a question haunted those around him: Was he addicted to risk taking, seeking thrills beyond his control?

The question was already the stuff of barracks chatter when three Taliban captured him. As they drove him to their camp and, no doubt, torture and a nasty death, he attacked the driver, forcing the small car over a suicidally steep embankment. When the dust settled, Ambrose had killed his captors and walked away. Debriefed later, he explained simply, "Ya gotta believe."

Maybe he saw no other way to survive. Maybe others would have taken the same gamble. In any case, when Ambrose passed up another tour with Delta Force, even his gung-ho superiors exhaled in relief.

"How does 'Ya gotta believe' fit with him being so damn smart?" Bly asked. "Smart people usually don't take blind leaps of faith, certainly don't turn those leaps into a mantra."

"Not sure, but while he's a world-class risk-taker, his record doesn't show him putting others at risk – making others nervous, yes, but not injured or killed. Until he started taking hostages.

"FYI, he's been very low-key in building the NPM. I had heard of some group in western Michigan that we needed to catch up with, but nothing about his brother having a chapter in the Southeast. I suspect he and Alexander were happy to grow slow, pick the right people, not the chest-thumpers looking to party. You're no doubt right about them being dangerous. Terrorists usually aren't disciplined or well-trained or as smart as these guys. Hell, they even hung back when the Capitol was stormed. At least, they're not on security video showing the first invaders."

"If Ambrose did signal something to that Armor woman, what was it?"

"Specifically, I haven't a clue," Little answered. "But let's assume they want an uprising, to help the President or for something bigger. The brothers will go to the strength of their followers, who likely aren't a bunch of computer nerds, into hacking or cyber warfare. They're blue-collar, guys who hunt – read that guns – and work with their hands – read that knowing how to blow things up. Already, we've seen too much of that. Clearly, some of them have military or police training, but few will be a match for our SWAT guys. Knowing that, the Dancers want to be force multipliers – get people into the streets, turn them against the government. Stuff like that."

CHAPTER 31

JANUARY 8TH

Most mornings, snow under the near-full moon would have made them visible from the street, even in the protective shadow of a massive Norway spruce. But the thin cloud cover at three o'clock was a friend, giving Mike and Stoney just the light they needed.

Their boots cushioned almost silently in new snow as they entered an alley behind the ranch style house. Parked half a block away, their driver watched for trouble, his phone on the seat. He gave quiet thanks for the heater in Stoney's pickup, called into service when his own began coughing and wheezing. Damn cheap gas.

The fifteen-degree Michigan temperature worked through Mike's light gloves, his fingers stiffening as he scored the windowpane with a glass cutter. Stoney lightly pressed adhesive tape on the glass and tapped the pane free. Mike reached in for the lock.

Climbing inside, they clicked on small direct beam flashlights. Stoney knew the house from delivering paperwork to First Sergeant Major Nathan Hall, the ailing commander of National Guard units near Grand Rapids. He led the way to a bedroom door. They exchanged glances through three-hole ski masks. Ready.

Mike turned the doorknob slowly. Unlocked. He pushed the door open gently and Stoney aimed his torch where he remembered the bed. Nathan Hall bolted upright, squinting with alarm. Four hollow points from silenced Glocks ripped into his chest. He slumped back on his pillow without a sound.

"Knew he was single," Stoney said. "Glad he was sleeping alone."

"Let's get out of here," Mike told him.

Other NPM members carried out similar deadly missions in nearby Kalamazoo and Raleigh, North Carolina. Killers from Baldwin's Freedom Country Coalition struck in suburban Salt Lake City. Their targets were local commanders of units judged ripe for mutiny.

After trading texts to confirm the executions, Mike and his counterparts called police dispatchers in Detroit, Raleigh and Salt Lake City. Everyone's goal: Get the news out quickly to put the revolution's best foot forward on a seminal day.

Dispatchers tried to keep the callers on the line, hoping to get a patrol car to GPS locations. Mike's response was typical: "Sorry dude. You've got what you need. Check it out."

He nodded to the driver, who had driven to a bridge spanning the Grand River. Crossing it, Mike threw the burner over the rail. He opened the glovebox for another as they drove.

"Gotta love these things," he said, punching in the number of an all-news radio station. Stoney was alerting the media, too.

News of the executions was breaking as people on the East Coast sat down for breakfast or headed to work. The shock of Guard commanders being murdered in their own beds was palpable, but the Dancer brothers and Baldwin hoped for an additional reaction: disgruntled guardsmen in other units piling on. If that happened nationwide, the uprising would be energized. From ample stockpiles, guardsmen would supply it with everything from small arms to heavy machine guns, gas masks to grenades, even howitzers. Plenty of munitions to arm a revolution.

Sydney Armor backed that appeal into a message from Ambrose

she posted on Facebook and Twitter and on dark sites reaching the underbelly of social media. Some site managers pulled down the posts quickly. But Armor also alerted television networks, particularly those on the right, and the AP. They responded, primed by Brent Wilfrid's slaying to report anything involving Ambrose Dancer. Concerns the press might have had about fanning revolution were outweighed by competitive instincts and, of course, the people's right to know. News was news.

Soon, Ambrose's message was out in full:

"Welcome to the revolution. This morning we began taking control of National Guard units across the country. Freedom-seeking brothers and sisters from coast-to-coast and border-to-border are joining us. Rise up, Americans, for the sake of your country, your way of life.

"We have a President who knows our needs, this country's needs, and is protecting our way of life. He has hit the reset button against socialism and the Deep State. He has uttered an emphatic no to opening our borders. He has restored Christian values. He is making America great again.

"But as the President warned would happen, warned time and again before the election, he has become the victim of corruption on a scale never seen before. A landslide election has been stolen. The will of you, the people, blocked. Nothing less than freedom and democracy are being pried from us.

"We must rise up and seize power. As you listen, that is happening within the National Guard. But freedom lovers everywhere must take control at every level. Police, take control. Firemen, take control. From city halls to the courthouses to statehouses, we must take control. It will be hard. It will be dangerous. But take control.

"And take heart from this: We know the President is on the cusp of using the Insurrection Act to allow the military to restore order. That would halt the leftists in their tracks. Other militias would be empowered to join us – and you – in the defense of freedom."

"Until then, here in the United States Capitol, we will continue to hold out against a corrupt Congress that is denying our President his victory, denying us our victory. Ultimately it will be up to true Americans of every stripe to rise against the leftists flooding our streets. Up to you to stand against the invasion of our borders. Rise up and, together, we will take back our country."

After anonymously alerting police and the media to the execution of their Guard commander, Mike and Stoney dropped their driver at his home. At an all-night diner, the triggermen toasted each other with coffee while wolfing steak and eggs.

"That was hard," said Stoney. "Really doing it, I mean. I wasn't sure I'd even hit him, the way my hands shook. I don't know if I could have done it if you hadn't shared that joint."

"You did good," Mike assured him. "It's like making money. The first million is the hardest, or so I'm told."

"You've done it before?"

"In Iraq, with a contract security outfit. We'd kick in a door and open fire because we knew the ragheads would resist, just flat knew it." He laughed. "Then the boss would put in for extra hazardous duty pay. Sometimes we got it."

Stoney looked at Mike with new-found respect. "Well," he said, "I don't think I'll be making a million."

Lights in the cavernous Guard armory were already on when they pulled into the parking lot. A handful of fellow militants in the unit had heard news reports and were eager for details. They stood in uniform near the twenty-four-cup coffee maker, nervously shifting from one heavy boot to the other.

"Corporal Mike! Stoney!" a lanky guardsman called. "We've been waiting for you."

"No shit, and good to see you, too," Mike answered. "If you've heard the news there's not much more to say. We're putting out the call for first responders. I'll talk when enough get here. Just remember this: We have no idea who killed poor Nathan. But – listen up, this is important – this is our chance to take control of our unit, to keep our President in power and retake our country."

"But how did it go?" the lanky guardsman persisted.

"Not going there, are we Stoney? You guys know the media doesn't always lie. Enough said. We need to get to the locker room to change. As troops come in, talk up the great opportunity we have, but nothing else. Got that?"

When they returned in uniform, several dozen guardsmen were milling about, roughly divided between those shocked by Nathan Hall's death and those claiming to be. As more drifted in, the militants became a distinct minority.

Buck Smothers, the second in command, hadn't shown up. All the better, thought Mike, to make sure we head in the right direction. He got people's attention and called for a moment of silence to honor Commander Hall.

"Thank you, ladies and gentlemen. You all know what happened at the Capitol and you know why. Leftist extremists determined to deny an honest count of electoral votes shamefully turned a peaceful rally into a riot. Some protesters loyal to the President tragically paid the ultimate price. Now those bloody leftists are having an executioner's heyday in our own backyards. Besides our beloved commander, others have died – on the East Coast, in the Southwest – the radio is reporting. An unconfirmed report has the commander in Kalamazoo being executed, too."

A stirring of "Oh my god" and "What the hell?" greeted that news. Mike let conversations in the still-growing crowd die down, knowing newcomers were being filled in.

"Some media say the President is about to use the Insurrection Act to call out the military. I expect our mission will be to put down civil disobedience. No specific orders yet, but we need to be ready to deal with a riot. Be ready with firearms, gas masks, shields, vests, the whole nine yards. It's time to lock and load, gentlemen and ladies, be ready to follow the commander in chief."

"Excuse me, Mike, er, corporal." A small man, his hair suggesting recent intimacy with an electrical outlet, waved his hands. People knew better than to ignore Bulldog Willie.

"Yes, Willie?" Mike said gruffly.

"I been channel surfing at home, to keep up on things, you know, and I been checking my all-news radio since walking in here. Nothing new but the killings, and not even a tiny iota about the President sending out troops, even on Fox. How do you know about the President, er, sir?"

"I can't remember, exactly," Mike answered slowly. "I've been up a long time and know I heard..."

"Well, Corporal Mike, you know how secrets won't stay put. There's scuttlebutt about members of this here guard being really unhappy with things, and now poor Nathan gets killed. You been unhappy, Mike?"

"Bulldog Willie, I resent that. I am probably less unhappy than anyone, but I am concerned about the country, and I am ready to support whatever the President tells us to do. All of us need to be ready. That's all I'm saying, said that to Stoney over breakfast a couple hours ago. Be ready to stand..."

"Hold up, corporal!"

Mike turned to see Buck Smothers, red-faced with anger, thirty years of military presence bristling, stomp past Stoney, whose eyes went wide.

"Who are you to be calling up this unit?"

"Just doing my job, sir, as the senior corporal when the meeting needed to start, in response to an emerging national emergency."

"So you say." The armory was tomb quiet as Smothers outstared Mike, then snapped at Stoney, "Did you enjoy breakfast, son?"

"Y-yes, sir."

"Now corporal, who issues first responder orders?"

"I think that normally would be Commander Hall...excuse me, would be you now, sir."

"Who else?"

"The governor or the state commander, sir."

"And who issued this morning's order."

"I did, sir."

"You, a corporal?"

"Given the circumstances, all the news and the threat to the commander in chief, this unit needed to be ready as soon…"

"Shut up, corporal. Answer my questions. No debate, no speeches. Admitting what you have, in front of all these witnesses, I could drum you out right now, court martial your sorry ass," Smothers growled. "No one but you seems to know the President might invoke the Insurrection Act. You and that bunch holding hostages. They've brought it up. What do you know about them, corporal?"

"Nothing, sir," said Mike, wishing he had sent a team to hit Smothers, too.

"And you, the corporal's breakfast companion, what do you know about the National Patriot Movement, I think it is?"

Stoney shrunk in his chair. "N-nothing, sir."

"Where did you have breakfast?"

"Sir?"

"You heard me. Breakfast! Where?"

"S-Sherlock's. S-Sir."

"Only Sherlock's I know is a good half-hour south. That it?"

"Y-yes, s-sir." My voice sounds like a mouse, Stoney thought. Damn.

"You and Mike live north of here, right? And Sherlock's is most of the way to Commander Hall's house, right private?"

"I w-wouldn't know, s-sir."

"Are you lying or forgetful?"

Sweat tickled Stoney's spine. He hoped his face was dry. Then a drop ran down his nose.

"I d-don't understand, s-sir."

"I was the one who sent you to Commander Hall's house with some papers to sign, when he was sick."

"Oh."

"Did you drive here in your puke-green pickup?"

"I remember taking the papers, sir, d-driving in my pickup. A while back, sir."

"No, I mean this morning!" Smothers barked.

Stoney's face turned ashen. His greasy breakfast threatened to come up. His mind flashed to his pickup, clearly in Smothers' sights. He could see Mike putting their guns in the console – "if the takeover gets hairy and we need them." Now they were the last thing they needed. The pickup will be searched, there will be ballistics tests, no matter my answer, Stony realized.

He felt unsteady, his knees turned to mush, and he collapsed to the floor of a Guard unit not to be counted in the rebel's column.

CHAPTER 32

T hough spread thin, the three small militias tried to make their reach appear broad. Working from blueprints the Dancer brothers had crafted earlier, they attacked all the levers of government they could, at whatever level, relentlessly and with discipline.

Walter Fostoria, who answered to "AC," watched patiently as an NPM recruit set heavy-duty bolt cutters to the chain link fence, then peeled it back. Slipping through the opening, the men, both tall, stooped to stay below the utility substation's electrical field; standing upright would get them fried.

They stopped at a gray box, the size of an office supply cabinet, with stubby legs. AC, retired from utility company maintenance jobs, knew it housed the crown jewels – isolators, capacitor banks, conductors – that made substations hum.

Each man took a three-stick bundle of dynamite from his backpack. "Follow my lead, like we practiced," AC said, setting his bundle on end and securing it inside a cabinet leg with electrical tape. A timer topped the bundle.

"You good so far?" AC asked.

"Yeah, right with you."

"Okay. We'll set them for an hour. Ready? On two. One, two."

In an hour, an explosion would bring the substation down and, with it, electricity in a slice of lightly populated Johnson County in southern Illinois.

Though a small disruption, militia leaders knew people took the electrical grid for granted. Suddenly losing power quickly got under their skin – or worse. When traffic signals or building elevators failed, or people unexpectedly found themselves in the dark, injuries and deaths followed. Those in authority got blamed.

The Dancers and Baldwin initially planned to target liberal cities like Ann Arbor and Madison; sticking it to socialist bastions would feel so good. Then they reasoned: better to stoke anger with attacks in conservative areas. Not only would authorities and the lefties get blamed, but the President's base would be riled up, some enough to revolt. Like in most red states, they were a force: The President carried Johnson County with seventy-eight percent in 2020.

Charges set, AC and the recruit drove north on Interstate 57 to plant dynamite at a substation in nearby Jefferson County, another conservative stronghold.

"I would have knocked out power in socialist places," AC allowed, "but this seems to make more sense in a devious way."

To drive the narrative of nationwide attacks, NPM teams targeted substations well outside their home territories. Ambrose also sent saboteurs across Iowa and South Dakota, and Alexander dispatched a team down Interstate 10 to hit substations from Mobile to west of Houston.

Three men sat on a ridge beneath high-voltage lines carrying power from the Bonneville Power Administration's hydroelectric dams on the Columbia River. They relaxed against the legs of a gigantic transmission tower after hiking uphill from an Oregon state highway north of Eugene. Grateful for a break from January's usual drizzle, the men smoked as they watched the sunrise bring into view other steel towers, stretching north and south through logged strips of mature Douglas fir.

Days before, they had climbed this same ridge in the Cascade Range to sight in their high-caliber rifles. The two young men had hunting rifles, but their team leader, Harrison Strawberry, carried a Barrett M82. It fired a larger load than today's work demanded but was the former Marine sniper's weapon of choice.

Months after being discharged, he was shocked when the precision rifle showed up at his house in Tucson, special delivery from a phony address in Boston. Costing thousands of dollars and blatantly stolen from Uncle Sam, Strawberry bet the M82 came from someone whose life he saved with a shot from afar on one of his Mideast tours.

Strawberry looked north to the third tower, standing a hundred feet high and, the challenging part, a full half-mile away. Three conductor lines ran through bread loaf-size insulators, carrying electricity to points south in Oregon and for export to California users – part of a system serving millions.

The insulators were his targets. Back in the day, knocking them out would have been a cinch. Now, with sporadic practice and squinting through early-stage cataracts, not so much. But Strawberry was confident; a ten-shell magazine emptied from a semi-automatic performance weapon with a 10X scope was a lot of firepower.

The sun rose high enough.

"Okay, one more time," he said. "I nail all three insulators on the third tower before you start firing. That way, the closer insulators you knock out won't be live and we won't have hot wires whipping at us. With power already out, we'll be giving the bastards more to repair. When I yell stop, you haul ass, no more shooting."

He moved to a flat spot and set up his tripod, placing another magazine in easy reach on a flat rock. The younger men took prone positions, too, one facing north, the other south.

Strawberry nailed the three insulators with five shots and thought, not bad. "Fire at will," he yelled, and thirty seconds later their work was done. Scrambling several yards, they turned to shoot out insulators on the tower where they had set up – more repair work for the bastards.

They knew the Bonneville Power Administration was immediately aware of the outage and its location. Power lost on a grid built to withstand mountain winds instantly raised the specter of terrorism. Any law officer in the area would already be on the way.

Strawberry's five-passenger pickup was parked on an old logging road. As they approached, an Oregon Highway Patrol car, lights flashing, wheeled in, bouncing up the road. "Run for it," screamed one of the young men, panicked. Instead, Strawberry unholstered his .45 Sig Sauer and dropped to a knee. With the windshield a glare in the morning sun, he centered on the driver's side and fired three times. The patrol car veered off the logging road, hurtling down an embankment.

"Now let's get to the Interstate," he said.

Strawberry's team was one of several Seth Baldwin dispatched to bring down high-velocity lines of the BPA, which supplies electricity as far east as Montana. Other rifle teams of his Freedom Country Coalition targeted hydro projects of the Western Area Power Administration serving states as far east as Iowa and Minnesota. Selecting remote targets, close to interstate escape routes, their attacks were coordinated with Strawberry's, disrupting millions of lives. Most people only lost power, but food in refrigerators went bad, businesses couldn't open, ATMs didn't work. Once repaired, life went on. But for some, inconvenience turned deadly – or nearly so.

In Salt Lake City, Dr. Clyde Benson had opened the heart of a fifty-year-old man to replace a dysfunctional aortic valve with one from a pig when the lights dimmed, then went out. Backup generators failed. Benson's patient died. Other faulty generators – not used for years or maintained – plagued nursing homes, too. Patients died after losing oxygen and medication drips.

When suddenly without lights, people who happened to be on stairs were left fearfully groping in the dark. In Redding, California, Lucretia Jeffers felt her way down until losing her balance on a turn and falling into the stairwell. Landing on concrete two stories below, her neck broke at the second vertebrae. "Almost certainly, she'll be a quadriplegic," a doctor told her family.

In Idaho Falls, Herman Walks On Fire suffered an anxiety attack when his apartment house elevator stopped between floors. He was going to breakfast to celebrate his ninety-seventh birthday with friends. With power not restored for three hours, he could be heard kicking and pounding on the elevator door – until he couldn't. A younger person likely would have survived.

Failed traffic lights were blamed for hundreds of fender benders and three crashes causing five deaths in Southern California and Seattle. Road rage led to dozens of fights. In Las Cruces, New Mexico, a car with members of a cartel plowed into a squad car. A shootout followed. Four of the drug dealers and a police officer were killed and a second officer wounded.

Much worse was the explosion at a railroad crossing near Wichita, Kansas. When safety arms failed to lower, a tanker truck carrying anhydrous ammonia was struck by a train. Besides killing the engineer and the truck driver, the blast tore through a nearby mobile home park. The coroner set the death count at eleven and rising, with more than a dozen victims in critical condition.

In Phoenix, William Fleet, an elderly janitor, was sweeping his way along the top row of auditorium seats after a Christian music concert. When the lights went out, he tried to navigate the steep aisle and fell, breaking both wrists.

Perry Winkle, forever teased for his parents' sense of humor, was answering a call of nature in his basement rental in Boulder, Colorado. He turned the wrong way in the pitch-black darkness of a bathroom he had used thousands of times, smashing the glass shower stall. He bled to death.

Alice Tomlinson was approaching a low-water bridge near Mountain Rest, South Carolina, when she heard a strange rumble. Those bridges, built without railings to let trees and other debris to easily wash over, can turn deadly if a motorist challenges even a few inches of rushing water.

As Alice neared the bridge, it was dry. But it sat around a sharp curve in the creek, and she was blindsided by two feet of rushing water as her car crossed. Alice never reached the hospital where she was a nurse's aide. Nor did her three-month-old son make it to daycare. Their bodies were recovered from her overturned car, a stone's throw below the bridge.

The short-lived flood on the unnamed creek came from a hydro-electric dam, one of ten targeted by the NPM that are among thousands designated "high hazard" by the federal government. Heavily concentrated in the Midwest and Southeast, the dams are at least a half-century old, small and have minimal security.

Still, they largely defied the NPM's demolition skills. Seven of the early morning attacks failed – the multiple dynamite charges proving to be too small. The others were deemed a success, the explosions flooding downstream areas and one small town. A few thousand people lost power and, besides Alice Tomlinson and her baby, five people were killed. Three were in the same family, their streamside house washed away as they sat down for breakfast. There was a sixth death, a dam security officer, shot when he pulled a gun to confront a demolition team.

Elaina Leslie and Billie Hanks, retired nurses, were resting on a bench with steaming cups of black tea after jogging five laps around a mall near downtown Detroit. Proud of exercising in the face of Covid-19, the women enjoyed only a couple sips before an innocent-looking shopping bag at the end of the bench exploded. Both died.

In Savannah, Georgia, Mike McDonald made his regular delivery at a fish restaurant, also in a mall. On his way out he walked past a green recycling container as it exploded. He died, too.

News of those deaths had been woven into a terrorism story Harold "Butch" Cardin watched on TV before stepping from his shoe shop in a Boise mall for a cigarette. "This place looks like a ghost town," he said absently, dropping his last-ever Marlboro in a plastic ashtray as it blew up.

The attacks on dams and electrical lines paled next to the random slaughter caused by single sticks of dynamite timed to blow in five minutes – enough time for an indiscriminate killer to walk from a mall to a car and drive away. Shortly after malls opened, explosions in open areas found victims like Leslie and Hanks, McDonald and Cardin. Innocent-looking sacks left in supermarkets and restrooms worsened the carnage. Lady Luck picked her victims.

Curious employees found two deadly sacks. A grocery clerk managed to toss the homemade bomb into a broom closet before it exploded. But a mall janitor's discovery came fatally late.

By morning's end, twenty-three explosions had claimed sixty-one victims, with thirty-four dead and many in critical condition. Had Covid not kept people at home, surely more would have died.

Militia leaders prioritized seizing radio stations, but finding NPM or FCC troops proficient at a control board was a challenge. When Larry Fetermann stepped up, even with his checkered record, he was welcome.

Most recently, "Super Mouth" Fetermann worked for a small station near Pinehurst, North Carolina. He enjoyed hosting talk radio in the morning, still well-fueled by meth from the night before. Alexander Dancer knew Super Mouth was a user but didn't drum him out, enjoying the digs he took at liberals.

Trouble followed when the guy cooking Super Mouth's meth changed his recipe. The Mouth, totally stoned, went on-air and blabbed local gossip about a county official seen banging a high school cheerleader on a boat dock at Seven Lakes. It was Super Mouth's last broadcast.

Damage done, Alexander still didn't boot him, seeing value in keeping a glib tongue in the wings. It was a good call, with Super Mouth now heading back to the station that had fired him – this time with a rebel's voice.

When the early shift engineer unlocked the station, a gun was at his head. Instead of canned music and local ads, listeners were treated to the Mouth's return. After noting NPM control of the station, he repeated the salacious gossip about the county official, adding a vicious rumor that the cheerleader's father had watched. Only then did he improvise from Ambrose's message:

"We have a President who is protecting our way of life. He has hit the reset button on socialism and the Deep State. It's our time now, our time to step up and reclaim our country ..."

More people – angry or fearful, looking for trouble or committed to political upheaval – were hitting the streets. There was more rioting than the day before, more buildings torched, more stores looted. Clashes of activists grew more violent, liberals egged on by antifa, conservatives stirred up by right-wing militias. Arrests climbed sharply. Emergency room wait times got longer, with more serious injuries to treat. The death count multiplied.

As usual, local leaders urged residents to stay home and remain calm. Several governors threatened to call up the National Guard, then retreated to wait and see. California and New Jersey did activate units to restore order.

In a Pittsburgh suburb, Mayor Timothy Novak ignored frigid weather to headline an outdoor press conference. Hours earlier, an explosion at a mall killed an elderly woman resting on a bench, knitting, and her granddaughter. A passerby recalled seeing a Target shopping bag under the bench, moments before the explosion. The local Chamber of Commerce office had been bombed the day before.

"I'm calling on the governor to bring in the Guard and put an end...," were Novak's last words. He crumbled with a massive head wound; the vest police ordered him to wear of no help. Police later determined the shot was fired from the roof of a high rise several blocks away, where a shell casing was found.

By mid-afternoon, a mayor in South Carolina and a police chief in Georgia had been shot dead, also at outdoor press conferences. On the central Oregon coast, a county supervisor was critically wounded from long distance as he walked from his car to the courthouse for a board meeting.

"Four assassins doing their deadly worst in less than two hours," said the WTAE-TV anchor in Pittsburgh. "The FBI has issued an urgent notice, saying investigations indicate high-powered rifles fired at long range were used in all four shootings. Local officials are urged to take extra precautions: No outdoor appearances. Tightly vet everyone at press conferences. Increase security."

"Damn," said Sydney Armor. "That was going so well."

She and counterparts in Alexander's and Seth Baldwin's regions had dispatched teams to search city, county and state websites for outdoor events. Militia rosters were scoured for shooters deemed good, bold and cold enough to assassinate. More than thirty opportunities were identified. Usually, shooters couldn't get there in time. A Detroit city councilman was saved by heavy traffic. But Mayor Timothy Novak and three others were not so fortunate.

Armor's phone chimed God Bless America. "Hi, Jake."

"You remember the crazy who's been stalking the Michigan governor?"

"Sure. He ready to go?"

"He done gone. Took his shot and missed."

"He was to get my okay."

"Yeah, negative that. The good news, I'm thinking, is he's dead. Got spotted at the top of an apartment house and shot it out with the gov's bodyguards. Gov's not talking but an ambulance was seen leaving the apartment house in no hurry or siren and such."

"Good indeed. Has he ever called you?"

Silence. Ames could sense Jake mentally catching up. "Yes."

"If they got his phone, which is likely, they'll be coming for you soon. Fucking destroy that phone, Jake. Burn it in that wood stove of yours, then tape what's left to a brick and throw it in the river. Where it's deep."

"Where it's deep," he said.

"Then you get off the street. No more stirring up Black Lives Matter in Lansing. You're just a Ford maintenance guy. Don't know from NPM. Got it?"

"Don't know from NPM. Got it."

Super Mouth Fetermann took a call from the county sheriff, threatening to cut power to the station.

"No, you listen," said Super Mouth, riding smooth on meth. "I keep broadcasting, or we shoot the engineer. Him dead or alive, I'll take my chances. I'm headed to the slammer for sure, but this state ain't done an execution in fifteen years."

After putting a gun to the head of Darien Grayson, the three NPMers backing up the Mouth had duct taped the engineer's hands at his knees and locked him in a closet. Worried about the army of law officers surrounding the station, they prowled its windows, expecting at any second a barrage of shots and SWAT teams bursting in.

Super Mouth blathered on happily about the revolution, confident that as reporting crews arrived outside and tension from the standoff built, more people were tuning in, sending his ratings stratospheric.

"Check it out folks, check it out," the Mouth urged his listeners. "The revolution is here. The real deal. Surfing the TV I see people in the streets, revolting against a fraudulent election. The courts ignored overwhelming evidence, folks. Overwhelming beyond doubt. Now the spineless VP and Congress have failed the President, failed us. But we control the Capitol, holding the Speaker hostage. Our patriotic militias are facing down the entire federal government. Think about that. Incredible! Now we're taking control of the streets, but we've only made a dent. Succeeding means more people on the streets. Means controlling city halls and court houses and statehouses. Running the elites and the Deep State into their holes, like scared prairie dogs. Now is the time, Americans. Take control, take control. Keep your President in the White House. Take back America!"

As national media picked up Super Mouth's rant, he quickly became the voice of the revolution, issuing a call to arms that excited the militia leaders listening in the House Dining Room, building confidence that Super Mouth could ignite populist timber.

When media researchers dug out file photos of Larry Fetermann, he became the charismatic face of the rebellion, handsome with a strong chin, full head of dark hair and a disarming grin. Digging into the story of his firing and drug addiction, perceptions changed as quickly as they had taken hold. Suddenly, he was a mouth with no balance beam, the hawker of unhinged ramblings. With the speed of a clot-causing stroke, the rebellion's voice lost its authority.

In the closet, Darien Grayson knew none of that. When his captors patted him down, they missed the phone in his floppy cargo pants. It took him until afternoon to chew the duct tape enough to free his numb hands. He painfully texted a 911 message with stinging thumbs: Grayson here. Okay in closet. Charge.

Outside the station, the deputy commanding the sheriff's SWAT team was hungry and tired and a Democrat fed up with Super Mouth's rants. When a dispatcher relayed Grayson's text, the deputy told his men with a wink, "If they resist, defend yourselves."

Battering rams hit the station's doors as the Mouth was exhorting people to "step up! The revolution means putting your life on the line for the President."

The gunfire was intense, but one-sided. Grayson was rescued. Super Mouth threw up his hands in surrender but ended up walking his talk, he and the other mutineers exiting in body bags.

Theodore Wormsley finally had his target, one destructive enough to make a difference. To make him a significant lone wolf contributor to the revolution. His search had not been easy. For too long he failed to look within his arbitrary safety buffer, wasting a day. Still unsure if the revolution was real, he kept checking the news and found assurance in reports of assassinations, rioting and other violence. Then he went back to pouring over maps and lists of iconic places – and searching his mind.

Frustrated, he had driven to the chilly solitude of his treasured Boston Mountains, seeking fresh perspective. He vigorously hiked a familiar trail, then propped himself against an ancient sugar maple to watch the sun setting behind scattered cumulus clouds.

Within a minute, he said aloud, "My god, how could I be so blind?"

His solution was only a four-hour drive west on Interstate 40: the U.S. Federal Building and Courthouse in Oklahoma City, built after Timothy McVeigh bombed the Alfred P. Murrah Federal Building in what then was the deadliest terrorist attack in the nation's history.

"Perfect," he murmured, fishing his phone from a pocket of his cargo pants. Luckily, he was in a spot with coverage, and a search reminded him that when McVeigh's rental truck, loaded with an ammonium nitrate bomb, exploded, it killed one hundred sixty-eight people, including nineteen children. Another six hundred eighty people were injured, and three hundred twenty-four other downtown buildings were damaged, with property loss set at six hundred fifty-two million dollars.

"Perfect," he said again, noting that McVeigh, like himself, was an Army veteran, and the new federal building, completed in 2008, sat close to the Murrah building memorial site. The media will take all of that – except for knowing he is a veteran – and spin a haunting narrative with the message that no one is safe, that nearly four decades after McVeigh the revolution is alive and well.

He saw the bombing was at 9:02 a.m. on April 19, 1995. "Can't do anything about the date, but tomorrow I can match the time if I hustle. That will feed the drama."

After gassing up his Ford F-150 pickup, Wormsley drove home to load his arsenal. He put a Standard .40-caliber Glock in the seat console for quick access. Two more Glocks fit in custom-made spaces of a metal chest, along with an AR-15 rifle and large capacity magazines of ammunition, one a drum with one hundred rounds.

The guns were all purchased legally but not the bump stock that converted the AR to fully automatic – a four hundred round per minute killing machine. Illegal, too, was his favorite weapon – an RPG-7 rocket-propelled grenade launcher – that also fit in the chest, which was strapped securely under the cover of the short bed pickup.

Years earlier, as he soured on militias to become a lone wolf, he had rented a room in the Little Rock home of a retired history professor. Wormsley learned the professor, though living independently, suffered confusion suggesting early dementia. Grasping the opportunity, he managed to assume the aging man's identity and navigate the year-long federal background check for legally buying an RPG. Clearing that hurdle, he found an early, 1966 version of the Russian-made grenade launcher costing two thousand dollars, plus grenades for five hundred dollars each.

Every couple of years he went to a remote mountain valley to fire the RPG and make sure it was operable. His supply of grenades was down to five – likely the most he could fire in a minute and still avoid capture, if his nerves held up.

He planned to find a quiet street near the federal building to retrieve the RPG and the AR-15 from the custom-built chest, then find a spot well within the RPG's maximum range of 900 yards. Ideally, he would be in the shadows of another building and hard to detect.

CHAPTER 33
JANUARY 9TH

With little time for sleep and too much adrenalin pumping, Theodore Wormsley was on the road at 3:00 the next morning, sipping coffee, cruise control set two miles per hour under the limit. He switched from one radio station to the next, snagging reports of attacks that read like a police blotter, but offered no perspective on the revolution. That the militias still held hostages was promising. He punched off the radio to think, mildly unsettled by never having seen his target and having to quickly stitch together his mission. Fort Smith slipped by, roughly the halfway point.

Thirty miles from Oklahoma City he stopped to refuel, should he need to suddenly put a chunk of miles behind him. Back on the interstate, Wormsley turned on the radio and chanced into earlier remarks by the President-elect, accusing a few small right-wing militias of causing "senseless deaths" in an "barren venture" engineered by "whack jobs" and "traitors."

The words stung and pushed up doubt. He searched other reports to make the case the President-elect was wrong, that the revolution was a reality and his mission not in vain. He realized he was grinding his teeth and starting to sweat. He snapped off the heater, forced himself to stay calm, positive, anxious for the GPS to announce his downtown exit. It's barely seven o'clock, he told himself, plenty of time for reconnaissance, to find the best vantage point for unleashing the RPG's fury. Maybe even time for breakfast.

Nearing his exit, Wormsley sighed with relief that interstate traffic had been light, that an accident or road construction had not slowed him. Then he chanced on a PBS report: "By comparison, this morning is off to a quiet start. The insurrection may be over – except for the hostage crisis, of course – or this may be the lull before the storm. FBI sources insist a few small militias brought all this on and those extremists are being rounded up. If that's true, and my independent reporting suggests it is, the storm has been weathered."

Wormsley's appetite was gone when he took the offramp for the short drive to the federal building on N.W. Fourth Street. Immediately he had the sense of being alone, of having the street virtually to himself. Except for a woman walking her dog and an elderly man sitting on a bench, reading a newspaper, sidewalks were empty. "Did the GPS lady get lost?" he asked.

Then there it was, his large target, in bland contrast to the architecturally imposing Murrah building McVeigh had leveled. As he began looking for a vantage point for firing the RPG, he noticed boots protruding from the shadow of a business awning. He slowed upon seeing a National Guardsman at the next corner, a rifle slung over his shoulder. The young guardsman eyed him with suspicion. An armored vehicle was parked at the next intersection, two soldiers squatting on the front bumper, one pulling on a cigarette.

Shit, Wormsley said silently, turning the corner. Another armored vehicle was at the end of that block and across the street, two more guardsman. I wasn't the only one who remembered the Oklahoma City bombing, he thought wryly.

He turned on an eastbound street, headed toward Arkansas and safety. Could have gotten off one grenade, maybe two, he thought, but would have achieved nothing McVeigh-like. Nothing to lead the news let alone drive the revolution before guardsmen cut me down.

He was not suicidal or into martyrdom. Escape, live to fight another day. A cog in the most dangerous terrorism threat facing the nation. Do not lose the status, however anonymous, of being The Lone Wolf.

Then it struck him, why the streets were empty. "This is Saturday!" Wormsley yelled. "This is freaking Saturday!"

He kept driving slowly, looking for interstate signs to spirit him away from his private, but total, humiliation.

"My god," he asked himself, "how could you be so stupid?"

The comeuppance of Wormsley, and the sudden rise and demise of Super Mouth, proved symptomatic of the rebellion. The mutineers could boast of energizing millions of people to their cause, gripping millions more in fear. They had turned out zealots – and a lot of ordinary citizens – enthusiastic for civil war, ready to toss democracy aside. Government at many levels had tottered.

But the republic was not toppled. By the fourth day, most of government was back, services, too. A multitude of work-around repairs restored electricity. Dead public officials and National Guard commanders had been replaced; their responsibilities assumed. Fires were out and looted businesses boarded up. Only a few extremists roamed the streets, and if they encountered other troublemakers and fought, no one cared. For most people, fears calmed to jitters as violence slowed to a trickle.

Most political leaders, even those on the right, condemned the carnage and destruction, though claims of election fraud persisted. Thoughts and prayers for the dead became a reliable verbal crutch, paired with appeals for business as usual. No politician of note had called for invoking the Insurrection Act. Military leaders were mum. The President, too, apparently could not find a likely path for holding power.

But the President-elect had issued a statement, one that had disturbed Theodore Wormsley : "This senseless violence – causing the needless deaths of innocent, loyal Americans – cannot continue.

To all the families who have lost loved ones, I offer my deepest sympathy.

"These days of destruction have been without purpose – a barren venture, the pointless thrashing of whack jobs fueled by baseless grievances. They have failed to overturn an honest election. Based on a briefing by the FBI, I am convinced these wanton attacks are the work of a few small right-wing militias. Rejecting the collective judgement of our democratic system, they chose to destroy it. Claiming to protect our way of life, they sought to dismantle it. They are traitors, nothing more, nothing less. I implore you – reject their delusional mutiny, completely and totally. That is how we will protect our way of life."

"That asshole," Ambrose muttered as the TV anchor continued, "And here is a just-released statement from Ambrose Dancer. As you likely know, he is the leader of one of those right-wing militias holding the Speaker of the House and others hostage."

"Today we struck blows for righting a stolen election and keeping our country on its true course. We – you, in fact – defied the evil forces of tyranny and corruption. You turned out to guard your way of life against oppression, against Deep State elites backed by socialist militants. In that effort, heroes have died, but we have not faltered. You will not falter. This revolution will continue tomorrow and beyond. We will prevail."

"Strong words," said the TV anchor, "but nothing helpful regarding hostage negotiations. The government hasn't offered anything new, either. As far as we know that tense situation remains at stalemate."

Sydney Armor toned down my script, kept it realistic, Ambrose thought. As he reached to shut off the TV, it flashed Special Report and a reporter said, "Nathan Hall was, unfortunately, not the only National Guard commander killed."

She named the others – in Kalamazoo, Michigan, Phoenix, and Asheville, North Carolina – as their photos flashed on the screen.

"Let me put those tragedies in perspective," she continued. "We told you earlier the killers of Nathan Hall have been arrested. Our reporting shows the other slayings also failed to get the results the killers wanted.

"In Asheville, an extremist from the National Patriot Movement appealed to Guard colleagues to seize the unit's munitions and join the revolt. That mutineer hasn't been identified, but during his spiel, Private Jeneane Cedar walked up and without ceremony clubbed him with a wrench. 'Who else is a traitor?' she demanded. That ended the Asheville revolt.

"In Kalamazoo, on the slain commander's cul-de-sac, a neighbor, in the dead of night, looked out his bathroom window and saw a pickup truck idling suspiciously. The neighbor, who refused to go on camera, got a partial license number and, upon learning of the commander's murder, called police. They tracked down the pickup's owner, who crumbled under interrogation and fingered the shooters. They were arrested without incident – and before getting to their armory to preach revolution.

"And in Phoenix, a guardsman who also belongs to the Freedom Country Coalition, argued for attacking a rowdy left-wing crowd, in violation of orders. 'In our hearts, we know what the President wants,' audio of the guardsman's appeal shows. 'More is at stake than squashing these rioters. It's our time to lead the way back to sanity and freedom.'

"Another guardsman shouted back, 'Our dead commander went by the book. Disobeying orders won't honor him. We need to stand by.' Only a few guardsmen, presumably other FCC extremists, briefly stepped up before slinking away.

"According to law officers, emerging evidence shows the NPM and FCC militias are behind the executions of the National Guard commanders. Bottom line, those militias' leaders, Ambrose and Alexander Dancer and Seth Baldwin, acting on the advice of Guard infiltrators, badly misjudged the appetite rank-and-file guardsmen have for revolution. The huge majority of men and women in the Guard view their oath to the Constitution as far more sacred than allegiance to any politician. Protecting their families and neighborhoods is more important than keeping any politician in office. Exit polls showed they sharply split their vote on Election Day, but then accepted the overwhelming evidence of a fair election. Voting for the President didn't sign them up to be party to murder. Or to sink the country into revolution.

"That was what the bulk of Guard personnel told us. Here's the caveat: A troubling minority said they would have rebelled if the big militias had led the charge. Put another way, that minority would have joined if they thought the revolution could have succeeded. That's a huge red flag should this country face a similar challenge in the future."

Ambrose shut off the television, biting on a small hangnail. Until the reporter got to the caveat, he had blamed Sydney Armor and others in the field for misreading Guard units. But maybe they hadn't. Maybe the responsibility was his, for misjudging the big militias. Anyway, the result was the same.

He turned to Baldwin. "What's your take on how things are going?"

"As that all-American war hero John McCain once said, 'All hat and no cattle.' We have caused a hell of a buzz but not what we need most – the prez ordering in the military. That's nothing against our guys. They did good, breaking hell loose in all four directions. If what we've done hasn't been enough for him to step up, I'm afraid he's not going to."

"Alexander?"

"I agree. All the great man should have needed was an excuse, not even a good one. We more than gave him that. He didn't even tell governors to step up and take control or, by god, he would, like he did during the Portland riots last summer. Compared with that, we made things a lot worse in a lot more places."

"Maybe the generals pushed back," said Ambrose. "They've got this thing about the 'optics' of troops putting down civilians."

"Maybe," said Alexander, rubbing bloodshot eyes. "Some of them have as much as said he lost the election."

"He did lose the election," Ambrose said hotly. "Shit, he knows that. We know that. It didn't stop him from trying to stage a coup – or us from jumping in. For us, this has never been about the election. It's been about the opportunity he created by riling up his people to the point of busting a gut, something he started before a single vote was cast. It's about taking the anger of voters who felt cheated and channeling it into a rebellion."

He exhaled, feeling spent. The trio sat hangdog, wrestling with where to take the conversation, or the revolution. And what to do with the hostages – and themselves – if the country didn't explode soon. They felt small and outmatched.

"So far the other militias are staying in their holes," Ambrose muttered repetitively. "I'm sure I saw some of them on TV, raising hell. But we needed, hell, we have to have much more."

Ending another long silence, Alexander said, "The big militias needed a push from the President. He had to show he had the balls for a revolution. Otherwise, they knew he would make them fall guys once he regained power – us too. Feed us all to the generals who he would convince were his best buds."

Alexander was pacing now, his analysis crystalizing and, with it, a sickening realization of doom.

"It's come clear, at least to me," he said, "the great narcissist only has the balls for a palace coup, not a real one with his dick on the block. He pushed others to do his dirty work and, when that failed, turned loose his mob, acting all innocent of course. Not to be dramatic, but he hasn't the guts to look down a gun barrel and not blink."

"Are we out of the woods yet?" FBI Agent Elizabeth Bly asked. Agent-in-Charge Little managed to keep a straight face.

"No, Ms. Bly. Look, we don't know what Ambrose Dancer and his crowd will do tomorrow. Don't know what the President is planning or how his followers will react. Or whether the main militia groups might still weigh in. Hell, we can't be sure what regular folks might do. A lot of frightened people out there could still flood the streets."

"But things have quieted down so much," she insisted. "And we're rounding up the bad guys."

Indeed. As soon as the Dancers and Baldwin were confirmed as leaders of the militias holding hostages, the FBI launched a full court press. Bureaucracies being what they are, it came too late to prevent the worst day of attacks. But court-authorized searches of militia leaders' homes and offices turned up membership rosters. Police and sheriff departments were immediately enlisted. After only a few arrests, word got out and militia members scattered. Most could capably live off the land – from forest to desert – but each one who was tracked down yielded new leads. Within hours, evidence-backed cases were built against the militia hierarchy, key soldiers like Sydney Armor. And against the most vicious troops, led by the executioners. When cornered, some of the extremists resisted and were killed. A few law officers and bystanders died, too.

"A few hours ago," Bly said, "I thought the country would explode, that we were going to have 1776 all over again and the government would be hated like George the Third's. Now that gloom and doom seem to be fading and the main thing, again, is freeing the hostages. Right?"

"We're on two tracks," Little answered. "One is saving hostages, as many as we can. The other is bringing in the treasonous bastards before they somehow fire up another bloodbath, one we can't control."

CHAPTER 34
JANUARY 10TH

The next day the Dancer-Baldwin militias attempted one assassination, a miss. They brought down a couple of electrical substations. Four dynamite packets exploded in malls, but people had learned to steer away from unattended packages; only two minor injuries were reported.

Fires and looting did worsen in a few cities. Two more governors sent in the National Guard to restore order. There was street violence, largely pitting Proud Boys against antifa, with fatalities. But for most people, if the crazies killed each other, all the better.

Absent were activists who earlier turned out to march and wave signs but were not into cracking heads or smashing windows. Gone were meaningful numbers of average Joes – from suburban moms to public employees and service workers. Shopkeepers holed up, armed and ready to defend their property.

Hindsight offered this clarity: Average Americans initially turned out by the tens of thousands because of concern that violence put them in harm's way, not to back a cause. With evidence that only a few small militias were involved, people stayed home. They condemned the mayhem but left dealing with it to law enforcement.

The bulk of people found repulsive the militias' horrific ploys to make them pawns in a revolution.

That revulsion appeared to grow in pace with each new report of a death. Two young sisters, suffering massive injuries from an explosion in a northern Indiana mall, didn't make it. Neither did a dam operator who suffered a heart attack when terrorists burst into his control tower. The wife of the assassinated mayor in North Carolina suffered a heart attack and died within hours. The power grid attack in Johnson County, Illinois, cut electricity to a nursing home and two elderly women, deprived of supplemental oxygen, died.

The reaction on Twitter and Facebook and other social media was mixed. While foes of the revolution dominated the sites, extremists deviously stirred the pot of rebellion with likes and views and other web tactics. Many of the President's loyalists, casting the violence as tragic but predictable given a stolen election, abetted that deception.

The media's ubiquitous man on the street interviews had great impact, overwhelming any notion of public support for the rebels.

"Bunch a White guys show up in the hood talking revolution," a Black man in Saginaw, Michigan, told a Sinclair reporter. "Wrong neighborhood, bro. We're not into a revolt. Those guys just want to stir up shit for the TV. Damn them for the fires and looting."

"I'm for the President, but I couldn't figure out what all the killing and the bombing was about," a woman from Dallas told CNN, hoisting a toddler on her hip. "I decided it had nothing to do with the President, so I bailed."

"Nothing about the election justifies a modern-day Boston Tea Party, let alone Revolution 2.0," a silver-haired stockbroker from Bangor, Maine, told NPR. "My worry is surviving Covid. I have no interest in taking on another war."

"A lot of us out here in Indianapolis are ready to help the prez," a man wearing a hardhat told Fox News. "But now we're just milling around, not knowing what to do. Prez told folks in D.C. to go home in peace. 'Til I hear different, I'm not going on some rampage, breaking windows and stuff."

Meanwhile, arrests piled up.

Security agencies in the malls freely shared security video of men, and a few women, leaving dynamite packets behind. Other terrorists were filmed walking – some calmly, some nervously – to their cars. Zooming in on license plates, investigators identified suspects. Some talked. The sabotage of dams and electrical services supplied other leads. The dragnet tightened.

Investigations into the assassinations of the four public officials – the Oregon county commissioner having died – moved slowly. But sketchy leads offered by uncertain witnesses gradually panned out. A person of interest in the commissioner's death was publicly identified – and tied to Baldwin's FCC.

Elizabeth Bly sat in Little's temporary office, passing him field reports.

"Shit meet fan," she said. "Tomorrow's going to be a big day. Nets are closing on the bastards."

"Do we have extra agents in place for interrogations in Detroit, Raleigh and Portland?"

"In place or on the way, I'm told."

"When we catch more of the militia boys, they'll be talking – a snowball rolling downhill. Call the lawyers for me once more, please, and stress how important it is in the hostage negotiations to know all we can about the arrests."

"How many arrests do you expect?"

"Ah, Ms. Bly. Call it more than a few and probably a lot."

She saw a crawl on the muted television and said, "Another Ambrose Dancer statement is coming up."

"... from the insurrectionist leader holding hostages in the Capitol," a blond woman said cheerfully.

"The revolution continues, with courage and determination, gaining strength against the ballot box corruption of November's election. The Steal slapped at more than seventy-four million citizens doing their sacred duty. Now, some who defended that right have paid the ultimate price. Many others are being wrongly arrested. But those deaths and arrests have been in a patriotic cause. People continue to flood the streets, recognizing the stakes. We demand the Steal be reversed and all Americans be freed from Deep State oppression. Join us in building a new America. Long live the revolution!"

"Perhaps Mr. Ambrose is right," the announcer said drily. "Our reporters can't be everywhere. But our reporting – and that of other media – strongly suggests he is wrong. His revolution is not gaining strength. According to the FBI, the terrible violence we have witnessed has been led by Ambrose Dancer, his brother and another man, each leading a small extremist militia. Our reporting had found little public appetite for revolution and a huge gap between unhappiness with an election and willingness to destroy democracy. Another gap exists between controlling a political party and support for dictating an election outcome – so far, at least.

"Again today, there's nothing new from the White House, FBI, Capitol Police or others in government about the status of hostage negotiations or how the hostages are holding up as their captivity slowly drags out."

I've had nothing new, either, groused Ambrose, watching the broadcast. In two calls from Agent Little, he had asked how the hostages were doing, said to call when we were ready to free them, and hung up.

Ambrose admitted to himself that the announcer, unfortunately, got it right. Sydney didn't help my credibility with that statement, either. Glad she kept it short, but no matter. No one will remember what I supposedly said. It will be forgotten when everything is over tomorrow or maybe the next day. One way or another.

He yawned, welcoming sleep that did not come.

CHAPTER 35
JANUARY 11TH

By the next day the revolution could not be found. A few antifa wastrels still stalked the streets, bent on trouble. So did Proud Boys and their ilk. But the nation was focused on the uncertain fate of the hostages and the manhunts for militia insurrectionists.

Eighteen arrests had been made, from the Carolinas to the Upper Midwest and points West. Under aggressive interrogation, most of the militants cracked like pistachios. Each confession swelled the list of suspects and all-points bulletins seeking turncoats considered armed and dangerous. Car chases, suspects on the run, shootouts, standoffs and surrenders dominated the news.

While there's no federal law against domestic – as contrasted with international – terrorism, crimes calculated to influence government by intimidation or coercion or for ideological goals are considered terrorist acts.

For January 6th and its aftermath, that umbrella stretches from disrupting Congress and storming the Capitol to destroying private property, kidnapping, assassinating public officials and murder. Never had FBI agents and Department of Justice lawyers enjoyed such a field day or held the spotlight on so many stages.

One stage was shared in Muskegon, Michigan, by Sydney Armor

and FBI Agent Constance Costello. Armor had, of course, felt the curtains closing, her militia's successful attacks hollowed out as public support went south.

Then came the paralysis of being exposed: "This just in as we wrap up this hour's update on America in Revolt," intoned a baritone on Fox Radio. "An arrest warrant has been issued for Sydney Armor, thought to be the field commander for Ambrose Dancer, leader of the terrorists holding the House Speaker and others hostage."

Armor could hear her heart beating and her face went numb. With her troops being tracked down, it had to happen, she knew, but hearing it was like the shock of a parent's long-awaited death. The last few days, always on the move, she had used and immediately ditched cheap burner phones – for her last call with Ambrose, for getting his messages out, for issuing orders. But she held onto the cell she had used for months, making thousands of calls. It was filled with numbers she still might need.

She knew someone likely ignored her order to dump a phone or got arrested or killed with her number in it. Suddenly in a panic, she realized the FBI, without doubt, had tracked her just-finished call to Pine Street in Muskegon. The Scottie on her lap whined, feeling her alarm as she steered across the street and flipped her phone into a storm sewer.

"Let's get to Detroit," she said, scratching Yappy's head. "It's easier to hide there. This soldier is gonna hunker down."

Immediately, she felt better, taking comfort in her pickup having stolen plates off an F-150 like hers that was gathering dust in a far corner of a parking garage.

But it was too late. Agent Constance Costello, off duty, was nearly to a friend's house when the GPS location of Armor's cell was broadcast, not two blocks away.

Turning onto Pine Street, she saw a pickup matching the description of Armor's coming in her direction. As they closed to forty yards, Costello braked, turning sharply to the left to block the street. She leaped out, protected by her car, gun drawn, already barking into the microphone.

"You in the pickup, step out slowly, hands high and empty."

"Fuck me," said Armor, options flashing. Give up; no. Ram the car; from this distance, she'd be shot. Run; the cop would chase, call in help. The .45 in her left hand felt good, and she was left-handed. Lowering the window, she heard sirens, still in the distance.

"Step out now!" Costello demanded. "You are under arrest."

Armor didn't move. Early evening light on the street was poor and she imagined the cop looking into the glare of her headlights. She thought she saw a form where the windshield and door frames met, where a cop would crouch. She leaned out the window, the .45 firm against her door, right hand holding her forearm steady, and cut loose three shots.

But the FBI agent had eased into a shadow at her car's front bumper. After Armor fired, Costello squeezed two shots over the F-150's steering wheel. Air shooshed past Armor's head as the windshield spiderwebbed. A loud whelp, then "Oh, my god! Oh, my god!"

The pickup door swung open, and Armor piled out, right arm wrapped around a silent form.

"You killed my fucking dog," she wailed. "You killed my fucking dog."

She fired at Costello's car, staggering forward in grief and anger. Costello hesitated, yelled, "Stop!" Armor shifted direction toward the command. A shot ricocheted off the pavement to Costello's left. She answered twice. The terrorist pitched forward, gripping her Scottie.

Ambrose was channel surfing when CBS reported Armor's death in a single sentence. "Damn," he said quietly. She had become a good friend, second only to Alexander, good as any he fought alongside in Delta Force. Bedding her had entered his mind more than once, but he wasn't sure how she rolled and hadn't wanted to jeopardize their relationship. Then everything got political, so swollen with opportunity... He raised his coffee cup in a silent salute.

"Ambrose, you okay?"

"More or less, bro. Just heard Sydney was killed in a shootout with some FBI bitch. That's all they said. Killed in a shootout. No other details."

"I'm sorry. I know you were tight, and that you could count on her." Alexander paused.

"My rough count makes more than twenty of your people dead or arrested," he continued. "I'm at fifteen, Baldwin about the same. And it feels like the FBI is just clearing its throat. Not much is going to be left of the NPM or the FCC.... Have you talked to Little?"

"Same o same o. He says call him when we're ready to turn Madam Speaker and the others loose. Then he hangs up. I guess that's what the FBI calls negotiating but, truth is, I don't know how to get off square one. They want us to just walk out and let them cuff us?"

"Point well taken," said Seth Baldwin, walking into the kitchen. "Very well taken, actually."

He leaned against a counter, wanting to talk, searching for a starting point. The brothers said nothing. All were weary past description, the price of tension and near-sleepless nights from a standoff they never expected to last so long. Ambrose's nails were chewed to the quick. Alexander's over-the-counter pain killers were failing to keep his headaches at bay. Baldwin claimed to sleep soundly, at least a few hours each night. But his tanned face was washed with gray, his cheeks slightly sunken. His clothes hung a half-size large on a shrinking frame, abruptly a failing old man on a steep downhill.

Baldwin sighed heavily. "I haven't paid much mind to the stores," he said lamely. "Are we all right?"

"Seth, we could eat ourselves fat and still go months," Alexander told him gently.

"My men seem all right. Your guys, too, near as I can tell. Letting them pop some beers helped," Seth went on. "At first that worried me, but no one is getting crazy hammered."

The Dancers nodded agreement, letting Baldwin reach his comfort zone.

"I just spent some time out there, watching. Madam Speaker made her rounds, talking to each of her little charges like she does, even the old senator. On my way out I walked by and said, 'Ma'am.' That's all I said, just greeting her, but she fixed me with a stare that wouldn't quit. Then she says, 'You're interrupting,' like she's presiding over the House and I'm out of order. Then she goes back to drilling me with those big eyes. I left, but it was more like backing off. Spooky."

"No doubt she's a tough one," said Alexander.

The silence was running oppressive when Baldwin said, "Only one talkative was that Squelch guy. He kind of motions me out of earshot of the others and tells me again how tight he is with the Proud Boys. Claims he can call the White House anytime we want to. Maybe we should let him."

Ambrose ran a hand over his forehead, trying to clear his mind. "I talked to the good Mr. Little first time you told me that, Seth. He shot it down, like I told you. Said any call would leak to the press and there'd be non-stop second guessing and what-ifs. I'd give a nut to have Squelch or any of us talk to the President. But if we did get through, do you think we could get him to call out the military?"

"No, I don't. I'm afraid that train is gone... But let's go back to Squelch. The new thing for that conniving prick was he'd help us take out the hostages. 'Think you know who to start with?' I asked him. 'Yes,' he said. 'Start small, to show you mean business, one or maybe a couple, work up to the Speaker. Do her and the commie libs would be in the streets. The other militias, too. The President would have to order in the military.' That's what he said, as if he wouldn't be popped.

"But I was glad he pulled me aside so I could hear the prick out, to be sure I wasn't missing anything," Baldwin explained. "Anyway, the rest of Squelch's pitch was that our attacks hadn't hit people hard enough. We struck fear but, his words, 'didn't grab 'em by the balls.' He thinks taking out the Speaker would do that. He thinks the left – not only the extreme left but some Dems and even independents – would go nuts. The prez would have no choice.

"Personally, I don't buy that. I think the Speaker is more a lightning rod for the right than a thunderbolt for the left. The left admires her a lot, some even love her. But she's not warm and cuddly. I doubt her death would fill the streets the way we need."

"And what was Squelch's reason for keeping him alive?" asked Alexander, making a leap.

"I was coming to that, oh wise one," Baldwin smiled. "He reminded me again of the suck he has with the prez. He ticked off half a dozen names I sort of know, people in the White House and Cabinet. Then he says, 'If you set things up so the President stays in office, I can flat guarantee a pardon before he leaves.'

"At that, I laughed and walked away."

"That turd can't guarantee water is wet," Ambrose said. "As for starting slow with killing hostages, I believe Agent Little when he says the SWAT guys will hit us when we roll out the first body. Squelch would give up his mother to save his sorry ass."

"I do keep wondering," Baldwin said, "if some of the men will do what's expected, if we get rushed."

"Some will, some won't, also as we talked about earlier," said Ambrose, not unkindly, respecting the pressure Baldwin kept bottled up.

Getting no hint of revolutionary fervor from news reports, the hostages' fate was now the fulcrum. Could they – or at least Madam Speaker – spark rebellion, as Squelch argued? Bring out people all along the political arc, left to right? Or would the President's cult bow out, horrified by the executions? Would the big militias finally grab a chance to keep their hero on the throne? Anarchy finally reach a pitch demanding a military response? Once deployed, the President could declare federal troops crucial – indefinitely – to maintaining order. Or the generals might find power irresistible.

To various degrees, the Dancers and Baldwin had explored those scenarios since the standoff began. All saw potential, but Ambrose most clearly. Baldwin and Alexander were conditioned to figure odds, weighing chances for a new spark, a repulsive one at that, reversing the dynamic of terrorism having failed so far. Ambrose was wired another way, his mind always seeking a path to success. He easily ignored past failure if another catalyst, repulsive or not, offered promise.

"But Seth," Ambrose continued, "It's unlike you to ramble on with nothing new but Squelch's bullshit. What's on your mind?"

"Trying to figure things out, as I'm sure you boys are, too. My Aunt Bertha said a thousand times, 'Don't choose failure when success is an option.' Good words."

He grabbed a chair, straddling it to form a comfortable triangle with the Dancers. "I keep watching TV to get the President's strategy, one that might give us a good option. It's hard to think he gave up."

"As I've said," injected Alexander, "he doesn't have the balls to rock and roll on his own. We gave him great reasons to send out the troops and he blinked. Hell, he shut his eyes. Only thing different now is time getting short. If the inauguration happens, he's done."

"Back up a minute," said Ambrose. "You're right about time being shorter. That's huge. The prez may be feeling cornered, about ready to find his gonads."

"I think Alexander was right first time 'round," said Baldwin. "Fair-haired narcissist won't risk getting his ass shot off. He wants a political route where he can rely on his mouth. Which reminds me of what a, experienced lady once told me, 'There are spitters and there are swallowers, and that's all you need to know about a person.' He's a spitter."

The Dancers chuckled, Alexander making loud spitting sounds.

Baldwin continued, "All right, that helps. Now, back to the hostages." He looked to the brothers, but neither took the lead.

"Here's what I see," Baldwin forged on. "Congress will figure out a way to go ahead with the inauguration. That done, the feds can wait us out forever, at least until our food is gone. They might even give us more food to continue the waiting game. In other words, they keep the ball in our court.

"So... We can wait and see what happens. Or we can release Madam Speaker and her little ones and surrender to sit our lives out in prison. For someone used to open spaces, that is really the pits. Or we can shoot the hostages, one at a time on some grotesque schedule or all at once, whatever. If it's one at a time, chances are we won't use up many bullets before SWAT busts in to save who they can. They'll probably see all of us resisting, even if we're not, and that will be that.

"If you see any other scenarios, I'd like to hear them."

The Dancers were silent. Ambrose had seen Madam Speaker and her entourage as a bona fide opportunity and had grabbed it. Alexander and Baldwin had gone all-in, the lure of revolution too great to resist. Their bets – on the White House, average Joes led by the President's base, the other militias – had been losers. Now they smacked of a camper in a blizzard, down to one match, at wits' end for a life-saving fire.

"We are a good team, gentlemen, that I believe," Baldwin said, slowly getting up and shuffling away with a listless wave.

"It's hard to make a case against him," said Alexander.

"Maybe. Or he may be leaving a chip on the table," said Ambrose, turning back to the TV, looking for news, more about Sydney, anything about the President. He was still surfing when a gunshot filled the kitchen, echoing loudly off its hard surfaces.

"Attack!" screamed Alexander, wheeling toward the dining room. "Attack!"

More shots rang out, militants doing their duty, putting down their assigned hostages, or a SWAT team?

Confused faces greeted Alexander as he rushed into the dining room, Ambrose at his heels. Hostages and takers alike were on their feet, wide-eyed, fearful.

But all was quiet at the main door. No battering ram pounding. No one – faces blackened, weapons blazing – crashing through the tall windows. No stun grenades exploding. No tear gas. The room was clear.

"Don't shoot!" shouted Alexander. "No more shooting!"

Two young men, aides to the Speaker, lay on their backs, shot in the head. Marie Wilton, grabbed on her first day as chief of staff to Representative Gonzalez, was on her side, blood soaking her blouse.

Willard Hart of the NPM and one of Baldwin's men stood over the young men, holding their guns.

"I thought ..." began Hart.

"You vicious assholes! You vicious assholes!" screamed the Speaker, looking older, haggard from the ordeal. "And you, killing a woman!"

In three swift strides she was on Eldon Weber, chipped red nails branding his neck before she was pulled off.

"I was following your orders, Ambrose, what you said," protested Weber, putting a hand to the bleeding claw marks.

Madam Speaker wasn't done. "Have the decency to cover them," she ordered.

There was a shout from the kitchen as Ambrose's phone chimed. "See what's up back there," he told Alexander.

Agent Little was excitedly demanding to know what was happening, rambling enough for Ambrose to collect his thoughts.

"I understand your concern," he lied easily. "Everyone's fine. One of the boys got too far into the sauce and fired off a couple rounds... Okay, Agent Little, four if you say so."

Hearing the sobs of distraught hostages, he cupped his phone – too late. "Yes, people are upset... No, I'm not letting you in to check on things... Nothing has changed, Agent Little. We had a minor incident, and some people are upset. That's all."

A loud argument broke out and Ambrose turned to see Madam Speaker toe-to-toe with Representative Squelch. "A couple of our fine charges are at each other. I'm going to get them under control," he said, hanging up. Instead, he walked to the kitchen.

Alexander was kneeling, head down, in front of Baldwin, who sat upright on the floor in a corner, legs splayed. Several insurgents stood nearby, a few still looking, most having turned from the ghastly scene.

Baldwin had pulled a black plastic garbage bag over his head, down to his waist. His ploy to keep his grisly death private had largely failed. The bullet from his large bore revolver, traveling straight up, had ripped away most of his face, exploding the black plastic, now draping his shoulders like a tee-peed tree. The gun rested loosely in his right hand, nosing out of the bag.

Looking at each other, the brothers knew they were sharing a thought: Baldwin had lightly signaled his end – his take on negotiations being pointless, trading his precious open spaces for a prison cell, the suicide of defying a SWAT team, the futility of hanging with a spitter.

The militants dutifully set about moving four bodies to the walk-in refrigerator. Earlier that day one of their own, Lawrence – wounded in the shootout with Madam Speaker's security detail – had been deposited there, dead of a suddenly raging infection.

Ambrose and Alexander took the lead on Baldwin, wrestling fresh garbage bags over him, head and foot, grateful someone found heavy cord to lash the bags tightly closed.

Back at their kitchen table, Alexander wondered out loud how soon decomposition would set in, even with the temperature set on cold.

"Maybe that won't matter," said Ambrose, sitting down with coffee, feeling spent. His phone ID showed Agent Little calling. Motioning Alexander over, he answered on speaker.

"I've got news for you, Mr. Dancer. Bad news and it's not about your mother, assuming you weren't hatched. The argument before you hung up, after insisting people were upset. Through the marvels of telephonic spying or deep dives or however the experts pick up background chatter, we know one party was the Speaker. We're pretty sure the other was Representative Squelch. Most important, we know people are dead."

Ambrose said nothing, at a loss. Physically and mentally, his systems were on overload, in need of time and quiet. Instead, he had Little.

"This changes everything. You are going to give up the hostages, Mr. Dancer. You are going to surrender without firing another shot. This is over, sir. Over."

"It changes nothing, Agent Little," Ambrose said slowly, forcing his voice to be firm, summoning a bravado he did not feel. "Nothing is over. There was an unfortunate incident. One of my men is dead. But we still have the hostages. Two men are assigned to each of them. Don't cause their deaths."

He hoped revealing the death of Baldwin, unnamed, suggesting hostages in revolt, might renew negotiations. How or to what end he had no idea. He was too tired.

"You are lying, Dancer, bald faced lying. We picked up the Speaker saying, 'killing a woman' and 'decency to cover them.' That means at least two hostages, not any of you traitors. Tell me how many hostages are dead, Dancer. Three? Five? More? We heard four shots, but there are many ways to kill people."

Ambrose went silent, searching for a way to exploit this new terrain. To get the feds to back off or, at least, give him time to pull together his wits.

"This is not a debate," Little said finally, quietly. "It is past time for you to give this up and release the hostages. Please give that some serious thought, Mr. Dancer. Don't make things worse. I'll get back to you."

"Aha," Ambrose told Alexander after hanging up. "We can still negotiate. What other reason for chewing things over before busting in here?"

"How soon do you think Little will call back?"

"Soon, probably. For all they really know, a woman from the NPM died. They don't know who needs to be covered. They aren't sure the dead are hostages. If they were, they would demand names. That's how gov'ment works, getting worthless details for touchy-feely stuff like notifying kin," Ambrose rattled on. He paused. "When they call back would you take it and put them off? I want to talk to the men guarding the hostages and rest a bit. I need to think."

When Special Agent Little called, Alexander told him, "Ambrose is sleeping, but wants you to know he talked to the teams on each hostage, including Madam Speaker. They have their orders if we're attacked. Give Ambrose a couple hours."

"Okay," said Little. "One more call. Then all bets are off."

CHAPTER 36

The brothers felt lucky that only three hostages had been killed, Madam Speaker not among them. And that most of their captors figured out they had not been attacked and disobeyed orders. "We – not a SWAT team – need to own the death schedule," said Ambrose.

Alexander wasn't sure what that portended, but his concern deepened when he overheard Ambrose seeking assurance from hostage guards that they were up to pulling the trigger. "Next time you hear a shot, it will be SWAT," he repeatedly said. "Put your hostage down. Don't hesitate."

The words chilled Alexander. Tormented, he went to the kitchen corner he had claimed on the first night and arranged his bedding of confiscated tablecloths. He settled in, savoring transient rest as he explored from every angle whether killing the hostages could somehow be a winning chip. "Ya gotta believe" was fine for inspiring an individual leap of faith. But to justify executions to spark revolution? No, sadly, Alexander decided. Their opportunity for revolution had fallen short. Sure, killing Madam Speaker and others would provoke outrage. Their followers would demand justice. So what? Killing Squelch and the old senator would not inflame the President's base. Hell, most on the right would find them a mighty fine trade for the Speaker. And with the President and other militias sitting on their hands... No, killing the hostages would not bring civil war.

Alexander pondered when the SWAT assault would come. Would they kill us, claiming we had resisted, or be satisfied to lock us up? He tried to imagine spending the rest of his life in prison. Maybe it wouldn't be so bad. Build a life, somehow. Be a jailhouse lawyer? He was smart. Lord knows prison injustices could keep him busy. Be a model prisoner and create opportunities for himself, doing good. Write or be a speaker or filmmaker explaining prison life to the outside world. Or an artist or musician, inspiring other prisoners. Alexander instantly wanted to slap himself, tell his weary mind to get real. His crimes – horrific slaughter on top of traitorous insurrection – left no room for opportunities. Years – maybe in solitary – would pass before redemption was even remote. His fate would be life in maximum security, spelled in all caps. Locked up with the hardest cases, men without hope, with nothing more to lose by slitting another throat. Shit, I'll get a freaking body building liberal for a cellmate, he thought. Be gang-raped in the shower until I'm eager to be anybody's bitch. Maybe Seth was right. One pull of the trigger. No one else hurt. Failure admitted. He rejected the thought as it surfaced. He was too selfish – cowardly? – for suicide. Bottom line, a SWAT team and live hostages gave him better odds than igniting the spark Ambrose held dear.

Then a solution struck Alexander like a sickening potent. Ambrose was his way out, horrific but real. Doubtful he could do it, Alexander prodded the unholy option into focus. Killing Ambrose would end the standoff. No one in the militias – NPM or FCC – would embrace the revolutionary mantle without his leadership. With Ambrose dead, most, if not all, of his NPM comrades, those in the FCC, too, would not kill hostages. They would refuse to create the spark driving Ambrose, Alexander felt certain. They would choose surrender and prison over suicide by SWAT. The hostages would live. Release from prison might be possible, someday, for others, if not himself. The now-vapid search for revolution would end. All that with Ambrose gone. But only with Ambrose gone. Cradling his aching head, Alexander's heart raced with dread at shouldering the sinful mantle of Cain.

Down the wall of the large kitchen, on his own makeshift pallet, facing a SWAT team or prison were not on Ambrose's mind; he wrestled with the threat of failure. *Options are not as dire as Seth Baldwin made them out to be*, he insisted to himself. Anger rose against his dead colleague as he went over the cards he held: *The President's unbridled, immoral thirst for power. The clock, each tick stoking pressure on the commander in chief to invoke the Insurrection Act. His loyal cult, far more potent than its raw numbers. Big militias hungry for legitimacy. And, of course, the hostages.*

Seth had lacked imagination, trapped by obstacles instead of ferreting out ways around them. And damn him, his suicide hit the men hard, sapping their morale. Blowing off your face is no way to lead.

Ambrose wanted to remind the men, Alexander too, that early on it was he who saw the President's potential – to win election and lead in the right direction. *It was he, Ambrose, who saw how the rally might spin out of control, protesters morph into a mob, storm the Capitol of the United States. Only he had recognized hostages as game changers – and had the balls to kill for them. Holding Madam Speaker and the others had frozen Congress for – how long now? – and halted the vote count for president. Never, never had that been done. Three small militias rocked the nation, rocked it more than since the Civil War. History will show I saw the potential for all of that. For a revolution to right this government. Nothing less than to right this nation.*

Sadly, history will also show I put too much confidence in the President, Ambrose admitted. *I saw him as a risk taker in revolution, as he had been in politics, as he had been as President, ruthlessly bending norms, dismantling the Deep State, realigning outdated global alliances. He was a risk taker until it really mattered. Then he retreated to his political cocoon. Always the fearful germaphobe, he* couldn't bear to touch an actual revolution, fearful of leaving his DNA for history's harsh judgment.

I was wrong, too, in thinking big militias would fill the void of the President's inaction. Sure, they plotted and gathered arms, brought troops to town. The Proud Boys even led the charge on the Capitol. But then they melded into the mob. At their core, the big militias lacked the resolve to go bold, independently. That said, I believe they could yet grasp what history offers. I can imagine Baldwin back in the fridge, advising: My granddaddy on the Cohen side always insisted that failure doesn't rule the future.

We mistakenly waited for an opportunity to turn an assault on the Capitol into an insurrection, Ambrose reflected. When the President declared the election stolen, before votes were even cast, that early, we – no, I – should have seen the potential for insurrection. Seen it and planned – big militias be damned.

Sure, I put a bunch of angry people in the streets, tens of thousands actually, bent on mayhem. Antifa and Black Lives Matter pitted against a lot of free-thinking militia troops who were pissed at waiting for a thumbs up from their dick-less leaders. Yes, they blew up shit, struck fear, screwed up government for a couple of days. Brought out regular folk on both sides, briefly. But I failed to see that those attacks weren't gut grabbers. Then the fires were out, power restored, stores reopened. Folks going about their business.

The reason for the revolution's looming failure unexpectedly struck him: The targets. Assassinating Guard commanders and low-level public officials. Igniting kill-whomever dynamite in malls. Blowing up dams and electrical substations. In hindsight, those targets were impotent against the challenge of inflaming a nation. Not enough people died, not nearly enough to reroute the course of history, ignite the civil war we needed.

The key was – is – death, he told himself. Not deaths that are faceless to all but the families. They get singalong thoughts and prayers from braying politicians, a pablum after every school and nightclub and church shooting. A litany so common that outrage has been anesthetized, even for decent people. Outrage must be revived.

We need targets filled with gut-wrenching pain: Set off explosives in crowded theaters. Fly armed drones into packed stadiums. Blow up dams sitting above populated valleys. Execute governors and senators and icons of entertainment and business and religion.

Clearly seeing such a string of devastating attacks, true game changers, Ambrose gasped for breath. Forget pissant disruptions angering people against government. Insert the high death counts that make people hate government. Render it helpless. He closed his eyes and was swamped by images of the President's devoted cult bubbling with hate, demanding release from their consuming grievance of a stolen election. Outrage revived.

Drenched in sweat, he realized he was mentally overheated, his judgment suspended. But he couldn't slow the march of his mind. Belatedly, much too belatedly, it opened dark passages he should have entered sooner. Passages keying success, planting him in a role the country and the President desperately needed.

A pathway – a solution teasing his subconscious for days – boiled up: Madam Speaker and the rest of my hostages – yes, my hostages – still can awaken dormant outrage. Civil war. Revolution. Four or more years of an unbound presidency.

The spark from executing Madam Speaker would be hotter, more targeted, than all the attacks that failed.

To anyone doubting – comrades in the militias, the cult, even the President – I tell you this: Madam Speaker is as hated as she is loved. She is the unabashed defender and public face of misguided values – abortion rights, open borders, gender identity, so much more. Take the Speaker down and this week's violence will smack of a dreary chess match.

Madam Speaker's minions will forget about gun control and defunding the police and abolishing the death penalty. Touchy-feely PC will flee their commie minds. March with signs? Hell, they will come with guns. They will take heads, literally. Feminists – men and women – will taste blood and thirst for more, antifa and Blacks egging them on. And in return, the President's millions and all the militias will happily oblige, confident, knowing most soldiers and cops will back them. Since 1861, this country has never been so divided, so ready to be ignited. The Second Civil War will be fucking glorious. Pardon me for that prissy word, glorious, but fucking glorious it will be.

Ambrose was short of breath, his excitement at a pitch he last felt killing Taliban. He wiped sweat from his eyes, straightened against the wall. "Ya gotta believe" flashed by. I must work all the way through this, he insisted, mentally shifting to Squelch and the old senator. Forget Squelch's sway with the White House or Proud Boys, he's worth more dead. No one cares about the puke – maybe his mother. A shit all his life, but I'll make him a hero in death, a symbol of all the culture war bullshit the President's lemmings hold dear. Bullshit the lemmings exploit in their frenzied struggle to hold onto a lost era. Squelch will be the White majority's new poster child for the American way of life. We will grieve for him, a red-blooded martyr shielding us from Madam Speaker's heathens.

As for the old senator, his worth pales beside Squelch's. His boast of geriatric vigor is only good until he trips on a sidewalk crack. But what the hell, toss him on the martyr pile, value added in a few Midwestern states.

Yes, death of the hostages will tip us into revolution. And Madam Speaker will fire up both sides, infusing love or hate and taking away the middle ground. Are the odds long? Maybe, but mine were worse with the Taliban. Facing death, or bad options, odds barely matter. What matters is finding a way.

Everything depends, of course, on Alexander. Whether he goes all-in. He won't follow Seth's path. That's not Alexander. If he can't stand having the blood of revolution on his hands, he may see only one way to stop me. Could he kill me? Probably. Would I stop him? No, I can't kill Alexander. That would be the only way, and I can't. It will be up to Alexander. All up to Alexander.

CHAPTER 37

gent Little called a couple of hours before sunup. "You have thirty minutes to release the hostages," he told Ambrose. "I'm not saying we're coming in thirty minutes, but this is my last call. We're out of patience. Hostage families have had enough. It's time for you to do what is right."

Little hung up before Ambrose could say a word. Damn bureaucrats can't even order an attack without pussyfooting, he thought. We don't have much more than thirty minutes. They want to come in the dark, their fancy night goggles giving them an edge.

He saw no reason for an all-hands meeting. The troops would do their duty or not. Besides, only one conversation was needed. Though Alexander was breathing heavily, he woke up the instant Ambrose touched his shoulder.

Seeking privacy, they entered the walk-in refrigerator, trying to ignore the shrouded bodies. Ambrose leaned against a large butchers block, Alexander facing him a couple steps away.

"I don't see a reason to talk to anyone else before I talk to you," Ambrose said, recounting Little's call. "It's decision-making time, bro."

The pounding in Alexander's head got worse. He wondered if

Ambrose knew his mind, the choice he faced. From a mere option had sprung the most critical decision of his life. He fought to ignore the pounding, a reminder that not only the lives of hostages hung in limbo. Certainly, Ambrose believed Madam Speaker's death would open a civil war on par with the nation's bloodiest and then ignite revolution. But Ambrose could be wrong, grasping at an illusion, judgment heavily clouded by his passion for rebellion. Madam Speaker was probably not that spark, Alexander reminded himself.

He looked at his brother, seeking his eyes, but Ambrose stared intently at the floor, arms crossed, the picture of indifference. He's putting this all on me, the asshole, all on me.

Alexander's right thumb was hooked in a belt loop of his jeans, sweaty fingers touching the butt of his Glock. I need to dry my hand, he thought. His mind screamed, "Forget that you dumb shit, just pull it, use it, use it!"

Through the pounding he heard Ambrose say calmly, "Bro, the Speaker and Squelch both must go down if we are to strike the best spark, the one that will turn everything around. With them, there's no room for error. That means taking care of them falls on us."

Ambrose looked into his brother's eyes, seeing his life dangling. Alexander's inner voice kept screaming, "Do it now. It's hard, but the right thing. Do it now!"

Ambrose watched Alexander ease his thumb from the belt, his hand move toward the Glock, then drop to his side. Blood had won. Ambrose lowered his eyes, smiling inwardly.

The pounding worsened as Ambrose pulled the half-dollar from a pocket. Alexander heard the words coming from a far corner of a dark place.

"Loser gets Squelch. I call tails. Flip you for Madam Speaker."

EPILOGUE

Among those charged with murder were Hasty, for killing Private First Class Darrell Steele, and the old man who stabbed Amy Bondarenko. Her photos and videos led to many arrests, including that of Gary Evans, the South Dakota patrolman, for maiming Corporal Nick Swift. Madam Speaker, Representative Herbert Squelch and most of the other hostages were executed. Nearly all their captors, including Ambrose and Alexander Dancer, were killed as they resisted arrest. The FBI roundup effectively destroyed the NPM and FCC militias, but Jeffrey Lomax and his South Arising emerged stronger than ever. Special Agent Brian Little resigned under pressure from the FBI, which needed a fall-guy for the failed hostage negotiations.

The deaths of Madam Speaker and Squelch generated only a feeble spark. There was no Revolution 2.0. A new president was inaugurated on January 20th, 2021.

ABOUT THE AUTHOR

Norman Brewer is an award-winning reporter and editor who worked for The Des Moines Register and Tribune and for Gannett News Service in Washington, D.C. He also was Director of Employee Communications at the U.S. Transportation Security Administration. His experience has given him a powerful perspective on January 6, domestic terrorism and the US political landscape. He lives in Portland, Ore.

ALSO BY NORMAN BREWER

Killer Politics: A Satirical Tale of Homegrown Terrorism

Blending In: A Tale of Homegrown Terrorism